WILD
HORSES

Center Point
Large Print

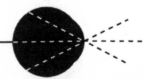

**This Large Print Book carries the
Seal of Approval of N.A.V.H.**

WILD HORSES

B. J. Daniels

CENTER POINT LARGE PRINT
THORNDIKE, MAINE

This Center Point Large Print edition is published in the year 2016 by arrangement with Harlequin Books S.A.

This is a work of fiction. Names, characters, places and incidents are either the product of the author's imagination or are used fictitiously, and any resemblance to actual persons, living or dead, business establishments, events or locales is entirely coincidental.

The text of this Large Print edition is unabridged. In other aspects, this book may vary from the original edition. Printed in the United States of America on permanent paper. Set in 16-point Times New Roman type.

ISBN: 978-1-62899-953-2

Library of Congress Cataloging-in-Publication Data

Names: Daniels, B. J., author.
Title: Wild horses / B. J. Daniels.
Description: Center Point Large Print edition. | Thorndike, Maine : Center Point Large Print, 2016. | ©2015
Identifiers: LCCN 2016008239 | ISBN 9781628999532
    (hardcover : alk. paper)
Subjects: LCSH: Large type books. | GSAFD: Western stories.
Classification: LCC PS3554.A56165 W55 2016 | DDC 813/.54—dc23
LC record available at http://lccn.loc.gov/2016008239

When I thought about who I'd like to dedicate this book to, my father, Harry Burton Johnson, came to mind. *Wild Horses* is about wild things and Montana. My father loved both.

The moment he saw Montana he wanted to live here. That's how my family ended up living in a cabin in the Gallatin Canyon when I was young.

He made us a zip line off the mountain, built us a log playhouse fort and piled up snow to fill it with water to make us a skating rink out front. He made rubber-guns and kites. There wasn't anything he couldn't make.

My father had such a joy for life and he passed it on to me. He loved Montana and he passed that love on to me, as well.

That's why this book is for him. Miss you, Dad.

WILD
HORSES

PROLOGUE

January 27

Life changed in an instant. Olivia Hamilton knew that only too well. One minute her mother had been alive. The next gone.

Tonight, one minute Montana's night sky had been clear, the next she found herself in the middle of a blizzard—fighting to stay on a two-lane highway in the middle of nowhere. Livie had driven in her fair share of winter storms, but this one was getting worse by the moment. She couldn't see more than a few yards ahead of her through the driving snow. Add to that, she didn't know the road or even exactly where she was.

All she knew for sure was that she was stopping at the next small town she came to and getting a motel for the night. She'd call home to let her family know where she was. As for calling Cooper Barnett . . .

Just the thought of her fiancé made her grit her teeth. If the man wasn't so damned stubborn they would have been married by now and she wouldn't have taken off after their latest fight and ended up on this road alone in the middle of Montana in the winter with the temperature dropping and—

The highway disappeared so quickly that she didn't have time to react. Through the windshield all she saw was blowing snow as the SUV suddenly jerked to the right. The tires caught in the deep snow along the edge of the highway. In a heartbeat, the SUV plunged into the ditch. Snow washed over the hood and windshield. Her head slammed into the side window an instant before the airbag exploded in her face. Then everything stopped.

Livie sat for a moment, too stunned to move. She was still gripping the steering wheel, her knuckles white. It had all happened so quickly that she hadn't had time to panic. Now, though, she began to shake, tears burning her eyes as she realized the desperate situation she'd put herself in. She could feel freezing cold air coming in around the cracks in the door. She hadn't seen a house or a light in miles.

Pulling out her cell phone, she hoped she could get a tow truck this time of the night. But she quickly realized that, like a lot of areas of Montana, there was no cell service.

At the sound of the engine still running, she told herself that her situation was dire enough without carbon monoxide poisoning. With the SUV's tail-pipe deep in the snow, it wouldn't take long before she was overcome. She quickly killed the motor.

A deathly silence fell over the car as she considered what to do. The car was buried in snow in the ditch miles from anywhere. She'd always been told to stay with her vehicle, but she could feel the temperature dropping and she'd foolishly left in such a hurry that she hadn't taken her usual precautions. She'd brought no sleeping bag or water or anything to eat and right now she had no idea how long it would be before anyone found her.

Cooper had begged her not to travel because the forecast called for a storm. But she'd been too angry with him to listen. She'd thrown her engagement ring at him and stormed out. All she'd thought about was distancing herself from him until she could cool down. She had a friend who lived in northwest Montana and, right then, going to see her seemed like a great idea. Let Cooper have a few days with her gone and see how he liked that.

When she'd left, the weather had been fine and she'd thought she could beat the storm. But when the skies darkened and flakes started to fall she'd taken a shortcut across the state. Except it wasn't long before she couldn't see the highway. She'd thought about turning around, but it was as bad behind her as it was ahead so she'd kept going. For the past twenty miles or so, she hadn't even seen another car on the highway. For all she knew the road had now closed to all but emergency traffic.

She felt something run down the side of her face. Turning on the interior light, she glanced in her rearview mirror and saw that she was bleeding from a cut over her left eye where she'd smacked her head on the side window.

But it was what else she saw in the mirror that sent her pulse hammering.

A single set of headlights appeared in a blur out of the storm.

She tried to open her car door. If she could get out and flag the person down . . . Her door wouldn't open, though, because of the snow packed around it.

Knowing that the driver of this car might be her only chance at survival tonight, she shoved as hard as she could. But the door wouldn't budge.

The lights were growing closer.

What if the driver didn't see her? What if . . .

What appeared to be a large dark SUV slowed, and the headlights washed over her. The SUV's flashers came on as the driver pulled to the edge of the highway directly behind the spot where she'd gone off.

She saw a man climb out and she began to cry with relief. Life could change in an instant, she thought again as she watched the man heading toward her through the storm. He appeared to be large, nice looking, wearing a cowboy hat and dressed in formal Western attire as if he'd been to a party somewhere.

Olivia "Livie" Hamilton had no reason not to believe the man had stopped to save her.

Chapter ONE

May 1
Three months later

Senator Buckmaster Hamilton stood on the second-floor outdoor balcony of the sprawling Hamilton Ranch house and surveyed the engagement party going on below him. Tiny white lights twinkled in the treetops as candles glowed on the cloth-covered tables around the provisional outdoor ballroom. A sea of Stetsons bobbed as a country music band played. The sound of clinking crystal glasses mingled with the hum of cheerful voices. It was a beautiful spring evening.

It should have been a perfect night since the party was to celebrate the first of his six daughters' engagements. All he'd ever wanted was for his daughters to be happy. That Olivia was the first to marry didn't surprise him. He'd seen the way she'd looked at the wrangler the first day he'd come to work on the ranch. Cooper Barnett wouldn't have been his choice for her, but what did he know about love other than it was blind?

He raised his own glass in a silent salute. No matter what happened after tonight, he couldn't have been more proud of his daughters, or as they were known around Beartooth, Montana, the Hamilton girls.

God knew he'd spoiled them after their mother died. In the twenty-two years since, he'd been overprotective, he'd be the first to admit it. There were stories that he'd met their dates on the front porch with a shotgun. He smiled. Although untrue, it had taken courageous young men to even dare to ask his girls out.

It was his fault, no doubt, that all six had grown into headstrong, hard-to-please women. Buckmaster sighed, although he truthfully saw nothing wrong with that. His girls had grown up with the run of one of the largest ranches in their part of the state. They had wanted for nothing, he'd seen to that.

Except for the mother they'd lost.

He took another drink to wash down the bitterness.

"One of our girls is getting married, Sarah," he whispered into the warm spring night. "You missed it all. Now you won't even be there to see Olivia get married." He let out a curse, furious with Sarah for leaving him. Even more furious with himself because he still ached for her after all these years, as if he'd lost a limb.

He didn't want to think about her. Not tonight. Focusing on the party instead, he surveyed the growing crowd and spotted his oldest daughter, Ainsley, gathered with four of her sisters near the bar. She'd been ten at the time of her mother's death and had become a little mother to the others. She even looked like her mother, a blonde beauty. Except that Ainsley was much stronger than her mother had been. She was the one everyone depended on, himself included.

His gaze moved to Kat, the daughter who'd taken after him the most. Strong willed, Kat had gotten his dark hair and his gray eyes. She looked rugged and unapproachable even as pretty as she was.

She'd been eight when Sarah had died. Kat, who'd become a photographer, was always in trouble growing up. He'd watched her pull away from the family first by becoming a vegetarian and demanding he quit raising cattle, and later by spending less time at the ranch and more time rebelling in every possible way. He worried about her and often wondered what it would take to make her happy.

He let his gaze take in the fraternal twins, Harper and Cassidy, and smiled. They were blonde, blue-eyed and adorable. He still thought of them as his babies since they'd only been a few months old when they'd lost their mother. They were both still in college and only home for their sister's engagement party.

As he found Bo in the crowd below, he realized she was the daughter who worried him even more than Kat. Kat was defiant and obstinate. Bo was the secretive one. She had been five when Sarah died. Even back then, Bo was the quiet one who seemed to move through the house like a ghost. Green-eyed with sandy-blond hair and freckles, she was also the smart one.

To his surprise, it had been Bo who'd wanted to take over the charity he'd started in their mother's name. The Sarah Hamilton Foundation had been a sentimental gesture he'd regretted the moment he'd found out the truth about Sarah's *accident* the night she died.

With concern, he now watched Bo down a glass of champagne as if it were water. He could tell it was far from her first. Something was going on with her. This wasn't the first time he'd noticed. He didn't know what it was and he'd been afraid to ask. Maybe he'd ask Ainsley, but not tonight.

He looked through the crowd for Olivia, his blue-eyed brunette, but didn't see her. Sarah had been a lot like Olivia—headstrong, spoiled rotten and too beautiful for her own good. Cooper, he feared, was too much like he'd been, stubborn and uncompromising. He and Sarah had been so young, and Olivia was only twenty-five.

At the thought of history repeating itself—

He washed away that terrifying thought with a gulp of Scotch. Behind him, he heard the balcony door open.

"I thought you might be here," his wife of fifteen years said. Angelina Broadwater Hamilton glanced at the glass in his hand. "People are asking about you downstairs."

Influential people in their political circle, people who had made him one of the youngest senators ever elected from Montana. People who could make him president, something he knew Angelina yearned for even more than he did.

Now, it appeared that there was a very good chance the presidency was his for the taking. He had an excellent voting record and, while a conservative, he was moderate enough to gain respect from both parties. He'd made a lot of friends on both sides of the fence. All the work that Angelina had done had paid off.

While he had always been ambitious, Buckmaster believed in his heart that he could help the country. He would be a good president. He would make Montana proud.

Below him, he saw his brother-in-law, Lane Broadwater, working the crowd at the party. In his midthirties, Lane was blond like his sister with the same blue eyes. Although he was eleven years younger, the two looked more like fraternal twins. Angelina had talked him into hiring her brother to handle the campaign when he'd run for senator. He'd been skeptical at first about Lane's abilities, but he'd proven himself to be good at the job. Also he was enough like his sister that he went after whatever it was he wanted. Lane and Angelina wanted to put him in the White House.

They'd proven to be very good at what they did.

He drained his glass and smiled as he turned to her. "Then we should get downstairs at once."

Angelina eyed him, clearly unsure if he was being sarcastic. She'd never been able to tell, but it didn't matter. He hadn't married her for her astuteness. While she was a beautiful blonde, tall, willowy, with a face that could have been carved from porcelain, he'd married her for her name. The Broadwater connection had definitely helped put him in the Senate and made him even richer. It would put him in the White House.

He could laugh about it now, but fifteen years ago some people were under the misconception that he'd married her so she could help raise his six daughters. Angelina wasn't mother material.

Fifteen years ago, he also hadn't particularly needed a wife—not in the practical sense—when he'd met Angelina. Which was good because there was also nothing domestic about her. He'd hired a staff to run the house and take care of his children since he spent a great deal of his time in Washington.

Angelina, though, was queen of her realm when it came to throwing parties. She attracted the right people, the kind who had made Buckmaster Hamilton one of the most powerful men in Montana.

Now, Angelina took the empty glass from his hand, smiling as she laid it aside for the staff to take care of later. Then looping her arm through his, she said, "You look very handsome tonight, Mr. Hamilton. Ready for our grand entrance?"

"Why not?" He smiled, though most women would have seen through it. Angelina never looked past the surface. Because of that, she didn't know about the dark shadows he sensed at the edge of their lives. She couldn't imagine any problems that Buckmaster Hamilton couldn't fix. But then again, she didn't really know him.

Cooper Barnett walked along the side of the house to the ballroom floor that had been built for the occasion. Everyone who was anyone was here, which meant he didn't know most of the guests.

But he had to admit, it was some party from the tiny sparkling lights to the bubbly champagne and the imported caviar Buckmaster had flown in just that morning. No expense had been spared. It was the Hamilton way. Whatever it cost, money was never an issue.

He caught his reflection in a mirror as he passed through the house, and he straightened his tie. Wouldn't his family be surprised to see him now? He looked nothing like the old Cooper Barnett; he still felt a lot like the old one—except in nicer clothes. It was that old one who worried him.

You don't belong here. Worse, he feared that a lot of people at this party knew it. He shoved the thought away as he exited the house and walked among the crowd outside, anxious to find his fiancée. Stars twinkled overhead. A light breeze swayed the nearby pines and music filled the air. The Hamiltons couldn't have ordered a more beautiful night. Even the weather did what Buckmaster wanted, he thought with a wry smile.

Then he saw his bride-to-be and forgot all about his future father-in-law and the old Cooper Barnett. His heart did a little stutter-kick in his chest. Damn but Livie Hamilton was breathtaking tonight. She wore a burgundy-red dress that accentuated her rich olive skin and contrasted perfectly with her long dark hair. He still couldn't believe she'd fallen in love with him. How had he gotten so lucky?

Not that she wasn't a spitfire who fought him at every turn. Also he'd done his best not to fall in love with her. He'd been warned about the Hamilton girls and he'd wanted nothing to do with her.

When he fell, though, he'd fallen hard. He wouldn't admit it to her even at gunpoint, but her independent, mule-headed stubbornness and determination were part of her charm. But she was a Hamilton and that came with its problems.

He was headed for her when she saw him. Her face lit, making his heart take off at a dead run. The band broke into Livie's favorite song, just as he had requested. It was sappy, but when he saw her smile of recognition, it was all worth it.

"You look . . . amazing," he said, taking her in with his gaze, then his arms.

She smiled up at him, her blue eyes wide and luminous. "You don't look so bad yourself. You clean up nice, cowboy."

He pulled her out onto the dance floor, drawing her in closer. As he nuzzled her neck, he caught the scent of light citrus. Desire almost buckled his knees. Overhead, starlight glittered down on them from Montana's big sky. The night really was perfect.

"I am the luckiest man alive," he said as he drew back to look at her. He'd never understand why she'd fallen in love with him. If only she wasn't a Hamilton, he thought, and shoved the thought away. He wouldn't let anything ruin this night.

He'd never believed in luck. He'd gotten where he was through hard work. But he was afraid to jinx this, afraid he didn't deserve this woman, deserve any of this—and he knew he could blame his father for that.

Ralph Barnett had told him from the time he was a boy that he wasn't worth two cents and would never amount to anything. He's spent most of his twenty-eight years trying to prove the man wrong. But there was still that part of him that didn't believe he deserved anything, especially happiness.

"I'm the lucky one," Livie said.

Cooper pulled her closer, leaning down to

whisper, "I love you," against her hair. He relished the soft sweet moan she uttered in response. He ached with a need for her. The two of them had been so busy they had hardly seen each other for weeks. Once this shindig was over, he couldn't wait to get her alone.

As the song ended, she drew back to look at him, her gaze locking with his. He lost himself in her sky-blue eyes. Her dark hair floated around her bare shoulders, making his fingers long to bury themselves in it. No woman had ever made him feel like this and he knew, after Livie, no other woman ever could.

"I love you, Coop. Remember that always." She said it with such force that he felt a niggling of worry. She looked a little pale, he thought, and recalled that the few times he'd seen her over the past few weeks she hadn't been herself.

He'd been busy working on the ranch, getting it ready for when she moved in after they were married. Livie had also been busy, taking care of the wedding plans. He would have been happy to elope, but Buckmaster Hamilton wasn't having that. His first daughter to marry was going to have a huge wedding, no expense spared.

Cooper had gone along with it, knowing it was important to Livie. But he'd dug in his heels when it came to her father helping them financially, which had been a bone of contention between them, among other things.

He would also have gladly gone for a longer engagement, giving him time to finish the house he was building for them on his ranch. But Livie wasn't good at waiting for anything. It was her impulsiveness that he loved—but it also caused him concern. She often acted without thinking of the consequences.

Like last winter when, after a fight, she'd taken off with a storm coming and ended up in a ditch. Even though she swore her injury was minor, she hadn't been the same since, he thought now.

"Is everything all right, Livie?" he asked, his heart suddenly in his throat.

Livie met his dark gaze. She'd loved this man almost from the first time she'd seen him in the corral working with the horses. There'd been something special about him—a tenderness, a vulnerability and yet a strength like none she'd ever seen.

At the thought of losing him . . . Tears filled her eyes, blurring her vision. Not now, she told herself. *All you have to do is get through tonight.* "I'm feeling a little emotional, that's all." She could see that he was worried and wasn't going to leave it at that.

But fortunately, his future best man, Rylan West, cut in and whisked her away. Rylan and Cooper had been best friends since Cooper arrived in town. It was good to see him and his wife, Destry, at the party. Not long ago, Destry had lost not only her brother but also the baby she was carrying.

When the song ended, Livie quickly excused herself to go to the ladies' room. As she left the party, she glanced back. She saw Cooper in deep conversation with her father. Both men were frowning. Like her and Cooper, they were probably having the same argument. Her father wanted her to live in a nice house after they were married.

Because she'd insisted on a short engagement, she and Cooper would be living in his old cabin until he finished building their house. With her father's resources and a hired crew, the house could have been finished before the wedding if Cooper would only agree to it. But he was determined to do it all himself without his future father-in-law's help.

The music started up again, seeming too loud. She caught scents in the crowd—perfume, aftershave, appetizers and alcohol. It all made her stomach turn. She swallowed back the nausea and made a beeline for the patio bathroom.

Rushing in, she threw up. As she finished, she leaned against the cool wall of the bathroom feeling a little better. Once she'd gotten herself together again, she stepped back outside. The party was beautiful from here—all the lights, the sound of laughter, music and voices, the tinkling of champagne glasses.

Her stepmother had done an amazing job, but

then again, the woman had been throwing parties for years here on the ranch. Livie remembered the day her father and Angelina had walked into the house and announced that they'd gotten married. She'd taken an instant dislike to Angelina—just as her sisters had.

Fortunately, Angelina hadn't wanted anything more to do with them than they did with her.

Livie often wondered what their lives would be like now if their mother hadn't died. Had it really been twenty-two years? She'd been three when her mother had been killed after her car had crashed into the icy Yellowstone River. Sarah Hamilton hadn't been wearing her seat belt and had been ejected into the river, her body apparently swept downstream. Like a lot of bodies that went into Montana rivers, hers was never found.

Livie had little memory of her other than a few photographs she'd seen before even those had disappeared once Angelina had shown up.

But even with her senator father gone a lot, she and her sisters had never felt deprived of anything. And no matter what anyone said, they weren't spoiled. They just knew what they wanted, she thought, realizing Cooper would have argued the point.

Still feeling a little weak, she walked toward a stand of pines at the edge of the party to catch a breath of fresh air. Why hadn't she called off the party? She knew the answer. The party had been planned weeks ago. Also calling it off would have the whole county talking. She told herself that if she could just get through tonight . . .

Another wave of nausea hit her. She sat down on one of the benches that circled the outdoor ballroom, this one in the shadow of the pines. Reaching into the small clutch, she dug for the pills the doctor had prescribed for her. Her fingers brushed the letter she'd received just that morning.

She drew it out with trembling fingers. Like the first one, her name had been typed on the blue envelope in bold black. "Olivia Hamilton." She had stared at it, heart pounding, trying to tell herself she was wrong, until she hadn't been able to stand it any longer and torn it open.

It was exactly like the first blackmail note, except that note had demanded only ten thousand dollars. This one demanded fifty thousand.

Stuffing it back into her clutch, she felt even more light-headed than she had moments before. She looked out at the crowd who'd come to celebrate her engagement. Another wave of nausea hit her. She stumbled to her feet, but instantly felt woozy and had to grab the back of the bench for support.

"You look as if you're going to faint," her sister Ainsley said, appearing from out of the darkness.

"I'm fine," she protested even though she was far from fine.

Ainsley sat down next to her. "Talk to me,

Livie." Ainsley had been away at law school until this week. Livie had had the entire addition her father had built them away from the main house to herself but she'd missed her sister. She loved having Ainsley back home. Seven years older, Ainsley had been like a mother to her.

Livie fought to keep her stomach down while at the same time trying not to cry. Ainsley had always looked out for her. She had been the person she'd gone to when she had her first period, when she needed her first bra, when she got her heart broken the first time.

But this was something she didn't want to trouble her big sis with. This was something she had to take care of herself.

"Does Cooper know yet?" Ainsley asked.

Livie looked up with a start. "Know what?"

"Does he know you're pregnant?" her sister asked, lowering her voice even though the sounds from the party covered her words.

Livie shook her head as her eyes filled with unshed tears. "How . . ."

"I heard you throwing up the past couple of mornings."

"Does anyone else . . ."

Ainsley shook her head. "Don't cry. You'll ruin your makeup." Her sister handed her a tissue. "Why haven't you told him?" When Livie didn't answer, she asked, "Are you worried about his reaction?"

More than her sister could know. It wasn't just that Cooper had their lives planned for the next forty years, a baby under any circumstances would throw a wrench into those plans. *This* baby . . . All she could manage in answer was, "It's complicated."

"Oh, sweetie." Ainsley put an arm around her. "This is good news, right?"

"It's the worst thing that could happen."

Chapter TWO

Before Ainsley left her, Livie promised she would tell Cooper about the baby. "I just don't want to do it tonight at the party."

"He's going to find out and wonder why you haven't told him."

Just as Ainsley wondered why Olivia hadn't told anyone. As she left to find her other sisters, she couldn't help worrying. How would Cooper take it? And why did she suspect there was more going on than just the pregnancy?

"The vultures are circling," Kat Hamilton said as Ainsley joined her sisters.

"Pardon?" Ainsley said, realizing she'd missed something.

Kat motioned with her head to a spot across the dance floor. "Until that wedding band is on Livie's finger, all's fair in love and war, right?"

She shook her head. "Why can't our sister see it? That woman is trouble."

Ainsley spotted Delia Rollins working her way through the crowd toward Cooper. Delia had been Livie's best friend. She had lived down the road at a small hardscrabble place when they were kids. Buckmaster had seen her one day reaching through the fence to pet one of the horses. He'd insisted that the skinny little thing come down to the ranch so she could learn to ride. She was told she could ride whenever she liked.

She and Livie had hit it off because they both loved horses. They spent most of their childhood on the back of one. They'd made a pact when they were eleven that no matter where their lives took them, they would each be the maid or matron of honor in each other's weddings.

So come the wedding day, Delia would be Livie's maid of honor. Livie had been determined to honor the pact even though she and Delia hadn't been that close since Livie went away to college and Delia stayed to take over her father's lumberyard when he died.

To make the situation worse, Cooper and Delia had dated for a short time before he'd come to work at the ranch—and fallen for Livie.

"Livie says that Delia and Cooper are just good friends," Ainsley said.

Kat mugged a face. "Well, if I was Livie I'd be watching that woman like a hawk."

Bo shook her head. "Livie and Cooper aren't married yet. I say let Delia give it her best shot."

"You can't be serious?" Harper and Cassidy cried almost in unison.

"I'm trying to save our sister any more heartache," Bo said. "Come on, do any of you really think she should marry Cooper Barnett?"

Ainsley followed Bo's gaze across the ballroom to the stand of trees where Livie still sat alone. This was Livie's engagement party and yet she and Cooper hadn't spent five minutes together. Earlier he'd been talking to one of the ranchers, clearly in a heated discussion about buffalo versus cattle. It was a discussion he and their father had knocked heads over many times.

"Let's not forget that he is making her live in that little old cabin of his until he can afford to finish the house he's building," Bo said. "He can't expect her to wait just because his stubborn pride won't allow anyone to help him."

"He's working on the house night and day," Ainsley said. "It won't be that long before they're moved in."

"If they do get married, I give them six months max," Kat said.

"I'm betting they never reach the altar," Bo said.

They looked to Ainsley, the one they all seemed to think was the most levelheaded of them. *If they only knew,* she thought.

"Olivia has loved Cooper since the first day he

hired on at the ranch," she said, even though she'd be the first to admit Livie didn't seem happy.

"That doesn't mean she should marry him," Kat said reasonably. "She's been acting odder than usual lately. Don't tell me you haven't noticed." She glanced at Ainsley. "Has she said anything to you?"

Ainsley shook her head. Livie had always been good at keeping secrets. Ainsley was even better.

She looked to the edge of the party. The old Livie would have been glowing with excitement tonight and kicking up her heels on the dance floor—even with morning sickness. She'd waited for so long to marry Cooper. Even pregnant, she should have been radiant with happiness since this was her engagement party and the wedding wasn't that far off now.

"Maybe she's getting cold feet," Cassidy suggested.

"Not a chance. She's crazy about him," Harper said.

"Did you know Daddy offered Cooper three hundred and sixty acres of prime land on the creek for a wedding present," Bo said as she took a sip of her champagne.

"Let me guess," Ainsley said. "Cooper turned him down flat."

"Yep," Bo said.

"I think Dad admires Cooper for standing up to him," Ainsley said.

Kat shook her head. "Well, I think Cooper's pride will be his downfall."

"If we all don't think they'll ever get married, then why are we here tonight?" Cassidy demanded. The party had been put off until now because their stepmother wanted it outside.

"Because Livie wants to believe she can change Cooper," Bo said. "We're the only ones who know she can't. The wedding isn't going to happen, so I wouldn't get too attached to your bridesmaid dresses if I were you."

"Maybe Cooper will change his mind and make things easier for Livie by taking Daddy's offer of help on the house," Harper suggested.

Ainsley shook her head. "I know Cooper pretty well. He doesn't say something unless he means it. I wouldn't count on him changing his mind."

"Then we should try to talk some sense into her," Harper said. "Maybe if we tell her how we all—"

"It's Livie's engagement party," Ainsley interrupted. "Let her enjoy the night. We can preach to her tomorrow." The others laughed.

"I'll drink to that," Bo said as she flagged down one of the waiters for more champagne. Shoving a glass into each of their hands, she lifted hers. "To Livie, the first to take the plunge. *Maybe.*" They all laughed and drank.

"If they don't get married, it will break Daddy's

heart," Harper said. "Look how happy he is tonight."

"Speaking of *Daddy,*" Kat said. "Does he know yet that you've dropped out of law school?"

All of them looked at Ainsley.

"What?" Harper and Cassidy said in unison.

"I'm taking a break." That was the problem with living in a small town. Everyone knew your business, especially your nosiest sister.

Bo poked her and pointed toward their father. Ainsley recognized the town busybody, Mabel Murphy, talking to Buckmaster an instant before he scowled and looked in her direction.

"I'd say Daddy just got the news," Bo said with a laugh, and threw back another glass of champagne. "As for Livie marrying Cooper . . ." They all followed her gaze to see Delia with her hand on Cooper's arm and in deep conversation. "Delia Rollins is Cooper's Achilles' heel."

It wouldn't be Delia who would keep the wedding from happening, Ainsley thought. Olivia had bigger concerns than Cooper's former girlfriend.

Cooper spotted Olivia sitting alone in the pines and had just started for her when Delia grabbed his arm.

"Dance with the future maid of honor?" she said with a grin.

"I'd love to but I have to find my fiancée. Maybe later."

33

"I'm sure she's around here somewhere. Anyway, you have all night to find her. You might not have all night to dance with me."

He'd always liked Delia. They'd started out as friends when he'd first gotten to town. He wished now he'd left it at that. "Delia," he said, and sighed. The silly game she'd been playing of apparently trying to make Livie jealous was wearing thin for him.

"Come on, there is nothing wrong in two old friends sharing a dance."

"We aren't old friends and you're Livie's maid of honor."

"So I am," she said, and laughed. "I couldn't have been more surprised when she asked me. I'm sure you were, too."

He'd tried to talk Livie out of it. "Why would you do that?" he'd asked when Livie had told him.

"Because she and I were best friends for years. We made a pact when we were eleven to be the maid or matron of honor at each other's weddings."

"Livie, you're not best friends now."

"No, but I wish we could be better friends. I want to put the past behind us."

Now, he said, "Livie takes her promises seriously."

Delia scoffed. "Apparently. We were kids. I was the skinny, scrawny one. We've changed a lot since then," she said, and added with a wink, "as you know."

He removed her hand from his arm. "Like I said, I need to go see my fiancée."

"Promise me one last dance for old times' sake," Delia said.

"Maybe later." At least, he hoped there would be a later at the party. Given the way Livie was behaving, he had his doubts.

Sidestepping Delia, he headed for the stand of pines and his fiancée. From the moment he'd hired on to the Hamilton Ranch, there'd been Olivia. She'd hung around while he was working with the horses. He'd been captivated by her—her smell, her laugh, her intensity when she set her eyes on something she wanted. He'd never known a woman who'd been raised like her and couldn't imagine just snapping his fingers and getting anything he wanted.

He'd told himself to keep his distance. But even with him fighting it, within no time, she consumed all his thoughts, all his time, all his energy. He found her infuriating and irresistible, challenging and charming. He had fallen so hard for her that it scared him.

Unlike Livie, he wasn't impulsive. He planned. He worked hard for what he wanted. He thought things out. Like this engagement and upcoming wedding. Everything had been moving way too fast for him.

From the get-go, though, he'd been reluctant to get involved with a Hamilton girl. The boy from the wrong side of the tracks and a Hamilton? Once he fell for her, he'd wished more times than he wanted to count that she wasn't Buckmaster Hamilton's daughter.

As he approached the bench where she was sitting, he realized with a shock that Olivia was crying. Stepping to her, he knelt down in front of the bench. "Livie, what is it?"

"We have to talk," she said, hurriedly wiping at her tears. "Let's go into the house," she said, getting to her feet. "I thought this could wait, but it can't."

His insides turned to ice. "Livie, tell me what it is."

"Not here," she said, taking his hand and leading him around the edge of the ballroom toward the house. He saw several people at the party looking in their direction, Delia among them.

Delia had tried to warn him when he'd told her he was seeing Livie. "Oh, Cooper, you don't want to get involved with one of them, trust me."

It had been too late. He'd already fallen.

"Livie's not like that."

Delia had laughed. "She's Buckmaster Hamilton's daughter and she will always be his daughter. Do yourself a favor and run as far and fast as you can in the opposite direction." She'd made the same argument he had made to himself. "She isn't like you and me. We know what it's like to be poor, to come from the wrong family and have to pull ourselves up by our bootstraps. She's fascinated with you now because you're different from anyone else she's dated. But when it comes time to get married, she's going to want more than you will ever be able to give her."

Now he feared Delia was right as he and Livie worked their way around the crowd, away from all the noise, to the quiet of the house. "Let's go into Daddy's den. There is something I have to tell you," she said, making his heart begin to ache.

"Tell me what this is about," he demanded as they walked down the empty hallway even though he was afraid he already knew. She'd changed her mind. Just like that. She'd insisted on getting married sooner than he'd wanted, she hadn't been able to wait for the engagement party, and now she'd realized what she was doing and was backing out.

"Do we really have to do this now?" he asked as she led him toward her father's plush, wood-paneled den. He felt himself getting angry. "It's our engagement party, Livie, a party that you and your sisters and father insisted on, you might recall." He balked, stopping in the doorway to the den, digging in his heels as he had so many other times with her. "Just tell me."

Olivia knew the timing was terrible. The thought almost made her laugh. There was no good time for what she had to tell him.

"Would you please close the door and sit down?" she asked impatiently when he remained stubbornly standing in the doorway.

With obvious reluctance, he closed the door and seemed to brace himself. "Just say you don't want to marry me and get it over with. I've been expecting this."

She shook her head in astonishment, her emotions running as wild as the horses Cooper tamed. The man never ceased to amaze her. *"You've been expecting me to break our engagement?"*

"That's what this is about, isn't it? Your father reminded me again tonight that you're a Hamilton and that you require the finer things in life, things that apparently he feels I can't give you fast enough." Cooper's eyes narrowed. "It isn't as if you haven't made it clear you feel the same way."

Livie sighed. Every fight they'd had was over her father's offers of financial help. Buckmaster Hamilton lived for his daughters. He couldn't understand Cooper's stubbornness any more than she could. Coop had refused both land and money, both graciously offered. He was determined to do everything himself, no matter how hard it was or how long it took.

But none of that mattered now because Livie doubted there was going to be a wedding, anyway. "Please. Sit down. That isn't what I need to talk to you about," she said, fighting the ever-present nausea. Her head felt as if it were spinning. The last thing she wanted was to break her engagement, but she figured Cooper would do that once she told him about the note in her purse.

He stood for a moment longer before finally dropping into a chair across from her. Dangling his Stetson on his knee, he said, "Okay, let's have it. I've known something was going on with you for weeks now."

She nodded, although she was surprised. She'd thought she'd kept her secret better than that. "Remember back in late January? We had an argument. I left in the middle of the night not really knowing where I was going."

"I remember *all* of our fights. This one, though, I believe, you threw your engagement ring at me as you left."

She felt her face flame at the memory. If only she could go back . . . If only . . . She swallowed the lump in her throat. Her mouth had gone dust dry. Searching for the right words, she said, "I took a shortcut across the state, thinking I might go to Missoula or Great Falls. I didn't really know."

His dark eyes narrowed as he frowned. "You just took off because you were angry. As I recall, you got caught in a winter storm, went off the road and couldn't get home for several days."

Livie nodded and touched her temple where she had only a faint scar, a reminder of what had happened that night, as if she needed one. Her other scars ran much deeper.

"Where I went off the road was miles from the nearest town. There was no cell phone coverage. If a driver hadn't come along when he did . . ."

"What are you trying to tell me, Olivia?" Cooper asked, his voice dangerously low. His handsome suntanned face had gone pale. As pale and shaken as she felt.

"The driver who helped me . . . took me to his cabin that wasn't far from where I went in the ditch."

His voice dropped to a near-whisper. "You spent the night there?"

She knew she had to get this out as quickly as possible or she wouldn't be able to. For months she'd tried hard to forget. "He called to have my car towed so I'd have it the next morning. He seemed nice . . ."

Cooper was on his feet, his expression stricken. "What *happened?*"

She'd told herself not to break down, but her hormones were out of whack and she was so scared she was going to lose Cooper, the only man she'd ever truly loved, that she couldn't hold back the tears any longer.

"I woke up in his bed. I have no memory of—"

Cooper shook his head as he took a step back. "You *slept* with him."

"It wasn't like that. You have to understand. I

didn't want any of this to happen. If I hadn't been on that road . . ."

He raised a brow. "Are you blaming *me* for this?"

She swallowed. "We've both made mistakes."

He stared at her, his gorgeous face a mask of anger. "Is that what this was? *Payback?*"

"No, it wasn't like that."

"Some man saves you in a blizzard and you end up in his bed—how do you explain that, Livie?"

"That's just it. I can't." She wiped angrily at her tears. She could see herself sitting in the man's cabin, sunken into a deep leather chair in front of the fire, feel the heat of the crackling blaze he'd built, taste the wine on her lips. Red. The glass in her hand glowing like rubies as the music lulled her.

"It must have been the wine."

"The wine?"

"It was just one glass." She remembered him refilling her glass. "Maybe two. I was cold, the fire, the wine, I hadn't eaten . . . and I'd hit my head when I went into the ditch."

Cooper shook his head angrily. "And you don't know how you ended up in his bed." He let out a curse as he turned away from her and rubbed angrily at the back of his neck.

The man *had* seduced her, just not the way Cooper thought. She'd trusted him, believing he'd saved her when all along he must have been planning to do exactly what he'd done. "I think he might have put something in my wine."

"Are you saying he drugged you?" His jaw muscle jumped as he spun back around to look at her. "What else did he do?" Seeing her expression, he let out a curse. "So you called the sheriff, right?" When she said nothing, he let out a bark of a laugh and said, "Wouldn't a woman who'd been drugged and possibly raped have called the sheriff on the bastard?"

"I don't know if he drugged me or if the wine just hit me and I passed out." She shook her head and began to cry again. "I was too embarrassed to do anything but get out of there."

She'd blamed herself for being lured into thinking she was safe with the man. The next morning, she'd found that he'd had her car towed. It was out front, just as he'd promised. She'd quickly grabbed her things and left. Her plan had been to never look back. To never tell anyone, especially Cooper.

She would have taken the secret to her grave.

"You must have at least confronted the man the next morning," he said, studying her with an angry, disappointed intensity that made her squirm.

She hated to admit waking up to find herself not only naked in the man's bed, but discovering him long gone. "He'd already left."

"Left? Without a word? Slam-bam, not even a thank-you-ma'am?"

She said nothing. What could she say? She couldn't explain how comfortable she'd felt in the man's company the night before. How protected. She'd relaxed, let her guard down, drank too much wine on an empty stomach. But how she'd ended up in his bed . . . she didn't know. The drugged part sounded far-fetched, she had to admit. Maybe she just wanted to believe that over the alternative. She could tell Cooper certainly had his doubts about her story.

Cooper was still rubbing his neck, his face filled with anguish. She couldn't bear the pain she was causing him. Suddenly, he froze, his gaze slowly lifting to hers. "Why are you telling me this *now?* Assure me it is only because you don't want to go into the marriage with a lie between us."

She swallowed again, choking back sobs as she tried to pull herself together. When she met his dark eyes, she cringed at the way he was looking at her. "He's blackmailing me."

"*Blackmailing* you?" Cooper let out a curse, then a bitter laugh. "Of course he is. How could I forget for even an instant that you are Buckmaster Hamilton's daughter?" He raked strong fingers through his dark hair. "So if this man wasn't blackmailing you, you would never have told me about this, would you have?"

"I didn't tell you because I wanted to spare you," she cried. "That's why I didn't tell you about the first blackmail demand."

His voice turned deadly. *"First* blackmail demand? Are you telling me you *paid* this man?" He started to turn toward the door as if he had to get out of this room or he wasn't sure what he would do.

"You can't leave." She reached for him, needing to touch him, to feel the connection between them.

"Give me one good reason to stay here right now."

"There's more."

He turned, but took a step back out of her reach. *"More?"* His laugh was harsh. "You get a blackmail note and you don't come to me, the man you say you're going to marry? Of course not. You went to Daddy. You got the money from him, didn't you? Why would you go to the man you say you're going to spend the rest of your life with when you were in trouble?"

"I didn't go to Daddy. I used some of my own money."

"How much?" Cooper asked from between clenched teeth.

"Ten thousand."

"You paid the man who you say possibly drugged and raped you ten thousand dollars rather than come to me with the truth?" Cooper stared at her as if he didn't know her. "And now he wants more, right? What a surprise. The man must have thought he struck oil when you told him your name."

Livie hadn't told him her name, though. She'd given him the name of a friend of hers from college. She'd lied and even now she wasn't sure why she'd done that. She guessed she'd done it because that night she hadn't wanted to be Olivia Hamilton, daughter of Buckmaster Hamilton. And future bride of Cooper Barnett.

Apparently she'd been more angry with Cooper than she'd realized.

When she'd gotten the first note, she'd wondered how the man had found out the truth until she realized how easy it would have been for him to check her driver's license while she was asleep. Or knocked out.

As if suddenly too exhausted to stand, Cooper lowered himself into a chair. He looked defeated. She watched him drop his head to his hands for a moment before he looked up at her. She couldn't bear the pain in his eyes. "You didn't trust me to help you. *Livie,*" he said with a shake of his head.

The way he said her name was a knife to her heart. No matter what he thought right now, she loved him and couldn't imagine a life without him.

"How could you be so naive?" Cooper sighed. "Give me the blackmail note."

She reached into her clutch and handed him the envelope.

He opened it carefully as if to not get any more fingerprints on it than was necessary. His gaze flew up to hers when he saw the amount her blackmailer was now demanding. *"Fifty thousand dollars?* When did you get this?"* He didn't give her a chance to answer, as if he'd already read the answer on her face. "Today. That's why you had to tell me the night of our engagement party."

"I didn't tell you because I hated that I'd been duped like that. All this is my fault. I wanted to fix it myself. Also I was afraid you would never forgive me."

He pocketed the blackmail note and stood as if to leave.

"What are you going to do?" she asked, suddenly scared.

"I'll take the blackmail demand to the sheriff in the morning and let him handle this."

"You can't do that."

He turned back to her, his eyes narrowing again. "Why is that? Wait," he said. "Because of the bad publicity for your father, right? Can't have any of that for our next president."

"It's not just that." Being the daughter of a senator, she knew what bad publicity would do to her father's political career. But right now it wasn't her father she was worried about.

She had to tell Cooper everything, but her heart broke at the thought of dealing him the final blow. She didn't know what he would do. Or what she would do. "I'm pregnant."

Cooper looked as if she'd hit him with a sledgehammer. "But we were being so careful." His features suddenly softened as if he'd dreamed of the day when she would be pregnant with his baby. Then he froze, his face transforming into a mask of shock and disbelief as he realized what she was telling him. *"His baby?"*

Her words fell like stones. "I can't be sure."

Cooper let out an inhuman sound that tore at her heart. She reached for him again, but he side-stepped to avoid her touch.

"Please, don't walk away," she pleaded. "You have to understand—"

"I *do* understand. If it wasn't for the blackmail, you would never have told me any of this." He let out a curse. "You would have let me believe it was my baby."

"No, I wouldn't have. You have to know me better than that."

He shook his head, his look saying he didn't know her at all.

"I'm so sorry," she said, crying again. "I'm so sorry."

As he walked away, the echo of his footfalls sounded like a death knell. She'd destroyed everything. When the door slammed, she feared she'd never see him again.

Cooper stumbled outside, blind with pain. He hadn't known where he was going. Even when he reached the corrals, he didn't remember how he'd gotten there. Out here with the horses was where he'd always been at home so it didn't surprise him this is where his footsteps had led him.

He fought to catch his breath, feeling as if he'd been kicked in the chest by one of his wild horses. He could still hear music coming from behind the house, the engagement party continuing even without the future bride and groom. The future bride and groom. The thought threatened to rip out his heart.

It all felt like a bad dream. He felt poleaxed, incapable of rational thought or even movement. He stood, his face turned up to the billions of stars twinkling in the vast sky overhead and yet he saw nothing. This wasn't happening.

Olivia's confession had knocked him down. He'd known something was wrong, but he'd never imagined . . .

He cursed himself for falling in love with his boss's daughter. All his life he'd kept his distance from women like the Hamilton girls. Everyone in the county knew about them, beautiful but pampered and protected by their doting father, the great Buckmaster Hamilton. No man would ever be good enough for his daughters.

While Cooper had known all this, Livie had gotten under his skin. No matter how hard he'd tried to keep her at a distance, she'd still gotten to him. The rancher's daughter and the hired hand. What made it even worse was his family background. He'd worked so hard to prove that he was not only his own man, but that he wasn't like his family. That he was worthy. But worthy enough to marry a Hamilton?

He let out a bitter laugh at the thought.

To make matters worse, no one here even knew about his family and yet they all thought he was marrying Olivia for her father's money. It infuriated him. He'd turned down Buckmaster's gifts not just to prove everyone wrong, but also because he didn't want to be indebted to the man.

Now he wasn't sure which part of Livie's devastating news hurt the most. The bottom line was that she hadn't trusted him enough to tell him the truth when it had happened or even later when she'd gotten the first blackmail note and decided to take care of it herself rather than come to him.

But the pregnancy . . . He closed his eyes and tried to breathe. From the moment he'd fallen in love with Livie, he'd dreamed of the day they would have children. He'd seen himself with his hand on her swollen belly, imagined the feel of their child moving beneath it . . . *Their* child.

Not a blackmailer's and possible rapist's.

Now the bastard was demanding fifty thousand dollars? Cooper sure as hell didn't have it—as if he would ever consider paying it even if he did. Buckmaster would pay, though. Hell, he probably wouldn't even miss that amount. But Livie would ask her father for the money and pay the black-mailer over Cooper's dead body. He'd take care of the blackmailer himself.

But the baby . . . The ache in his chest made it impossible to breathe at even the thought of her carrying someone else's child.

At a sound behind him, he turned, expecting it would be Livie, the last person he wanted to see right now. Didn't she know him well enough to know that now wasn't the time?

"There you are," Delia Rollins said as she materialized out of the darkness. "I wondered where you'd gone off to. You promised me one last dan—" The rest of her words died on her lips when she saw his face. "What's happened?"

There was both worry and hope in those words. Delia had been his friend from the first time they'd met at the lumberyard. He'd liked her, sensing that they shared a similar background even before he'd heard about *her* family. Everyone in town said that the lumberyard would have gone under years ago if it hadn't been for Delia taking it over.

"Cooper? What's wrong?" she said, grabbing at him as he turned away. She caught the hem of his jacket. He didn't see the blackmail note fall from his pocket as he turned his back on her. Delia was the last thing he needed right now because it would have been too easy to turn to her for comfort.

"What is this?" Delia said behind him. He

turned as she held up a sheet of pale blue paper, squinting to read it in the ambient light of the ranch yard lamp. *"Cooper, who's blackmailing you?"*

"It's not mine," he said as he took it from her.

"Not yours?" Her eyes widened as she looked at the envelope she'd taken the paper out of—and the name printed on it. "Someone is blackmailing Olivia? Why?" She let out a curse under her breath as he took the envelope from her. "What has she done to you now?"

"Delia, please. I don't want to talk about this," he said as he put the blackmail note back into his jacket pocket.

"Someone is demanding fifty thousand dollars? How can you not talk about it? What are you going to do? You don't have that kind of money."

"I'm not *paying* the blackmailer and neither is Livie or her father. Delia, let it drop. I'm sorry you saw the note. You can't say anything about it."

She stepped closer. "You know I would help you any way I could."

He caught a whiff of her perfume, the familiar smell tugging at him. Drunk and angry, he'd made the mistake of going to Delia after a fight with Livie early on in their relationship. Things between him and Delia had always been easy—unlike his relationship with Livie. Delia accepted him for who he was. But that moment of weakness had almost cost him Livie.

He couldn't make that mistake again, even though it would have been easy right now to turn to a woman who understood him in a way he feared clearly Livie never could. Fortunately, he recognized how vulnerable he was right now, as vulnerable as he'd ever been.

He looked into Delia's concerned face and shook his head. "I can't," he said, pulling away from her comforting touch. It would be too easy to let her salve the poison bite of Livie's betrayal.

"If you ever need someone to talk to . . ."

He nodded, telling himself the worst thing he could do was compound his and Livie's problems by taking Delia up on her offer. Turning, he headed for his pickup. When he reached it, he looked back to see her watching after him.

Glancing at the house, he saw Livie standing at the window. She was crying, something he'd only seen her do once before tonight when her colt had died. That time, he'd taken her in his arms and held her. He hadn't been able to bear seeing her in pain like that.

He hesitated now, desperately wanting to go back, dry her tears, hold this woman he loved. What if it was true that some man drugged and raped her? What if none of this was her fault? How could he turn away from her?

If only she'd come to him right after it had happened. If only she had trusted him. If only he didn't suspect that there was more to her story than she was telling him. If it was true, what she'd said, then why did she act so guilty?

She must have seen his hesitation. Hope seemed to bloom in her beautiful face in the instant before he saw her hand go protectively to her belly. The baby. His heart broke all over again.

Chapter THREE

Livie had tried to call Cooper last night and again this morning. The calls had gone straight to voice mail. That's why she was so surprised when she heard his old pickup pull up out front.

In an attempt to keep his grown daughters close, Buckmaster had what he called bunkhouses built a few hundred yards from the main house. Each was a separate apartment with a communal living space as fancy as the main house.

Livie was the only one still living there with the twins away at college, Ainsley in law school, Kat living most of her time out of a tent on one of her many photo shoots and Bo in a small apartment in one of the historical buildings along the main drag of Big Timber.

Livie liked being on the ranch since she rode her horse most days. Also she liked being close to Cooper, who was the ranch's head wrangler and horse trainer.

At the sound of his pickup, she grabbed her

robe. She heard his pickup door slam and, a moment later, his insistent knock at her door. Quickly finger brushing her hair, she braced herself. She couldn't help being half hopeful and half terrified as to what this early morning visit meant.

As she opened the door, she knew what she must look like. Like a woman who'd just awakened, her hair a mess, her face still soft from sleep—the way he'd seen her numerous times when he'd awakened next to her.

Cooper stood on the front step, a scowl on his face, until he looked at her. For a moment, something familiar flickered in his dark gaze. Desire. But that moment of weakness quickly passed. "Come on," he said, his voice rough as if the desire had left his expression but it hadn't gone far.

She realized he might be planning to drag her down to the sheriff's office. She'd known Sheriff Frank Curry since she was a toddler. Her face heated at the thought of having to tell him her story. "Where are we—"

"Let's go find the bastard. Get dressed. I'll be waiting in the truck." He didn't give her a chance to speak before he turned and stalked off.

She watched him go back to his pickup, her aching need to be held by him an unbearable pain in her chest. She hadn't even been sure she would ever see him again. But what he'd suggested, going after the blackmailer . . . He couldn't be serious.

Livie hurriedly pulled on a pair of designer jeans, a light cotton rust-colored sweater and her cowboy boots. She knew she didn't have time for makeup so she quickly brushed her teeth and her hair, dabbed on some lip gloss and left.

As she climbed into the passenger's side of his pickup, she said, "I don't think this is good idea."

He cocked his head, eyeing her in a way that told her he was still furious with her and equally as hurt and disappointed. "How would you suggest we handle this?"

She didn't dare admit that she had thought about paying the blackmailer off. She wasn't naive. She knew that the man would try to bleed her dry. But now he had nothing to hold over her head. She'd heard her father negotiate all kinds of deals in his lifetime. Livie was sure she could make a deal so she would never hear from the man again.

But it would have meant going to her father since it was going to take more than fifty thousand dollars to be rid of him. She knew how Cooper felt about all of it so that option wasn't on the table.

"It's just that it could be dangerous," she managed to say under his intent gaze.

He laughed, surprising her. "Honey, before I became the man who was to marry Olivia Hamilton, I was capable of taking care of myself.

I can take care of you, too, for that matter. If you should ever decide to trust me." With that he turned the key. The old pickup's engine rumbled to life and he backed out, kicking up fresh gravel.

Livie bristled. She knew he thought her an over-indulged debutante, but there was more to her than just being Buckmaster Hamilton's daughter and damned if she wasn't going to prove it to him. If he gave her the chance.

Nettie Benton Curry, the new bride of Sheriff Frank Curry, had a problem that had been eating at her for days. If she didn't talk to someone about it soon, she thought she might burst. What surprised her was that there was only one person she could tell. That seemed shocking given that she had spent most of her sixty-some years spreading gossip. She was good at it. She listened, she watched, she knew things that other people didn't and she liked to share it.

But the one thing she'd never really had was a close friend she could confide in who would keep *her* secrets.

That's why it was ironic when she realized the only person she could tell was her old nemesis, Kate LaFond. Kate, now Kate French, was a good thirty years younger than her. Not that the age difference was the problem.

When Kate had come to town, Nettie had spent weeks spying on the woman, convinced that Kate was hiding something. Of course, she was, and Nettie had been bound and determined to get to the bottom of it.

What was surprising was that since the secrets had come out, Kate had become a . . . friend.

So now, unable to keep what she'd done to herself any longer, Nettie stopped by the Branding Iron Café to see its owner. It was late enough that the first round of ranchers who sat at the large table at the front was gone. Only a few touristy-looking people were still having breakfast.

The old mining town and near-ghost town of Beartooth was seeing a revival of sorts. The general store had been rebuilt as it was before the fire that destroyed it last year and work was continuing on the old hotel. It would never be like it was back in the late 1800s when it was a gold boomtown. But now it had a post office, café, store, bar and hotel.

What few other buildings remained were deserted, standing empty, the window glass long gone, leaving black holes where windowpanes had once kept out the elements. On the way out of town there was evidence of an old gas station with two pumps under a hip roof. Next to it, a classic auto garage from a time when it didn't take a computer to work on a car engine.

No one passed through Beartooth. It was as far off the road as a town could be. The pavement ended at the north end of town. From there a dirt road wound up into the mountains to fork off into numerous old logging or mining roads.

So it was amazing to Nettie and most residents that a few tourists were already trickling into town even though the hotel wasn't up and running just yet. But the general store was busier than usual.

Kate saw Nettie come into the café and motioned her to a booth out of the way. Nettie had just sat down when Kate appeared with two cups, a coffeepot and one of her large homemade cinnamon rolls. She put the roll in front of Nettie along with a fork and poured them both coffee before sitting down.

Nettie took a bite of the cinnamon roll. It was still warm, butter and icing dripping off the sides. Kate knew that she liked the center cuts because they were the gooiest.

"How are you feeling?" Nettie asked, now not sure she could bring up the subject that had caused her so many sleepless nights.

"Good," Kate said, grinning as she placed a hand over her huge belly. "Any day now. I'm trying to come up with names. Jack is no help. He wants to name her Falcon or River or Sunshine." She shook her head, laughing.

"You aren't working too much, are you?" Nettie asked in alarm. She knew that Kate had had several miscarriages in the past.

"I'm not working at all, really. I just can't stay

away from this place. That's why I'm glad you came in to visit this morning." She frowned. "Isn't it your day off at the store?"

Nettie had once not only owned Beartooth General Store with her former husband, but also she'd run it for years. When it had burned down, she'd sold out, lock, stock and barrel, but before long she'd missed working there. Fortunately, a local benefactor was behind the rebuilding of the town and had offered Nettie a part-time job.

"So if you're not working today . . ." Kate eyed Nettie. "What's wrong?"

Nettie started to deny that anything was bothering her, but saved her breath. "I did something." She glanced around to make sure no one was listening. "It's about Tiffany."

Like everyone else in four counties, Kate knew about Sheriff Frank Curry's daughter, Tiffany. The seventeen-year-old girl had shown up to surprise the father who hadn't known she even existed. The surprise was that she'd come to Beartooth to kill him after being brainwashed by her hateful mother.

"You know Tiffany is still locked up at the state mental hospital," Nettie said, and Kate nodded, waiting for what she didn't know. "The state did some testing when Tiffany was sent up there to see if she was competent to stand trial. They also did a DNA test and they sent Frank the results. I mean, his ex, Pam, was such a liar . . . What were the chances that she'd even lied about Tiffany being his child?"

"So is she?" Kate asked in a whisper.

"Well, that's just it. Frank never opened the envelope with the results in them."

"Nettie, what did you do?" Kate asked even though from her expression she already knew.

She sighed. "I found the envelope. I know I shouldn't have—"

Kate held up her hand. "Don't tell me. And you can't tell Frank, either. If he wanted to know, he would have looked."

"He's always felt responsible since the child was Pam's as far as we know and her hatred of him made Tiffany the way she is, so he didn't care if Tiffany was his or not."

"I know he feels guilty, but he shouldn't," Kate said. "Maybe Pam did poison the girl against Frank. But as psycho as Pam was, some of that also could be genetic in Tiffany."

"It still doesn't help my problem," Nettie said with a groan. "I wish I'd never opened that envelope. I don't know what I was thinking."

Kate smiled and reached across the table to cover her hand. "We both know what you were thinking. You wanted to know the truth. Now you do. And now you're going to have to take it to your grave." She met Nettie's gaze. "You know your husband. If the results of that test got out after he specifically didn't want to know . . ."

Nettie nodded. "But he held on to the envelope. If he really hadn't wanted to know, he would have destroyed it, right?"

"Where is Frank now?" Kate asked, clearly having guessed.

"He's gone up to the mental hospital to see Tiffany—just as he does every week," Nettie said with a shudder. "And every week that girl scares the bejesus out of him and breaks his heart just a little more."

There was little conversation on the drive north. Cooper stared straight ahead, his large sun-browned hands on the wheel. He'd dressed in a chambray shirt and jeans, both worn, a straw cowboy hat on his head and scuffed boots that looked as old as his pickup.

She suspected he'd purposely dressed like the working man he was not just to show her but also the man he would be confronting. He wore his blue-collar background like a chip on his shoulder. What he didn't seem to realize was how proud she was of him. While he'd never told her much about his family background, she gathered that he'd often gone to bed hungry as a child. She also knew that he'd never had much. It was one reason he took pride in the cabin he'd built shortly after going to work for her father. She loved him because of it, not in spite of his background that had made him the man he was.

A wave of nausea hit her. She concentrated on the scenery, surprised she hadn't noticed how everything had greened up after the long winter. Nor had she realized what a beautiful day it was. The vast Montana sky was a deep blue, making the cumulus clouds over the mountains even whiter. The peaks were still snowcapped and would be through most of the summer months at high altitude. It was a sight she'd never tired of.

Livie breathed in the day, trying not to fidget. The thought of coming face-to-face with the man who'd rescued her last winter made her anxious, and not just because she feared what the man might do.

She looked over at Cooper. Just the sight of him always made her smile and her heart lift as if filled with helium. Her love for him was a constant ache that often left her feeling breathless. She wanted this man, needed this man, didn't think she could live without him. What he didn't understand was that she would have followed him to the ends of the earth.

It was her father who'd balked at the thought of her marrying him before the house Cooper was building for them was finished. Daddy had wanted her to have a brand-new house as a wedding present, which of course Cooper had refused. Her sisters had chimed in. That was the problem with having five sisters like hers.

"Seriously?" Kat had asked. "You won't last a

week in that tiny cabin before you come home. When is he going to have your new house finished?"

"I don't know. Doing it all himself takes time. You know how he is."

"Where would you put all your stuff?" Harper had wanted to know.

Even Ainsley, who seemed to like Cooper, asked, "Is he just trying to make a point by insisting on doing it all himself?"

"Of course he is," Bo had butt in.

Livie had stood up for Cooper, saying, "He wanted us to wait to get married until he had the house finished. I'm the one who doesn't want to wait any longer. I will be fine in the cabin. This way, I can have more input on the house."

Her sisters had exchanged a look. Cooper's stubborn pride was legendary at the ranch and even her sisters thought he was wrong.

If only living in a tiny rustic cabin for a while was her biggest problem, she thought now as she looked out the pickup window. For weeks, she'd been playing the "if-only" game. If only she and Cooper hadn't fought. If only she hadn't taken off that night into the storm. If only . . .

Sometimes she couldn't breathe she was so scared that she was going to lose him. Now, though, she was more afraid *for* him. Afraid not only what the man who rescued her would do— but say. What if he told them she had initiated the

63

sex that night? What if Cooper believed it? Worse, what if it was true since she couldn't remember what had happened?

"I don't know what you have planned," she said tentatively. "But I'm worried about you."

He shot her a look. "Don't worry about me. After everything you told me at our engagement party, how much worse could it get?"

"He could shoot you." This was Montana. Homeowners owned guns and knew how to use them. "I just don't want to see you get hurt."

Cooper let out a bitter laugh. "Nothing could hurt me any worse than I'm hurting right now. Unless there's something more you haven't told me."

She shook her head, her gaze going back to the blur of pine trees out her side window. They weren't far from the spot where she'd gone off the road. Like that night, she hadn't seen another vehicle in miles. No houses. Nothing but wild Montana country.

"Then let's just see what this man has to say for himself," Cooper said.

"The turn is up here just past that bridge." Livie saw the area as it had been that January night—covered with snow—even though spring had come here. Only a few snow piles melted under the shade of the pines. It was a different kind of cold that settled inside her as Cooper slowed to turn.

· · ·

As he drove, Cooper thought back to Livie's return after that January fight. She'd been distant. He recalled that when they'd finally gotten together, she'd wanted the light out when they'd made love. His heart sank. What if she was telling the truth and this man had drugged and raped her?

It was what she wasn't telling him that made him doubt her. He knew this woman too well. Whatever she was keeping from him weighed on him. He needed to know, and yet he feared it would be his undoing.

He also knew he should have gone to the sheriff and let him handle this. He'd considered doing that, but only for an instant. He had to handle this himself. He couldn't face himself if he didn't. He needed to look this bastard in the eyes before he beat the crap out of him. But, of course, he also had his reasons for not wanting to go to the law for help. Going to the sheriff would be a last resort and one that he knew he would regret.

Following Livie's directions, he turned up a mountain road with a sign that read Private. He could see nothing ahead but trees with a towering peak as a backdrop. Private road?

Livie had said the man took her to his cabin in the middle of nowhere. It was definitely in the middle of nowhere, all right. He thought of his own cabin, the one he and Livie had planned to live in until the house he was building was finished. His cabin was small, neatly laid out, because he'd built it himself, but it was primitive compared to how Livie had always lived. And yet, he was proud of it. The cabin sat on the first land he'd ever owned.

So he was expecting a cabin much like his own as he came around a bend in the road. But what came into view through the pines wasn't anyone's idea of a cabin, except maybe a Hamilton. The rambling huge structure was log—that much was true. But other than that, the dwelling was as ostentatious as any he'd seen, except, of course, the main house on the Hamilton Ranch.

Cooper shot a look at Livie. She was staring at the house as if seeing it for the first time. Or seeing it through his eyes, a man who'd grown up dirt poor in the true sense of the words. He was half hoping she would say they'd made a wrong turn and that this wasn't the "cabin."

But he could tell by her anxious expression that there had been no wrong turn. This was the place the man had brought her to that night in January.

Livie had often accused him of having a chip on his shoulder when it came to anyone with a lot of money. He'd always denied it, even to himself, until now. Seeing this place, he hated this man even more than he thought possible.

Cooper parked next to the owner's large black shiny new SUV. Cutting the engine, he sat looking at the massive front door of the "cabin" and realized he'd done something he'd always prided himself on never doing. He'd lied to Livie. He was scared as hell to meet this man, fearing that what waited beyond that door could kill him. Not the way Livie thought. Hell, at this point he'd almost welcome a bullet.

His greatest fear was that Livie had wanted the man behind this door. Wanted what even a stranger had to offer over what Cooper could give her.

"Let's get this over with," he said, and climbed out.

Livie tried to still her trembling as she opened her pickup door and stepped out. Her legs felt like water under her. She wobbled, light-headed and nauseous, and prayed she could hold it together.

It was colder up here in the mountains, but her real cold was the ice that had compressed her heart at the thought of what could happen in the next few minutes. She shouldn't have let Cooper come up here. Not that she had a choice. Had she refused, he would have thought she was protecting the man.

She crossed her arms over her chest. She could do this. She was Olivia Hamilton, a woman who prided herself on her strength and determination. She could face this man who was set on destroying her life.

And yet, she had lived in fear of what had really happened that night for the past three months.

There was no doubt that the man had seduced her. He'd rescued her, brought her to his beautiful home, made her feel grateful and protected. The truth was, he'd lulled her into a feeling of security with his graciousness and his beautiful home. Not to mention his expensive wine.

She'd fallen into his trap because she was Olivia Hamilton, the pampered, protected daughter of Senator Buckmaster Hamilton. It never dawned on her that he might want something from her. In her relief at being rescued, she'd trusted a total stranger because he had looked the part and had said and done all the right things—at least until she'd passed out.

That's why she blamed herself.

For months she'd regretted taking off her engagement ring and storming out that night. If only she could go back . . . If only . . . At the back of her mind—and she knew Cooper's, as well— was the question. Had the wine been drugged or was that her way of deceiving herself?

Cooper, his back ramrod straight, mounted the steps to the huge wooden door. He grabbed the bear-shaped knocker and pounded hard on the door. No sound came from inside. He pounded again. Still it took a few minutes before the door opened.

Chapter FOUR

Livie thought she was braced for when the man opened the door. But she was wrong.

The man who stood on the threshold was taller than the man who'd rescued her that night. He was also heavier and more full in the face, less athletic in build and a good thirty years his senior. He wore a cable-knit sweater over jeans that had the hems rolled up to expose boat shoes. Everything about him, including the expensive watch on his wrist, said privilege and money—just like the man who'd rescued her.

"Yes?" he said as he took in first Cooper and then her before returning his gaze to her companion.

"Is this him?" Cooper asked, looking over at her as if nothing would surprise him.

This man was old enough to be her father. "No," she said, a little too defensive. She was still reeling from the fact that she'd never seen this man before in her life. For a moment she'd thought she had the wrong house. Then she looked past him into the living room. No mistake. This was the house—just not the man.

"We're looking for the owner of the house," Cooper said.

"I'm the owner. What is this about?" the man asked.

Knowing that Cooper wasn't leaving until they got answers, Livie said, "We're sorry to bother you, but may we come in for a moment?"

A woman appeared at the man's elbow. She was Livie's age, yoga-class slim, blonde and classically pretty, dressed in jeans and a pale blue sweater. What struck Livie was that there was something vaguely familiar about her. The daughter of the man she'd met?

Livie realized her mistake as the woman put a possessive hand on the man's arm, her huge diamond glinting on her ring finger.

"Howard?" the woman asked as she eyed Livie and Cooper with concern. "Is anything wrong?"

"If you can give me a minute," Livie said. "I would be happy to explain why we're here."

Neither moved.

"Who was staying in this house this past winter?" Cooper demanded, cutting to the chase. "That's the person we need to speak with."

Howard frowned. "No one was staying here. The house was closed up for the season. I think you have the wrong—"

"There *was* a man staying here the end of January," Cooper said.

Livie quickly explained. "My car went off the road in a snowstorm and the man brought me here."

"That's impossible. It couldn't have been this

house," Howard said, and started to close the door on them.

"I'm Olivia Hamilton from Beartooth," she said as Cooper reached to stop the man from closing the door. "I know this all sounds—"

"*Hamilton?* From Beartooth, Montana?" The man studied her. "By any chance are you related to . . ."

"Senator Buckmaster Hamilton?" Cooper said with a slight chuckle. "She's his daughter." He said it in a way that made clear he hadn't meant it as a compliment.

The man quickly brightened and stepped aside. "I know your father. A fine man. I was so glad to hear that he's running for president. I'm sorry, please come in. I can't imagine how I can help, but I'll certainly try."

Cooper put his hand in the middle of her back to urge her forward. His touch, while fleeting, sent a pleasurable shiver through her. She realized with a longing that this was the first time he'd touched her since her confession.

"Your daddy said his name could open doors for me," Cooper whispered next to her ear as they entered the house. "I guess he was right."

The interior of the "cabin" was as opulent as Cooper had expected after seeing the exterior. No expense had been spared. He could understand how Livie would have felt at home here. She would have felt safe because this was what she was used to, only the best of everything.

"I'm Howard Wellesley," the man said, extending his hand. "And this is my wife, Amelia."

"Cooper Barnett," he said, taking the man's hand.

When he said no more, next to him, Livie added, "Cooper is my fiancé."

Both Howard and Amelia offered congratulations and invited them into the living room. The open-concept living room and kitchen made the room with its high log ceilings feel even larger.

"Could we offer you something to drink?" Howard asked after they were seated in the leather chairs in front of the fireplace.

When they declined, Amelia said, "I met your father last summer. It was at a party not far from here."

"Small world," Cooper said under his breath, not surprised the Wellesleys would know Buckmaster.

"Yes," Howard said. "As a matter of fact, he came back here for drinks after." He waited a heartbeat, then asked, "Now what is this about someone using our cabin last winter?"

Cooper noticed Livie looking around. She was pale, as if she might be sick at any moment. His heart went out to her before he remembered where they were and why, and also that the baby might not be his.

Howard cleared his throat to get Livie's attention.

Startled out of her thoughts, she looked up. Cooper could see that she was reliving that night. With that other man. He ground his teeth.

"I'm sorry, what did you ask?" Livie said, and then told Howard that she'd changed her mind. She would love a glass of water if it wasn't too much trouble. The trophy wife stepped into the kitchen and returned with a glass of wine for herself and a crystal glass filled with water and ice for Livie.

Cooper watched Livie take a drink, seeing how upset she was. What was she remembering? When she finally spoke, though, her voice was controlled.

"As I told you, my car went off the road near here. A man driving an SUV much like the one parked outside rescued me and brought me here. He led me to believe that he owned this house."

"I can't understand this." Howard glanced to his wife, who was looking intently at her freshly manicured fingernails. "The cabin was closed up for the winter. At least, I thought it was. This happened in January, you say?"

"The twenty-seventh."

Amelia looked up from her nails. "I'm sorry, but I have to ask. Why are you concerned about it now, months later?"

"The man who used your cabin is blackmailing Olivia," Cooper said. "I came here to put a stop to it. I have to assume that whoever he is, he knows you. Perhaps a relative or a friend who knew you would be gone?"

"No, no," Howard said, clearly insulted that Cooper could suggest such a thing. "No one I know, let alone am related to, would be involved in blackmail. That's preposterous. What did this person say his name was?"

Livie couldn't help remembering. The living room looked exactly as it had that night. The fire crackled in the large rock fireplace. The deep leather chair next to the fire had the same feel to it as she had sunk into it now.

Mostly, she remembered being so relieved and grateful to be out of the storm. She could have frozen to death in her car if he hadn't come along when he did.

What scared her was that her life outside of Beartooth, Montana, had seemed so far away that night. Was that also why she'd lied about her name? Or had she just wanted to be someone else that night and not think about Cooper and their problems? For weeks, she'd felt exhausted by their arguments, his stubbornness and her hurt that he wouldn't give an inch. She'd been so tired of making excuses for him to her family.

As she now took in the room, she knew why she'd felt safe here and she figured Cooper did, too. She would have been comfortable here because it was what she'd grown up with. And she'd trusted the man because she'd thought they'd had that in common.

Why hadn't she sensed that things weren't what they seemed? Or had the man who'd pretended to own the house also wanted to be someone else that night?

She could feel Cooper's gaze on her. She'd seen the way he'd taken in the cozy scene in front of the fireplace. From his expression, she knew what he was seeing—her here with another man.

And it had all been a lie from the start.

Add to that the connection between the Wellesleys and her father. They had not only met him in this area of Montana, but also had him back to this very house for drinks. It all seemed surreal and yet too real. Her father had always warned his daughters about people who might want to take advantage of them because of who they were. No, she thought now. Because of who *he* was.

"Howard asked you what the man's name was," Cooper said, bringing her out of her reverie. It surprised her that Cooper wasn't the one who'd asked before this. Apparently he hadn't cared. Not that she'd thought the name would have meant anything to him since it hadn't her.

"Hank Wells." It sounded as fake as it probably was now that she'd said it out loud. So why hadn't she questioned it that night?

To her surprise, Howard gasped.

"You know him?" she asked.

"Hank Wells was the name I went by when I played in a band," he said.

"It was a long time ago," Amelia said as if she'd heard the story too many times. "The band only played a few years and hardly anyone has ever heard of them since they had only one minor hit."

One minor hit? "The man played me a song. He said he wrote it for the band. 'Wandering Ways'?" Livie asked.

"Appropriate," Cooper said under his breath.

"That was it," Howard said, and Amelia took a drink of her wine. He had paled and now appeared even more upset and confused. "I don't understand this."

Livie hadn't noticed the beat-up inexpensive guitar in the corner until that moment. "That guitar . . ." She got to her feet. The battered guitar had seemed out of place that night, so much so that she'd asked the man about it.

Howard started to say something, but quickly rose to hurry over and take the guitar from her, as if it was a priceless vase.

"The guitar . . ." She looked to Howard in confusion. "It's *yours?*"

"It's my first guitar," he said, his expression softening with both self-depreciation and fondness. "It was all I could afford at the time. I spent many hours playing this when I used to travel with . . ."

"The Sidewinders," Livie said.

Howard nodded slowly as he put the guitar back where it had been.

"The man who brought me here told me about the band and what it was like traveling from town to town playing noisy bars." She could feel Cooper's gaze on her.

"What did this man look like?" Howard demanded as he took his seat again on the couch next to his wife.

Livie described him. Blond, blue eyes. So different from Cooper with his dark hair and eyes. "He was tall, athletic, mid to late thirties." What she didn't say was that his thick hair curled at the nape of his neck, that his eyes were a deep blue that invited her into his confidence, that when he talked or sang, his voice was low and soft, making her think he'd known sorrow.

She'd felt close to him that night with the storm raging outside. It was as if the two of them were the only people left in the world, she thought with an inward shudder. A part of her *had* been attracted to the man. The admission rattled her to her core. She might never know what she did that night.

"Handsome, I take it?" Howard asked.

Livie merely nodded, aware of her fiancé watching her closely, reading more into her words than she wished. Cooper had his head cocked to the side in a way that told her he wasn't just angry, he was hurting.

But neither of them could leave things as they were. They had to know who the man was and stop the blackmail, even if they could do nothing about the past.

"Was he one of your band members?" Even as she asked it, she wondered about the age difference.

Howard shook his head.

"That's a pretty generic description," Amelia said. "It could be anyone."

"But it *wasn't* just anyone," Cooper said, his voice sounding cold and hard as the granite rock on the fireplace. "It's someone who had access to your . . . cabin, probably that rig out front and your husband's guitar and the stories that go with it, not to mention the hit song."

Howard glanced over at his wife. A look passed between them. Livie could feel the increased tension in the room.

"Look, you have to know this man," Cooper said, "since he knew his way around your house, where to find your good wine." Howard winced at that. "And he appears to have made himself at home."

"I can't explain this," the husband said in exasperation. "I have no idea who this man might have been."

Amelia got up to refill her wineglass. "It's obviously someone who's been to one of your parties and heard your band stories you're always telling, Howard."

"Who has a key to your house?" Cooper asked. "He did open the door with a key, didn't he?" he asked, and looked over at Livie.

She had never seen Cooper's eyes so dark. He shifted in his chair with obvious impatience. She tried to remember that night, a night she'd spent the past three months fighting to forget. She had seen the man open the door with a key, hadn't she? Or had he only pretended to? She'd been hurt, cold and still shaken and scared from going off the road in the storm. Looking back, she'd been more vulnerable than she'd known.

"I can't be sure. I thought he did," she said finally.

"This man told you he owned the house?" Amelia demanded. She'd come back into the room with a fresh glass of wine, but she hadn't taken her seat next to her husband on the couch again.

Had he? "I guess he only let me believe he owned the house." She realized with a start that the reason Howard's wife had looked so familiar was because she'd seen her before. There had been a photograph of her on the mantel that night. Just as there was now. The man hadn't said the photo was of his wife, but he'd let her believe it was. Just as he'd let her believe he'd lent her his wife's clothes since hers had blood on them from the wound on her temple.

Without thinking, she touched the small scar. Her fingers felt as if she'd burned them as she recalled the gentle way the man had cleaned the wound and put a bandage on it.

"Who was watching your place?" Cooper asked as he got to his feet. "I'm sure you have a caretaker. I think it's time to talk to him." The husband still looked confused. "If your caretaker was doing his job, then wouldn't he have known someone was using the house?"

"My thought exactly since he certainly never mentioned it to me," Howard said as he rose again from the couch. "This is all so . . . upsetting." He started toward the door where some winter coats hung along a wall; the hooks were the hooves of elk. He pulled down a quilted down coat. "My caretaker lives up the road. If you want to stay here—"

"We'll follow you," Cooper said, giving none of them a choice.

Howard stopped at the door to look back at his wife for a moment. Then he pushed out the door, pulling his coat around him, and headed for his SUV, Cooper and Livie at his heels.

Cooper felt himself seething as he slid behind the wheel of his pickup. He'd been expecting a fistfight. Never in his life had he dreamed things would go like this.

"So he played you a song on the guitar," he said without looking at Livie as she buckled up her seat belt.

She said nothing.

"Cozy little cabin, by the way." When he finally did look over at her, her eyes were filled with tears. He swore under his breath. As Howard's SUV roared to life and took off down the road, he followed the Suburban a short distance until the brake lights flashed and Howard swung to a stop in front of a modular home tucked back into the pines.

Glancing back the way they'd come as he parked, Cooper noted that he couldn't see the Wellesley house from here. "Why don't you stay in the pickup?" he suggested as Livie opened her door.

"I'm the only one who can recognize the man," she said without looking at him, and climbed out.

"You have a point there," he said under his breath, and got out, slamming his door.

Howard was already on his way up to the front door by the time they joined him. He banged on the door and, a moment later, a heavyset man wearing gray sweats answered his knock. The man held a fried chicken drumstick in his free hand and was still chewing as if caught in the middle of dinner.

He looked from Howard to Olivia and Cooper, then back to Howard, his expression one of only mild interest.

"Is this the man?" Howard asked Livie.

Cooper tried not to laugh. Clearly he didn't know Buckmaster Hamilton's daughter. The man standing in the doorway also didn't fit the description Livie had given.

She shook her head as if unable to even answer such a ridiculous question.

"I need to talk to you, Bob," Howard said, and shoved his way into the house. They followed him into the cluttered house. It smelled of wet dogs, grease and stale beer. Cooper felt his stomach turn, thinking of the house he'd grown up in. When he looked at Livie, he saw that she'd grown pale again.

He took her arm. "Wouldn't you rather wait in the pickup?" he asked, figuring she'd balk again at the suggestion even though she appeared green around the gills.

To his surprise, she merely nodded and practically ran from the house.

"Is she all right?" Howard asked.

"Morning sickness," Cooper said, then wished he hadn't when he saw the man's surprised look. Neither he nor his wife had asked about the blackmail. The night Livie had been in their house was three months ago. It wouldn't take much to put two and two together now.

"What do you know about someone staying in the cabin last January?" Howard demanded of the caretaker. "Apparently whoever it was had a key, built a fire, drank my wine, slept in my bed . . ." He stopped, avoiding looking at Cooper. "I would have thought this would have been something you would have noticed."

He and Howard had followed Bob into the kitchen. A heavyset woman sat at the table. She didn't get up and the man didn't introduce her. She merely kept eating as if whatever was going on didn't hold much interest for her.

Bob put down his half-eaten drumstick on his dirty plate and took his time wiping his hands on his napkin. Finally he said, "That would have been January 27. Of course I noticed. I saw the tracks into the cabin the next day and went inside to investigate."

"And?" Howard demanded.

"It looked like it always did after you and the missus have been up." He tilted his head toward the woman at the table. "I told Patsy to go up and clean the place. I would have contacted you, but given the condition of everything, no sign of forced entry and all that, it seemed pretty obvious that you'd used the cabin yourself."

Howard let out an exasperated sigh. "What do you mean, 'the condition of everything'?"

"When Patsy checked the closet, she saw that your clothes and your wife's had been worn and left to be cleaned in the spot where you always leave them."

"She wore my wife's clothing?" Howard demanded of Cooper.

He said nothing, but he felt his jaw tighten. Apparently Livie had made herself at home, as well. Then he remembered. "She hit her head when she went off the road. She had a cut over her eye. There was probably blood on her clothing."

Howard didn't look appeased by this explanation. "I want to know who the hell used my cabin."

The caretaker looked at him just as calmly as he had when he'd opened the door, making Cooper wonder if this had happened before. "Then I suggest you ask whoever has a key. Maybe Mrs. Wellesley might be able to shed some light—"

"Mrs. Wellesley has no idea who the man was," Howard interrupted. Bob looked at the floor and said nothing in the heavy silence that fell between them. "I will get to the bottom of this," Howard blustered as he turned abruptly and headed for the door.

Outside the caretaker's house, Howard stopped. He was breathing hard. Cooper hoped the man didn't have a heart attack. He looked as if he'd aged since he'd opened the door to him and Livie.

"Whoever the man is, he's now demanding fifty thousand dollars in blackmail money," Cooper told him. "I'm thinking I should just turn it over to the sheriff."

"No," Howard said quickly. "Let me see what I can discover first before you do that. A few days can't hurt."

Cooper hoped the man was right. "Maybe you don't know him, but he knows you," he said, and added silently, *Or at least he knows your wife.*

"If you leave me your number," Howard said once he seemed to catch his breath, "I'll let you know what I find out."

He had a pretty good idea what Howard would uncover. He hoped the older man didn't do something he would regret. "I'll be in touch," Cooper said, making it clear that this wasn't the end of it. "I want this man's name."

As they parted, he still itched to kick the bastard's ass. Not that it would lessen his pain or solve the problem between him and Livie, he thought as he looked toward his pickup, only to find it empty.

After leaving the caretaker's home, Livie couldn't stand the confines of the pickup. Breathing in the cold spring air, she'd headed up the road toward the Wellesley cabin.

The men were still inside accomplishing little, she'd thought. If they really wanted answers they should have been talking to Amelia Wellesley.

The walk was short back up the road. It had

85

felt good to be moving, to be doing something, especially after what she'd learned. The man had duped her in ways she hadn't even imagined.

Livie knocked lightly, but didn't wait for Amelia to open the door. Stepping in, she found her in the kitchen. She had a glass of wine in one hand and a cell phone in the other.

Seeing Livie, she glared at her as she said into the phone, "I have to go," and disconnected. She took a sip of her wine before she said, "That's quite the story you told earlier. How long have you been seeing him?"

"I'd never seen him before in my life or again after that night."

Amelia raised a brow. "Would you be surprised if I told you that he's been taking my money, as well?"

"Not really. Who is he?"

"He said his name was Drake, but I suspect even that was a lie."

"But you know how to reach him," Livie said.

"His number's been disconnected." She took another drink of her wine.

"I don't believe you."

Amelia slammed down her nearly empty wine-glass on the counter. "I just tried to call the bastard. I thought I was rid of him and then you show up at my door. Do you realize what you've done coming here like this?"

Livie did. "I'm sorry if this causes you a problem."

"A *problem?*" The woman let out a bitter laugh and drained her wineglass.

"He called me that night. Yes, that's right, the night he was with you," Amelia said. "I was supposed to meet him here, but I couldn't make it. Nor could I give him any more money." She met Livie's gaze. "He sent me a photo of the two of you in *my* bed."

"Do you still have that photo?"

Amelia looked at her as if she must be mad.

"But if he was blackmailing you, I'd think you want to see him caught as much as I do."

She shook her head as if amused. "I'd never press charges against him and he knew it. Just as he knew you wouldn't tell your fiancé about that night."

"How could he know that? How could he know anything about me?"

She refilled her wineglass before she said, "The man preys on women like us. Women who don't want the bad publicity and can get their hands on money. In my case, a rich husband. In yours, a rich father. He seemed to know me so well that for a while I thought maybe Howard had put him up to it. That it was a test."

"How did he get a key to your house, to your SUV?"

The woman's smile had a bite to it. "What do

87

you want me to say? He played me, just as he did you. With me, he targeted me at a fund-raiser of my husband's, also pretending to be someone he wasn't. With you . . ."

"I was just in the wrong place at the wrong time."

"His good luck," she said, and raised her wine-glass in a salute. They both glanced toward the front door at the sound of vehicles approaching. The men would be here soon.

"What will your husband do?"

Amelia looked away for a moment. "Howard will be angry, but he'll get over it." Her gaze shifted back to Livie. "Your fiancé doesn't seem to be as forgiving."

She didn't want to talk about Cooper. She hesitated and then asked, "Is there a chance he could have drugged me that night?"

Amelia laughed. "Did he look like the kind of man who has to drug a woman to get her into his bed?"

That was the last thing she wanted to hear. Desperate, she pleaded, "If you know how I can find him . . ."

"I don't." She met Livie's gaze. "Don't worry. If you don't pony up the money, he'll find *you*. Because now he's your problem."

Chapter FIVE

Sheriff Frank Curry found himself in the sun-room at the state mental hospital thinking about how many times he'd stood in this very spot. Each time he'd been filled with anxiety and hope. Each time when he'd heard footfalls behind him, he'd turned praying that Tiffany would be better. Each time, she hadn't been.

Now as he heard the sound of her and probably an orderly approaching, he braced himself for the inevitable. If anything, Tiffany seemed to be getting worse. Her determination to get out of here left him terrified of what she might do if ever released.

Taking a breath, he turned. The sight of Tiffany always confused him for a moment. The girl was beautiful—blonde, blue-eyed and waif-like with a sweet innocent face. She always looked like a child, not the almost nineteen-year-old she was. He got a glimpse of what she could have been—had her mother not poisoned her with her lies. Had her mother not made Tiffany into a potential killer.

"Hello," he said, his voice breaking at the heartache he felt each time he saw her. He wanted to fix her mind, her soul, make her whole again, but he knew he was probably the last person on earth who could help her given her hatred of him.

"I'm glad you're here," she said in a small voice she used when she thought the hospital attendant was listening. "My doctor says I'm doing so much better and he's spoken with my lawyer." She took a step toward Frank, then another.

He tensed. So did the male orderly. Maybe the doctor thought Tiffany was better, but Frank and this orderly were still leery of her.

"I'm going to need your help, Dad." She smiled. It was her sweet smile, but it never reached the ice blue of her eyes. She only called him dad when she wanted something.

"You know I will help you in any way I can."

"That's what I told my lawyer. He's going to be contacting you. He thinks he can get me out of here, get me probation and no jail time because of all the time I've spent here."

Frank shuddered inside at the thought. But Tiffany had hired a high-powered lawyer with the money her mother had left her. And she would put on a good performance at her hearing. It was possible that she could get away with attempted murder, not to mention the charges against her when she'd broken out of the hospital last year and hurt several people.

"Just think it might not be that long before I can come visit you and your new wife," Tiffany said.

He heard the threat. Felt it at heart level. "Tiffany—"

"I'm better, really." She reached out to touch his arm and the orderly took a protective step toward him.

Her fingers felt warm, human, and yet Frank felt a jolt at her touch.

"I don't want to hurt anyone, especially you or Nettie." Her gaze met his and he felt the pull, just as a judge would. She seemed so sincere . . . How could someone not believe her?

Only if that person knew what she'd been like when Frank had told her that he was remarrying. Tiffany had been beside herself at the thought of him marrying Lynette "Nettie" Benton. She'd even threatened to kill herself, saying her dead mother, Pam, had been coming to her room at night and would kill her if he married the woman.

Frank had let Pam and Tiffany manipulate him, keeping him from the woman he'd loved for too long. A few months ago, he'd married Lynette and prayed Tiffany wouldn't follow through with her threat to kill herself. She hadn't.

He'd been pretty sure that if Tiffany was going to kill anyone it would be him and Lynette.

"I want to believe you, Tiffany. You have no idea how much." But she *did* know how much. It gave her the upper hand. She played on his guilt for not loving her mother enough, for turning Pam into such a bitter, vindictive bitch who would use her own daughter to get revenge.

"Believe me, Dad." Tears welled in all that blue, and when she stepped to him, he took her in his arms for a moment before the orderly insisted Tiffany step back. As he held his daughter for those fleeting seconds, he couldn't help but think about what could have been.

"My lawyer will be contacting you," she said as she let the orderly lead her away. At the last minute, she turned and mouthed, "Thank you." Then she was gone.

Livie tried several times to get Cooper to talk as they headed home, but the most she could get out of him was a grunt so she quit trying.

His big sun-browned hands gripped the wheel as he stared straight ahead. She could tell he was stewing because she'd seen his jaw muscles bunch, his eyes narrow. She could almost feel the anger coming off him. But the hurt and disappointment were worse.

"I love you," she said, her voice little more than a whisper.

"Don't."

"You can't give me the silent treatment forever."

He glanced over at her, his expression daring her to take that particular bet.

She swallowed back the lump in her throat and turned to stare out the side window as she fought tears. After what he'd seen back there, she couldn't blame him for not believing how she'd ended up in the man's bed. She still had her own doubts, even though the man had definitely played her.

She'd never thought about luck. If she had, she would have realized how lucky and privileged she'd been her whole life. It was as if she'd been raised in a large protective bubble that held the entire Hamilton Ranch, maybe even the county.

But when she'd taken off with a storm coming last winter, she'd stepped outside that bubble and a bad thing had happened. She suddenly felt more than unlucky. She felt vulnerable. It made her heart beat faster and chilled her to her bones.

What she'd learned from the Wellesleys had left her shocked. That the man she'd met had deceived her even more than she'd first thought shouldn't have come as a surprise. But it had.

"Didn't you once date some guy who played in a band?" Cooper asked out of the blue.

She looked over at him. "Why would you ask me that now?" When he didn't look at her, she said, "I told you. I'd never seen the man before." She stared at him, upset that he didn't seem to believe her.

"You said he wrote songs."

Her head hurt and her stomach was acting up again. She felt queasy and the motion of the pickup was only making it worse. She was having trouble understanding what he was getting at.

She also couldn't believe he remembered her

telling him any of that. She'd opened her heart to him one night out by the corrals. It had been one of those star-filled Montana summer nights, the air scented with fresh cut hay. The two of them had sat on the top rung of the corral fence, both staring out into the night, both still shy with each other.

She'd told him things she had never told anyone else and he told her a little about his family and how he had wanted to be different from them. The intimacy of the night had made them tell each other secrets they'd kept locked away and had brought them closer.

"Wellesley said that 'Wandering Ways' was the band's only hit and that he wrote it, but I got the feeling there was more to it."

She stared him. "You think the man I met wrote the song? He probably wasn't even born when that song was a minor hit!"

"It just seems a coincidence that the man knew not only about the guitar and the band, but also the words to the song." He glanced at her. "Had you ever heard the song before?"

Livie shook her head and then closed her eyes against the rush of nausea. Cooper was making too much out of a song. What had happened to her that night had nothing to do with her. The man had merely taken advantage of an opportunity that had presented itself. It could have been anyone on that road that night.

Opening her eyes, she said as much to Cooper, repeating what Amelia had told her.

"And you believed her?"

That he wanted to even question that made her sigh. "Sometimes you look at me as if you wish you hadn't fallen in love with me."

"My life would be a hell of a lot simpler, wouldn't it?"

They rode in silence for a few miles before he said, "I don't understand why this man pretended to be someone else."

She looked over at him. "Don't you? Haven't you ever wanted to be someone else?"

His smile was sad as he met her gaze for a moment. "You have no idea." He'd told her enough about his family that she thought he might understand about wanting to be anyone but who he was.

"There have definitely been times when *I* wanted to be someone else," she said.

That seemed to surprise him. "Do you realize how many women would love to have been one of the Hamilton girls?"

"I'll admit it's had its advantages. But it was like living in a fishbowl."

"I guess I can understand that," he said after a moment. "Your father is such a powerful figure in the state, hell, the West. Being his daughter maybe wasn't as easy as I think it was."

She smiled over at him, surprised that under

the circumstances he could even give her that. "Thank you."

He nodded and turned back to his driving as he neared her ranch. "I don't think you'll be hearing from your blackmailer again, but if you do . . ." He pulled up in front of her door. "I hope you'll let me know."

His look said he was doubtful, but she knew it would be a deal breaker if she took things into her own hands again. Worse, if she got her father involved.

"What now?" she asked, not wanting to get out until she knew where they stood.

"We wait and see what happens."

But time wasn't on her side. She was three months pregnant. Their wedding was only a few months away. By then she would definitely be showing. If there *was* a wedding.

"I know it's probably too soon to talk about us—"

"It is," he said, cutting her off as he reached across her and opened her door.

Love shouldn't hurt this badly, Cooper thought as he drove away from the Hamilton Ranch. He felt raw. He'd had a rotten time getting to sleep last night and had awakened this morning, heart aching. The visit to the Wellesley "cabin" had him even more angry and hurt.

If what Amelia Wellesley had told Livie was

true, then this man had preyed on both women. Cooper couldn't bear the thought that the man might really have drugged Livie and taken advantage of her. But he also knew that the man had seduced both women into trusting him. Wasn't that what hurt the most?

He thought the blackmail would stop because of their visit to the Wellesleys. He didn't believe that Amelia Wellesley didn't have the man's phone number or that she wouldn't tell him what had happened now that her husband was onto her.

When the man didn't get the money he'd demanded, he would realize it was over and skip the state. But Cooper wondered where that left him and Livie? All this had only made their differences more apparent. Love didn't conquer all.

He couldn't wait to get home. The only way not to think about any of it was to work. He'd thrown himself into work his whole life to escape. But before he could turn down the road to his land, he remembered he needed more two-by-fours and Sheetrock. That meant a trip into Big Timber to the lumberyard.

Not sure he was up to facing Delia, he considered bagging it for the day. Last night she'd seen how much pain he was in. He ached to pour his heart out, not that he thought it would make him feel any better. Delia would offer a shoulder and right now he could use some friendly comfort.

Unfortunately, Delia wanted more than to be

friends, no matter what she said. He didn't want to hurt her any more than he already had. Nor could he hurt Livie. But he also couldn't avoid Delia. And if he put off buying the lumber he needed, he would never get the house done. Work would be the only thing that got him through the next few months until the wedding.

If there was even going to be a wedding.

Delia Rollins heard Cooper's old pickup. She knew the sound of that engine like the beat of her own heart. She braced herself for seeing him again. It was always the same, the painful lurch of her heart. Her mouth would go dry and her chest would ache. And yet, seeing him made her day.

After last night, she wasn't sure what to expect, though. But when he came through the door, she saw that he looked worse, as if that was possible. What had happened? Another fight with his fiancée? Why did he keep going back?

He walked up the hardware aisle toward her looking like a beaten dog. When he saw her, he tried to hide whatever was wrong. But she knew him too well. She cursed Livie Hamilton. The woman didn't deserve Cooper, and if Delia had her way, she wouldn't have him.

"Hey," he said by way of greeting. "Need to get some two-bys, also some Sheetrock."

She reached for the two-way to the lumberyard at the back. "How many?"

He'd written it down on a slip of paper and she read off the order into the radio.

As he started to reach for his wallet, she said, "I'll put it on your account and send you a bill."

Cooper hesitated. He liked to pay cash, but she knew all the work he'd been doing on his place had to be leaving him close to broke. This would give him a month or so before he had to pay. She appreciated Cooper's pride, something Hamilton never could.

"You look awful," she said, breaking the silence.

"Thanks," he said, and gave her a faint smile.

"You missed a nice party."

"I'm glad you enjoyed it at least."

She had gone back inside. Being rejected by Cooper was something she should have gotten used to. Livie might have blinded him with the Hamilton sparkle of money and prestige that she'd thrown like fairy dust into his eyes, but Cooper would eventually see past it. He just needed to be reminded that he wasn't one of them and never would be even if he married Livie.

This was about Cooper's happiness. That's what kept her coming back for rejection after rejection. She was doing this all for him. She'd danced with every single man at the party and a few who weren't. She wanted it to get back to Cooper. He seemed to think she was waiting around for him. He needed to know she had options.

"Just take your pickup around back and George will load you up."

He gave her a nod and retraced his steps. She waited until George had him almost all loaded up before she went outside.

"Here's a copy of your order," she said, handing Cooper a manila envelope. He took it without looking at it. He was already behind the wheel, clearly anxious to leave, but she couldn't let him leave just yet. "If things get too rough, there's something in the envelope that might help." She smiled as she touched his shoulder through the open window and then stepped away, wondering how long it would take him to open the envelope. And then wondering what he would do when he did.

Russell Murdock stood in the graveyard, hat in hand, as sunlight speared down through the pines and his daughter cried softly next to him.

He'd thought nothing could break his heart like the loss of his wife of forty-two years. He'd been wrong, he realized as he thought of the tiny casket buried here and his daughter's pain at losing her unborn infant.

He'd known this was where he would find her since he suspected she came here every day about this time. Only a few months ago, the entire county had turned out for her brother's funeral.

Russell had worried then that she might lose the baby she was carrying. Her brother's murder by a serial killer had come as such a shock to everyone. Worse, it had been Destry who'd found his mutilated body. Russell couldn't imagine what that had done to her. She'd always been so protective of Carson.

As the ranch manager of the W Bar G Ranch, he'd watched both Destry and Carson grow up. Carson had never been strong. He'd hated ranching, while Destry had thrived in the same environment. Not that having Waylon "W.T." Grant for a father hadn't been hard on Carson. Destry had believed W.T. was her father, as well—at least until a few years ago when the truth had come out.

Russell hated that he'd remained silent all those years, but he'd believed it was best that Destry not know he was her biological father. No one had been more shocked when W.T., having found out that Destry wasn't his daughter, had still left the ranch to her. At the very end, the old bastard had realized if he wanted his ranch to survive he'd better leave it to the one person who loved it and wouldn't sell it before he was barely in his grave.

Destry now dried her eyes and put the small bouquet of wildflowers she'd brought on the child's grave, then she moved over to her brother's grave and fiddled with the arrangement she'd put there earlier.

He wished he knew how to comfort her. She'd been conceived in a one-time moment of weakness all those years ago. He knew nothing about raising children since he and his late wife, Judy, hadn't had any together, although they'd tried for years.

But Russell at least had gotten to watch his daughter grow up. He'd been the one who Destry had come to as a child. He'd taught her to ride, answered her questions about growing up and threatened to wash her mouth out with soap when he caught her cussing up a storm in the barn.

She turned to him now, her eyes swimming with tears, and stepped into his arms without a word. He held her, fighting his own tears. "I love you," he whispered.

She nodded her head against his chest and mumbled, "I love you," before leaving.

Russell stood watching her go, telling himself Destry was strong. She would survive this. But he knew there would always be a hole in her heart where that baby had been as well as the terrible hole her brother's death had left.

Walking to his pickup, he climbed behind the wheel and started the engine. He wasn't ready to go back to his empty house. Nor was he in the mood for company. He often drove back roads on the nights he couldn't sleep. As he headed down one narrow dirt road now, the sun high overhead, he was distracted by the loss of his grandchild and his concern for his daughter.

He didn't see the woman stumble out of the pines that lined the road until she was directly in front of his truck. Russell slammed on the brakes, fearing there was no way he could stop in time.

Chapter SIX

Russell jumped out and ran to the front of the truck, terrified he'd killed the woman. He'd gotten the truck almost stopped. But still he'd bumped her enough to knock her down. Now she lay on the ground with her eyes open as if gazing up into Montana's big sky. He knelt down next to her and was relieved when he felt a pulse.

Her blue eyes shifted, her gaze meeting his. He felt a jolt of recognition even as he told himself he was mistaken. He couldn't possibly know this woman.

"Are you badly hurt?" he asked, even more shaken now than he'd been when she'd appeared out of the trees directly in front of his truck.

"No," she said, and tried to sit up. He saw that she wore slacks, a blouse and impractical shoes for a woman who'd just come out of the woods. Her hair was a mess, her face and arms scratched up, several of the cuts bleeding, and her clothing was soiled as if she'd been wandering around in the woods for some time.

"Maybe you should stay right there for a moment until we're sure you aren't hurt," he suggested, but to his surprise, she sat up. He could see no sign that the truck had actually hit her, although he'd heard a soft thump as he'd gotten the pickup stopped.

"Are you alone?" he asked, looking around. "Where is your vehicle?"

"Can you help me up?" At her insistence, he helped her to her feet as he struggled with how familiar she looked.

"I'm going to take you to the doctor."

"That isn't necessary," she said. "I just need to see my babies."

"Your babies?" he asked, and glanced again toward the pines.

She smiled and shook her head as if he was being silly. "They aren't with me. No one is with me."

"Then how did you get out here?" he asked.

She looked around for a moment, confusion in her gaze. "I don't . . . know."

Russell tried to still his pounding heart. There was a retired doctor who lived not far up the road. He helped her into his pickup and tried not to stare at her as he got the engine going again.

He'd heard the expression "It was like seeing a ghost," but he'd never experienced it before now. He half expected the woman to vanish into thin air before they reached Doc Farnsworth's place. It wouldn't have surprised him any more than seeing a woman whose funeral he'd once attended.

After Cooper dropped her off, Livie had felt lost and restless. The only way she'd ever been able to clear her mind was on the back of a horse so she quickly changed and headed for the stables even though it was getting late in the day. From the time she was old enough to ride, she'd always escaped on horseback into the Crazy Mountains, or the Crazies as the locals called them.

She'd just saddled up and was about to ride out when she heard her father call her name. She walked her horse over to where he was standing by the corral. Livie had to stand on the bottom rail to kiss his cheek. Buckmaster Hamilton was a big man, tall and broad shouldered with a thick head of salt-and-pepper-colored hair that made him look distinguished. He carried himself like a man to be reckoned with.

But he didn't dress like the wealthy man he was unless he was going up to the capital or to DC to talk to "them bureau-rats" as he called them. This morning he wore a tattered flannel shirt and equally worn jeans and boots. This morning he looked like a Montana rancher.

"Wonderful party last night," he said. "I was surprised that you and Cooper left so soon, though."

"It was a beautiful party. I hope everyone had a good time," she said as she turned away to stroke the horse's neck.

Her father had never been one to make small talk or beat around the bush. "Why don't you tell me what's going on with you and Cooper," he said. "I'm not blind. Your sisters were taking bets last night on how long the marriage will last. Several of them are wagering it will never happen."

That didn't surprise her. She and her sisters had often done the same thing at friends' weddings. She flashed him her best smile. "Cooper and I are working things out."

"What has he done now?" her father asked, not unkindly.

Livie almost laughed. How shocked he would be to hear that the "trouble" wasn't Cooper and his stubborn independence. It was her own impulsiveness and naiveté. "I know you just want to help."

"You'd tell me if there was anything I needed to worry about, right?"

She nodded, fighting tears. "Cooper and I are both so busy with him working on the house and me finishing up the wedding plans." The lie stuck in her throat.

Her father eyed her for a long moment. "I heard he picked you up early this morning. You just got back?"

"We went for a drive. We needed a break." She could tell that he didn't believe her and what's more, he thought if anyone were to blame it was Cooper.

"I only want the best for you," he said.

"I know, Daddy," she said, and squeezed his arm before swinging up into the saddle. "I love you for it, but I'm a grown woman and pretty soon I am going to be Cooper's wife." Wishful thinking, she knew, but she had to believe it was true.

"Uh-huh. But you know you can always come to me, no matter what."

That was the problem. He'd always been there. He'd always been able to fix whatever was wrong. She'd depended on him to save her time and again over the years from little things, like writing her a note when she'd skipped school to covering her checking account when she'd overdrawn it.

It was time she stood on her own two feet, no matter what her father or her fiancé said.

Cooper cursed to himself under his breath most of the way home. It had been a day like none he'd ever experienced. He felt anxious and frustrated and still mad and hurt. Overhead, a flock of geese carved a dark V as they swept across the big sky. The faraway sound of them used to fill him with a sense of loneliness.

When Olivia had come into his life she'd changed that. He no longer felt lonely. If anything, being a part of her large family had given him little time alone. There was always someone stopping by to see how he was doing on the house—or to watch him break the wild mustangs he worked with in the corral.

Buckmaster had actually listened when he told

him he wanted to adopt wild mustangs from the range in Montana and part of Wyoming.

"They're amazing horses," he'd argued. "Because of their unique genetic makeup, they may be the most significant wild horse herd remaining in the country."

"Son, they're nothing more than local domestic horses that have escaped to the wild."

But Cooper had argued that they are direct descendants of the Barb horses with interesting bloodlines such as American saddlebred, Canadian, Irish hobby and Tennessee walking horses.

Also, he said, since they've lived in the Pryor Mountains since the late 1600s, it made them native. "These mustangs are a part of Western heritage. We can adopt them from the Pryor Mountains Wild Horse Range. They need to be saved and you need them on your ranch."

Buckmaster had been skeptical at first about bringing wild horses to the ranch. "I've heard stories about these feral animals. They tear up fences, cause trouble."

He'd finally won her father over and began adopting and training the mustangs on the ranch, as well as adopting some for his own place.

Buckmaster had been pleased with the results. He was a man who could admit when he was wrong. Cooper liked that about him.

He was often annoyed by Livie's family, thinking they were meddling into his business.

But at the thought of not marrying Livie—the thought alone made his heart and his chest ache—he realized how much he would miss being part of the Hamiltons. It was an admission and a realization that surprised him.

As he pulled up in his yard, the invoice Delia had given him—and whatever else she'd put inside the envelope—slid off the seat and skittered over to the far corner of the truck's floorboard.

He bent to retrieve it—and spotted something else that had apparently fallen off his truck seat.

It wasn't until he saw the pale blue envelope with Olivia Hamilton printed on it and nothing else that he felt a start. Confused for a moment, he thought this was the blackmail note that Livie had given him. But this envelope hadn't been opened. He stared at it, heart pounding. Who had put this in his truck and when?

He'd parked out on the street in front of the lumberyard. Anyone walking by could have tossed it into his open window while he was inside the lumberyard giving his order to Delia.

Ripping the envelope open, he quickly read what was typed on the sheet inside.

I'm not sure you know who you're dealing with. The price of silence has gone up. If $75,000 isn't sent to Hank Wells c/o General Delivery, White Sulphur Springs, within two days I'll be paying your fiancée a visit in

Beartooth. As you can see, I can get to Livie at any time I want.

Pulling out his cell phone, he quickly called Livie. The call went straight to voice mail. He tried the house.

"Have you seen Olivia?" he asked when the housekeeper answered.

"I believe she went for a ride. Her father mentioned he'd seen her down at the stables."

Cooper quickly disconnected, started the truck and took off toward the Hamilton Ranch. He told himself he was overreacting. But the black-mail note had left him shaken. He realized he hadn't taken any of this seriously enough. He'd been so sure they wouldn't be hearing from the black-mailer again.

Now, he wasn't sure what to think, but all his instincts warned him that Livie was in danger.

Russell paced anxiously as he waited for Dr. Farnsworth to finish his examination. He'd thought about calling the sheriff, but what was he going to tell him? The doctor had assured him that he hadn't actually hit the woman with his pickup. More likely he'd only knocked her over. Since she seemed to be all right—except for the fact that she'd been dead for years—the doctor had suggested he wait until he finished his examination before he called anyone.

Russell kept thinking about the stolen glances he'd given the woman as he'd driven down the road to the doctor's house. She'd seemed so at peace, gazing out the window. If anything, she appeared in awe of the waning spring day. Several times, she'd commented on how beautiful it was, how bright the spring colors were, as if she'd never laid eyes on this part of Montana before. Or at least hadn't for many years.

Doc Farnsworth, alone and frowning, came out of the room where he'd taken the woman. For a moment, Russell thought the doctor would tell him that when he'd gone into the room, there hadn't been a soul in there. That Russell had just imagined leading the woman into the room while Doc's wife had gone to fetch her husband.

"Well?" Russell said. He'd never been an impatient man—quite the contrary. But right now he was more than a little anxious to hear what the doctor had to say. "Is she all right?"

Doc took off his glasses and began to clean them with his shirttail. He'd moved here about ten years ago after retiring from a long practice in a small town over in the Bitterroot Valley. He had to be in his late seventies, but he didn't seem to mind seeing patients who for whatever reason couldn't make it all the way into Big Timber.

"Physically, she seems to be fine except for some cuts, scrapes and bruises," Doc said. "You said that she came stumbling out of the woods?"

"Yes, right before she stepped in front of my pickup."

"Well, that could account for most of the bruising and abrasions on her," he said thoughtfully.

"I heard her hit my truck, but by then I was almost stopped."

"Yes, she has a small bruise on her hip, another on her arm, that look newer, as if they might have just happened," he said with a nod. "You and your pickup are definitely not responsible for her state."

He couldn't hide his relief. "So she's okay?" No mirage. No ghost. Skin and bone.

"Physically. She seems to be suffering some memory loss and confusion. Do you know if she hit her head?"

"When she fell in front of the truck, she might have. She seemed to . . . faint. I still don't know where she came from. That spot up the road is in the middle of nowhere. I didn't see a car broken down anywhere along the road. I have no idea how she got there."

"She doesn't seem to recall that, either. When I questioned her, she became very agitated. I've given her a little something to rest. The wife and I are going to keep her here overnight. If she isn't better in the morning, then I'll call the sheriff."

"Let me know." Russell left, feeling strangely

spooked. It wasn't every day he stumbled across a ghost. He doubted he'd get a lick of sleep tonight, and if he did, he feared the dreams that might haunt him.

As the sun set, Livie rode up into the Crazies following a crystal-clear snow-fed stream that ran fast and furious down through the rocks. She breathed in the smells of spring in the mountains. Overhead, squirrels chirped from high branches and meadowlarks broke into song.

When she'd left the ranch, there'd been a breeze. The higher she rode, the breeze turned to a stiff wind that rocked the pine boughs as clouds scudded across a spring blue sky. This was her favorite time of the year. She'd almost forgotten with everything going on how much she loved riding up into the mountains as far as the melting snow would allow.

At the top of a rise, she stopped to look back at the ranch in the last of the day's sunlight. The view filled her with pride and a feeling of well-being. The huge white house contrasted sharply with the new green of the spring grasses. She could see the horses running through the pasture. Farther away black cattle dotted the hillsides.

Just the thought of leaving it made her sad. Everywhere she looked on the ranch she found glimpses of herself. The first time she'd been bucked off a horse. The first time she'd swam in the creek. The first time she'd kissed a boy. It had all happened on the ranch.

The first time she'd fallen in love, too, she thought. She'd promised herself she wouldn't think about Cooper and the trouble between them. But he had been in her heart for so long, it was only natural that when she thought of the ranch and firsts, he came to mind.

When she reached a meadow, she climbed off her horse. Snow still covered part of the creek this high in the mountains. She walked over to it. The snow-fed water made her fingers numb as she scooped up a handful to taste. There was nothing as sweet as the taste of icy-cold mountain water.

Sitting down on a large rock, she closed her eyes and tried to calm the growing worry inside her. Soon she wouldn't be able to ride without the chance of hurting the baby. The baby. She placed a hand over her stomach and prayed that it was Cooper's.

Livie saddled up again, hating that she would have to turn back because of the growing twilight. The air had cooled and the sun had sunk behind the mountains. Dark shadows hunkered under the pines. She started to rein her horse around to ride back down to the ranch when she heard a horse whinny below her on the mountainside. She pulled up short to listen.

She listened to another rider working his way up the mountain. By the way the rider was moving she got the feeling that he was tracking her.

Livie slipped the rifle from its scabbard, thinking about her blackmailer. Had he heard about her visit to the Wellesleys? Had he decided to show her that he meant business by paying her a visit? If so, then he had been watching the ranch. He would have to have seen her ride out earlier.

Her father had taught her to always carry the rifle when she went riding. Not so she could shoot something even though there was always the chance she might cross paths with a bear or a mountain lion or something might spook her horse and throw her. Three shots would signal that she was in trouble and could be heard for a great distance.

Fortunately, her father had also taught all six of his daughters to shoot. She raised the rifle. She could hear the rider's horse. Any moment horse and rider would be coming out of the dense pines.

Chapter SEVEN

When the phone rang just minutes after he'd driven home from the office, Sheriff Frank Curry figured it was official business, since it usually was. He reached for it, praying the call wasn't about Tiffany. The daughter he hadn't known existed until a couple years ago who was now locked up at the state mental hospital for trying to kill him was always his first thought when the phone rang. Especially when it rang in the wee hours of the morning.

When he thought about what his ex had done to the child, he still wanted to ring his ex-wife's neck. Someone else had killed Pam, fortunately for him.

Unfortunately, that seemed to have made Tiffany only sicker. He found himself always waiting for the other shoe to drop.

"Sheriff Curry here."

"Frank, it's Father McGregory."

A lapsed Catholic, he couldn't imagine why the priest would be calling. "Yes, Father," he said, and waited. Would the state mental hospital have called the priest?

"I'm over at Halverson's. Lester is asking for you. He has something he says he needs to tell you. I'd suggest you hurry. I've already given him last rites, but he is hanging on, he says, until you get here."

Livie slumped back in her saddle with relief as Cooper came riding out of the trees. She lowered the rifle and saw that he looked as glad to see her as she was to see him—at least for a moment.

"What the hell are you doing up here alone?" he demanded. She could see that he was scared for her as she slipped the rifle back in its scabbard, but his tone still made her bristle. "Damn it,

Livie," he said, dragging his Stetson from his head and raking a hand through his thick dark hair.

"I'm fine," she snapped. "I can go for a ride on my own—"

"Ranch," he finished for her.

"Even married to you, I will still be a Hamilton and part of this ranch," she said.

"Oh, you'll always be a Hamilton, all right. So mule-headed and obstinate that you'll put yourself in danger."

"If this is about—"

"You were followed."

That stopped her. She started to say that she was followed since he was right in front of her, when his next words stopped her cold.

"Someone was trailing you. I lost his tracks about a quarter mile back. I suspect he heard or saw me."

Her throat went as dry as dust. "Did you see *him?*"

Cooper shook his head. "But I'd recognize his horse's tracks if I saw them again. One of the shoes has an irregularity in it. I picked up his trail on Hamilton Ranch property."

Livie tried to make sense of what he was telling her. "Then it was someone from the ranch. You can't think this has something to do with the blackmail." She couldn't believe the man would do something so brazen as to come to the ranch, let alone wait somewhere and follow her. She took a ride most afternoons. He would have had to be waiting for her. Watching.

She shuddered at the thought and then remembered talking to her father before she left on her ride. "I bet Daddy asked one of the hands to make sure I was all right. I saw him right before I rode out. He was worried about me."

Cooper didn't look convinced. She could tell he also didn't like the fact that Buckmaster was worried about her. That meant that her father knew more about what was going on than Cooper would have liked.

"I don't believe it was my blackmailer," she said. "He wouldn't chance getting caught on the ranch. By now, he has to assume that I've gone to the sheriff."

Cooper looked at her askance. "If he's the kind of man you say he is, I doubt being caught trespassing would deter him from coming after you. This ranch is huge and abuts to forest service land." Cooper reached in his jean jacket pocket. The moment she saw the pale blue envelope with her name typed on it, she felt her heart drop. "I got another blackmail demand. It was apparently left on the seat of my pickup.

" 'I'm not sure you know who you're dealing with. The price of silence has gone up. If $75,000 isn't sent to Hank Wells c/o General Delivery, White Sulphur Springs, within two days I'll be paying her a visit in Beartooth. As you can see, I can get to Livie at any time I want,' " he read, sending a chill through her.

"He's bluffing," she said even though she feared he wasn't. From what Amelia had told her, this wasn't a man who gave up easily.

"He knows who you are, where you live," Cooper said. "There's no telling how long he's been watching you."

She didn't want to believe that. The "incident" had happened in late January miles from the ranch. She hadn't received the first blackmail threat until the middle of April, almost three months later.

Didn't that mean that he hadn't been planning to blackmail her? For all that time, he'd known her real name. If he'd traveled in the same circles as Amelia, then it wouldn't take much to figure out that she was Buckmaster Hamilton's daughter.

She said as much to Cooper.

"Who knows why he waited, Livie? Given what Amelia told you, he sounds like a man who uses every advantage. He could have been watching you this whole time, learning everything he could about you, letting you think you were safe before he struck."

Maybe he had been watching her all this time.

Lester Halverson lived like a hermit at the edge of the Yellowstone River, far from the nearest paved road. He was a thin, scrawny man who looked as tough as jerky. There'd been rumors that he'd once had a wife and possibly a child, but after a tragedy, he'd locked himself away in his shack along the river.

The sheriff had been called out to Halverson's on several occasions over the years because Lester hadn't taken well to visitors. "You have to quit brandishing a shotgun when someone happens on your place, Lester," Frank had warned him.

"Them trespassers ain't got no business on my land."

Whether the land was actually Halverson's was debatable, but Frank had never been interested in getting into it with the old man. Lester did no harm. That was the best that could be said about him.

Father McGregory was waiting at the side door to the shack-like house when Frank arrived. "This way," he said, and led him down a narrow hallway to an alcove that acted as a bedroom. "The sheriff is here, Lester," the priest said.

Frank saw what appeared to be nothing more than a pile of grayed blankets shift. When Lester's face materialized from the small pile, he realized he hadn't seen Lester for a while. The man had shrunk down to nothing.

"Lester, it's Frank Curry," he said, crouching down next to the narrow bed.

"Already confessed to Father McGregory," Lester said in a papery weak voice.

Frank shot the priest a look. *Confessed?* He couldn't imagine what sins the old man had to confess on his deathbed—not just to a priest, but to a sheriff.

"Can't keep the secret no more," Lester said. His cough was faint, no more than a wisp of dry air. "Come back to haunt me."

The sheriff looked to the priest, but Father McGregory's expression was solemn. "What secret is that, Lester?"

"Come right out of my ice fishing hole out front," Lester said, his voice sounding a little stronger. "Thought I'd drunk too much hooch. But there she were like a drowned kitten. Hauled her in, warmed her up as best I could. Near dead. Had a fit so I said I wouldn't call nobody." He gave a slight shake of his head. "Middle of the night I hear a door slam, engine rev. Gone, just like that."

Frank couldn't understand why the priest had called him out for this since it couldn't be anything more than the demented ravings of a dying man. He started to rise, when Lester's thin arm sprung from the bedding. Viselike fingers dug into his arm.

"Hamilton's pretty wife," the old man hissed. "That who she was. She done it on purpose, goin' in the river. Told me so. Said it was the only way out." Lester nodded and let go of his arm. "Weren't my place to say nothin', but now . . . Can't leave with this on me."

Frank looked over at the priest, but Father McGregory was looking at Lester. "He's gone," the priest said, and quickly stepped to the old man.

Frank moved back from the bed and then let himself out of the shack. He needed fresh air to try to make sense of what Lester had told him. Twenty-two years ago he'd gotten the call in the middle of the night. Sarah Hamilton's car was seen in the Yellowstone River, only part of the back bumper sticking out of the ice. Rescue efforts had turned up no sign of the woman. It was believed that because of where she'd gone off, her body had been swept downstream under the ice. Her remains had never been found but that hadn't been that unusual. Montana rivers claimed lives, the bodies never seen again.

Now with a jolt, he reminded himself that Lester Halverson didn't live far downstream from where Sarah Hamilton had gone into the river. Was it possible? Had Sarah survived? If true, who had picked her up that night?

Father McGregory stepped outside to join him. "I've called the mortuary."

"What do you make of all that?"

The priest shrugged. "He was so insistent, I called you."

Frank remembered the feel of the man's talon-like claws on his arm. If Sarah Hamilton had survived, then where had she been the past twenty-two years?

Chapter EIGHT

Cooper braced himself for when Livie opened the door the next morning. He'd felt such a mix of emotions over the past forty-eight hours. Usually when he saw her, only one emotion struck him, overpowering all others. Desire.

It had always been that way with this woman. Now as the door opened, he felt it kick him in the chest, taking his breath away. It would have been so easy to sweep her up in his arms, carry her into the bedroom and make mad, passionate love to her.

In the past when they'd argued, make-up sex was one of the ways he'd shown her he was sorry. Actually, like most men, he wasn't good at expressing how he felt about her. In the bedroom, he tried to show her.

But as strong as the urge was to do his talking with his body in the bedroom, he couldn't bridge the gap between them. Not yet. Maybe not ever. More than anything his anger was directed to the man who'd seduced her. He'd fought Livie from the beginning from denying his attraction to her to more recently refusing to give an inch when it came to doing everything himself. She was right. He was partly responsible for this mess.

"Hi," she said, smiling the smile that had broken down all his barriers.

"How are you . . . feeling?" he asked lamely.

One fine eyebrow shot up, but she said nothing as she stepped aside to let him in.

The lure of the bedroom was too strong. "Could we go for a walk?" he asked, even more uncomfortable with her here. Her apartment was so Livie, decorated in bright colors, so different from his cabin.

She looked both surprised and wary, but reached for her jean jacket.

Outside, the spring day was cooler than it had been, but clear and beautiful. She seemed to breathe in the fresh air as if she'd been locked up for a while.

"Did you find the horse from yesterday?" she asked hopefully.

"I did. It's one of ours . . . the ranch's," he corrected. He'd worked with the Hamilton horses for so long they felt like they were his.

"But we don't know who rode it, who followed me up the mountain?"

"Not yet." There were a good ten ranch hands who worked here, some of them new. "I thought you could get a list of them from Ainsley. She's still handling most of that for your father, isn't she?"

"You can't think that he's employed on the ranch," she said.

He glanced over at her. "Why not? He impersonated Howard Wellesley. You think he can't do the same as a ranch hand?"

She said nothing for a moment as they walked down a trail that led to the creek. He could smell the water before he heard the splash of the snow-fed stream rushing over the rocks. As they came out of the pines, a rainbow trout turned in the cool, clear creek with a flash of color before disappearing.

"I thought your dad might have seen someone since you said you saw him before you rode off, but apparently he's gone up to Helena," Cooper said.

They walked in silence for a ways before she said, "I called the Wellesleys to talk to Amelia again. I thought she might . . ." Her words faltered as he looked over at her in surprise. "I was told by their caretaker that he was closing up the house because the two of them were spending the summer in Europe."

He stopped walking to curse under his breath. "Definitely changed their plans, didn't they." He thought of the latest blackmail threat. What happened if they didn't pay? He knew Livie must be worrying about the same thing. If only she hadn't paid the man the first time.

Cooper walked on down the creek to stand under the shade of the pines. It was cooler down here and he needed it to calm down. He hadn't been able to sleep last night thinking about it.

"Until we find out who on the ranch might have followed you, maybe you should move into the cabin with me," Cooper said. He regretted the words almost at once. It would be hell being that close to her in the small cabin.

She looked too shocked to speak. "I—"

"Never mind, you're happier here. I shouldn't even have suggested it." He mentally kicked himself. It had been a dumb idea. Worse, it wasn't one she had jumped at.

"Wait, Coop, I—"

"We have to tell the sheriff about the blackmail even if it hurts your daddy's presidential chances. I can't risk that this lunatic might come after you if we don't pay. Maybe the sheriff can track him down and put an end to this."

"Are you sure that's what you want to do?" she asked, seeming even more surprised than when he'd asked her to move in with him. She had to know that, like everything else, this was something he'd wanted to do himself. What if he never got to confront this man?

It was a question he'd asked himself. He had thought of nothing else since she'd told him. This baby—maybe his baby, maybe not—how did he feel about it? Could he accept another man's child?

He'd told himself that if he could put his fist into the man's face, he could get past all of this. He wouldn't even need to have the man arrested for blackmail since he knew the scandal would hurt her father's political aspirations.

"I can't take a chance with your safety," he said as he took off his straw cowboy hat and raked a hand through his hair. Looking over at her, he saw her worrying at her lower lip with her teeth. He wanted to comfort her, tell her everything was going to be all right. But he couldn't.

His gaze went to her mouth again. Damn. Why did he have to feel the way he did about her? "We'll go to the sheriff after I get some work done," he said, and headed for the corrals.

Livie had been going stir-crazy after Cooper's visit that morning. She needed to ride her horse, but the thought of having been followed yesterday kept her in her apartment until she couldn't take it anymore.

She found Cooper out in the corral working with one of the mustangs. It broke her heart every time she saw him. Having him within touching distance was unbearable. Her fingers itched to smooth back the lock of dark hair that always fell over his right eye. She needed him like she never had before. If only he would hold her, she could believe that everything would work itself out.

It made her ache inside to be this near and feel the distance between them. Being pregnant with raging hormones only made it more unbearable. She needed to curl up in his strong arms.

She was still shocked that he'd suggested she move in with him. But he hadn't given her a chance to even think about it before he'd taken it back. He was the one who'd wanted to wait until after they were married to move in together. She'd never realized he was so old-fashioned and had been touched by it when she'd discovered he'd been worried about her reputation.

It had made her laugh.

"I want to do this right," he'd said as he'd cupped her face in his hands. "We have the rest of our lives together."

Now as she watched Cooper work with the wild mustangs he'd talked her father into adopting, she felt such pride in the kind of man he was. She'd always loved watching him work with the horses.

"The man has a way with horses," her fathe had said the first time he'd seen Cooper work with a problem horse at the ranch.

Had her father known then that she was falling for Cooper? Was he aware of the hours she spent watching him work? She knew he'd been worried about her since she was spending less and less time at the boutique she'd opened after college.

"What do you want to do with your life, Livie?" he'd asked her not long after Cooper had been hired.

"I want to get married and have babies," she'd said.

They'd been having a family dinner and were all seated at the large dining room table. Angelina had groaned. "Apparently she took after her mother."

"Is that all my mother had wanted, as well?" she'd asked her father.

Buckmaster had nodded. "Sarah loved being a wife and mother more than anything else."

She'd heard something in his voice beyond the usual sadness. And so had Angelina, who'd quickly risen from the table to make a phone call she'd said she'd forgotten to make earlier.

Now as she watched Cooper work with the mustangs she felt a little jealous. He was so patient with them, so understanding of their wild spirits. She wished he could be more like that with her.

Cooper wanted to tame her, no doubt about that. No, she thought, he wanted to break her to his will. She knew that wasn't fair. He was the one who thought she was trying to break him, saddling him with her father's land and money. And like the wild mustangs, he was bucking and snorting and fighting her every step of the way.

She watched him pick up a halter and move slowly toward a young mustang he called Blue. His love for the horse was evident in the way he stroked a hand down the thick neck. Cooper had told her he was training Blue for her to ride. Blue was typical of the mustangs. He stood fourteen hands high, weighed close to eight hundred pounds and exhibited one of Cooper's favorite colors, blue roan. The colors often ranged from bay to black, chestnut to dun and blue or red roan. Most were dun or grullo.

The mustangs had primitive markings such as dorsal stripes, transverse stripes across the withers and horizontal "zebra" strips on the back of the forelegs. The horses were heavy with strong bones.

She found them gorgeous and mysterious, a lot like she did Cooper.

"The reason you want these horses is because they are intelligent, strong, surefooted and have great stamina," Cooper had said the first time he'd brought back four of them.

It broke her heart when he'd told her that many of the wild horses had once been sold for dog food, before people had fought to save them. People like Cooper Barnett.

She thought now of the day he'd brought the first mustangs back to the Hamilton Ranch. When they were let loose in the corral they shied, avoiding any kind of human contact, and behaved like . . . wild horses.

Her father had shaken his head. "This was a crazy idea," he'd said, and walked away.

Cooper had stood at the edge of the corral smiling, unperturbed. "Don't worry. Give me some time with them. They can be ridden and trained to do anything that these other horses can do. They have a calm temperament. With all the riding you do in the Crazies, one of them will be perfect for you, Livie. They are alert on trails. On one of these, I won't have to worry about you."

She'd been as skeptical as her father and couldn't understand Cooper's need to work with wild horses.

Now, as she watched the other mustangs run in the wind, their long manes and tails blowing back, she thought of the evening she and Cooper had come down here after he'd brought the first mustangs home.

"They're like Montana," he'd said as they watched the horses run in the pasture. They had looked majestic and beautiful in the waning light. "How could anyone not want to ride one?"

"I'm not sure I will ever be able to trust one," she'd said, and he'd merely grinned at her.

"You trust me, though, right? I will pick one out for you and one day you'll ride him." Blue was that horse.

"Livie?" Cooper touched her arm. She felt a jolt. She hadn't thought he even knew she was there watching him. "Let's go see the sheriff now."

Sheriff Frank Curry listened to Olivia Hamilton's story, her fiancé, Cooper, adding bits and pieces as it went.

When they'd finished, Frank had a bad feeling there was more to the story than either was telling him. But two things were clear to him. Someone had targeted Olivia and she didn't want her father to know what was going on.

Buckmaster Hamilton wasn't a man who liked being kept in the dark. So the best plan of attack was to find out who was behind this and put an end to it as quickly as possible.

"So you don't know this man's real name?" Frank asked after he'd had the blackmail notes checked for prints. The only fingerprints on them were Cooper's and Olivia's. That wasn't too surprising. With all the forensics shows on television, even the stupidest criminal knew to wear gloves.

"His first name might be Drake. I'd never seen him before. I've been trying to remember our conversation that night, hoping he might have slipped up and said something." She shook her head, then let out a surprised sound. "I just remembered. He had a tattoo on his biceps. I got only a glimpse of it when he threw more logs on the fire. The initials D.C. So maybe his first name really is Drake."

"You just remembered that *now?*" Cooper asked, looking astonished.

She shot him an impatient look. "I've spent three months trying to forget. I just remembered the tattoo now. Amelia Wellesley told me that he called himself Drake."

Frank wrote down the information, including the description Olivia gave him. It could have fit a lot of men. "I'll give Howard Wellesley and his wife a call." He hoped she could provide more information or at least a better description.

"When I called back up there, I was told by the caretaker that they are in Europe this summer."

"I think this man is in the area," Cooper said, and told him about finding the latest blackmail threat in his pickup and someone following Olivia up into the Crazies the afternoon before. "The horse and rider were on the Hamilton Ranch. It was one of the ranch horses."

"Would someone other than a ranch hand have access to a horse?" Frank asked.

"I suppose if the person rode bareback, they could have taken one of the horses from the pasture," Cooper said. "Hamilton Ranch has a lot of horses."

Frank nodded and looked to Olivia. "Can you think of anyone who might want to harm you other than this man?"

Her hesitation made him realize that she didn't want to say in front of her fiancé. Frank asked Cooper to give him a moment alone with Olivia. He saw the cowboy's hesitancy to leave and waited until Cooper had closed the door behind him before he turned to her again.

"I know you're holding something back. So let's hear what's bothering you," he said, not unkindly.

She looked relieved, seeming to relax with

Cooper out of the room. "I honestly don't have a clue who this man is."

Frank glanced at the two blackmail notes she'd given him. "Neither of these mention the night in January. Is it possible they aren't from the man?"

"But they have to be," she said, frowning. "No one else knows about that night."

"What if it isn't about that?"

She stared at him as if stunned. She'd just assumed . . . "I can't imagine what else it could be."

"Well, give it some thought. You said that you didn't receive the first note until after you'd announced your engagement to Cooper," Frank said. "Is there someone who might want to stop the wedding?"

"Delia Rollins." The words seemed to come out before she could stop them.

He raised a brow.

She immediately looked embarrassed. "She dated Cooper before he and I fell in love. I hate to even say this since she is my maid of honor, but I don't trust her when it comes to him."

Frank smoothed down his mustache as he leaned back to study her and let her talk.

"When Cooper fell in love with me . . . well, Delia took it well enough, maybe too well. I think she would love to take him away from me."

He knew firsthand the lengths a scorned woman might go to. "There's someone else I might talk to, as well. Hitch McCray."

That seemed to surprise her. "Hitch?"

"I heard he's recently returned to town." Hitch had skipped town after his mother died and left her ranch to Jack French. Hitch had taken it hard since he'd gotten nothing but a few acres and the old farmhouse where he'd grown up.

"I recall he was especially enamored with you before he left town," Frank said to her. "I recall hearing about one altercation in particular where your father had him thrown off your property."

She scoffed. "It wasn't me he wanted. It was my father's ranch. Hitch wouldn't take no for an answer. After that . . . incident . . . he got the message."

Frank agreed to talk to both Hitch and Delia. "Let me know if you get any more blackmail threats or if you think of any reason someone other than this man might be sending them."

Cooper wasn't sure what had made him go around the block as he and Livie parted in the parking lot at the sheriff's department. They'd driven separate vehicles because she'd said she had errands to run. He couldn't help worrying about her since they had no idea what her blackmailer was going to do now.

That's why he noticed the blue pickup. It was parked on the other side of the street. As Livie pulled out in her SUV with her personalized Livie license plates, the driver of the blue pickup pulled out after her.

Cooper swung around and followed. He could see the back of the driver's head. That is, he could see the man's cowboy hat and only occasionally got glimpses of the man's face in the side mirror.

When Livie parked, the driver of the blue pickup started to park, too, but then he looked back and saw Cooper. The cowboy sped off, Cooper hot on his heels. At the edge of town, the man took a left, then a quick right, speeding through a residential area.

Cooper tried to read the license plate on the back of the truck, but it was covered in mud. All he could make out was that the plate appeared to be a Montana one.

He swore as, ahead, the truck picked up even more speed—and a car backed out of a driveway right into Cooper's path.

He slammed on his brakes, skidding to a stop only inches from the car filled with kids. Past it, he saw the blue pickup disappear around a corner.

When the sheriff answered, Cooper quickly told him what had happened. "It was a blue pickup." He gave him the make of the pickup, a Chevy, knowing how many blue Chevy pickups there were around. "I tried to catch him, but lost him. He was headed toward the West Boulder. I believe the plate was a Montana one, but I can't be sure."

"If you see him again, call me," Frank said. "Don't go after him yourself."

Cooper hung up and drove back to the main drag. Livie's SUV was gone. Good, he thought. She went home. At the ranch, she should be safe as long as she stuck close to the house. At least, he hoped so.

Frank decided to start with Hitch McCray. He drove out to the man's place in the shadow of the Crazies outside of Beartooth.

If it wasn't for Hitch's pickup parked out front of the old farmhouse, he would have thought the place was abandoned. The two-story frame house needed a coat of white paint and a good cleaning. Leaves had blown up onto the porch and now moved restlessly in the breeze. The faded curtains were drawn behind filthy windows.

As he got out of his patrol SUV, he could hear the tinny sound of what blades were left of the windmill vibrating in the wind. He walked toward the front door, mindful of rattlesnakes in the tall weeds that had grown in around the house.

"Sheriff," a male voice said behind him before Frank could reach the porch. He turned to find Hitch coming around the side of the house with a shovel in his hand.

"Hitch." He touched the brim of his hat, shifting easily on the soles of his boots as he took in the other man.

Hitch was big, broad shouldered and strong

137

looking. He wasn't bad looking. But he tended to rub people the wrong way. His mother had been a mean, penny-pinching, bitter woman who'd been hard on her son. Because of that, Frank had cut the man some slack in the past when Hitch had taken up the bottle.

This morning Hitch looked clear-eyed and clean shaven. Frank wondered if he'd quit drinking. That would definitely be a positive.

"What brings you all the way out here this morning?" Hitch asked as he leaned on the shovel. "You the welcoming committee? Or is the town planning to run me out on the rails?"

He supposed Hitch had reason to have a chip on his shoulder. What interested Frank more was the fresh soil on the blade of the shovel. "I heard you were back. Just thought I'd stop out and see how you were doing."

Hitch laughed. "I'm supposed to believe that?" He shook his head. "Jack French send you?"

Frank chewed his cheek for a moment. "Any reason Jack would do that?"

"Bad blood, Sheriff. You know he stole my ranch."

"I know your mother left it to him to make up for lying for years about killing his father."

Hitch tightened his hold on the shovel, digging the tip of the sharp blade into the hardscrabble in front of the house.

"What you been digging?" Frank asked.

"Buried a dead coyote I found out back because it was stinking up the place."

"You never said why Jack would want to send me out to talk to you."

"I might have seen him in town last night. I might have said a few things."

"You threaten him?"

Hitch looked away. "I was just shootin' my mouth off. I don't want any trouble."

"Well, Jack didn't send me." Frank glanced at the old house where Hitch had lived with his mother all those years. "What are your plans?"

"I came back to tie up some loose ends. I'm not staying."

"Is Olivia Hamilton one of those loose ends?"

Hitch reeled back a little in what could have been feigned surprise. "Livie?" He chuckled. "That stagecoach left a long time ago. Why would you ask me about her?"

"She's received some threats."

His laugh held no humor. "So of course it must be me." He shook his head angrily. "That's why I'm leaving and never coming back here. It would be just like the Hamiltons to blame me."

"Actually, it was my idea to come talk to you. Olivia is convinced it isn't you."

This time his surprise seemed sincere. "Really? Well, that is the first break *she's* ever given me."

"You haven't had it easy, Hitch. I'd like to see things turn out for you."

"I wouldn't hold your breath on that, Sheriff, but thanks for the thought," he said, and tossed the shovel into the back of his pickup. "Now, if that's all, I need to go into town for a few things."

After talking to the sheriff, Livie felt a little better. Cooper, though, had seemed nervous when they were at the sheriff's department. For a man who was so sure of himself, it had been strange. She wondered if he'd had a run-in with the law in his past.

She shrugged the thought off.

He'd wanted her to head straight back to the ranch so he would know she was safe. After a couple hours this afternoon with the sheriff, she needed some time to unwind. But she also hated the feeling that she was no longer safe, even in the small Western town of Big Timber.

"Just be careful," Cooper had said, meeting her gaze before they'd parted.

For a crazy moment, she'd thought he might kiss her. But instead, they'd both stood awkwardly looking at each other like the former lovers they were.

After he'd driven away, she'd gone downtown to run some errands before going to Hamilton's, the boutique she'd opened after college. Because she'd been so busy with the wedding planning, she hadn't spent any time at her business.

While she'd felt guilty about it, she hadn't been

worried. Fortunately, one of the smartest things she'd done was hire Lisa Anne Clausen. Lisa Anne was the dream employee.

"It's been a little slow, but summer is coming and the tourists love all the Western items that we carry," Lisa Anne said when Livie asked how things had been going and apologized for letting the woman handle everything on her own.

"I knew the shop was in great hands," she said. "You do such a great job. I've realized that I won't have as much time after I get married." She didn't mention the baby. "Would you consider taking over as manager?"

Lisa Anne stared at her a moment before breaking in a smile. "I would love it."

"Good. We can discuss your new salary later. It's late. Why don't you go on home. I'll close up."

"Livie, thank you." She stepped forward to hug her. "For everything. You don't know how much this means to me."

Livie thought she did. Lisa Anne had had a crush on Carson Grant for years and everyone, but possibly Carson, knew it. When he was killed, she'd taken his death hard. The job had helped, Livie knew, and was glad. She liked Lisa Anne and hoped that someday the attractive young woman would meet a man who would sweep her off her feet. She deserved a good one.

After Lisa Anne left, she looked around the

shop, pleased by what she had accomplished since she'd opened it. She'd been lost after college, not really wanting a career. The boutique, though, had turned out to be a great business and one she'd enjoyed.

She picked up a pair of silver earrings in a horseshoe design. She liked the weight of them and had a pair at home. Putting them back, she felt almost sad as she realized she might not be able to spend much time here—just as she'd told Lisa Anne. But she'd seen shops where there was a baby bassinet in the back. There was no reason her child couldn't be part of this.

Her hand went to her stomach. *Please let this be Cooper's baby. Please.*

Someone passed by the window in the darkness that had fallen over the town. Realizing how late it was, she locked up and stepped outside, only to collide with a solid form.

Hitch McCray grabbed her to keep her from falling and grinned down at her. "Well, if it isn't Olivia Hamilton."

Chapter NINE

Delia Rollins looked up as the sheriff came in the front door at the lumberyard. As he made his way to her at the back counter, she could see that he wasn't here to shop. Sheriff Frank Curry had a way of carrying himself when he was on duty that she'd come to recognize from the times he'd visited her parents' house looking for her younger brothers.

"Afternoon, Sheriff. How's that remodeling job going?" she asked, pretending he'd come in for material. Since his marriage, he'd been making some changes out at his house to accommodate his wife, Nettie. "She like that paint color you chose?"

"I'm here on another matter," he said as if he suspected she already knew that. He glanced past her to the glass-enclosed office behind her. "If you're not busy maybe we could step into your office for a few minutes?"

"Sure." She led the way. "What's this about?" she asked as she closed the door. She didn't offer him a chair nor did she sit. She had a feeling this wouldn't take long.

Frank removed his hat and held it by the brim in his thick fingers. "I need to ask you about Olivia Hamilton."

"Livie? Has something happened to her?"

"Why would you ask that?"

She couldn't help but laugh. "Because you're here. Did she tell you I'm her maid of honor? It was something we promised each other when we were kids."

"Olivia has been receiving threats."

Her eyebrows shot up. "What could I possibly have on her that would be worth blackmail?"

143

"I didn't say blackmail."

She smiled. "Cooper told me." That wasn't quite the truth, but close enough.

He looked surprised. "When was that?"

"The night of their engagement party."

The sheriff seemed to digest that for a moment. "When I talked to her, your name came up."

Delia smiled. "I'm sure it did. She's afraid I'm going to steal Cooper Barnett back."

"Are you trying to?"

"Sheriff, Olivia Hamilton isn't going to marry him and not because of anything I could do."

"What does that mean?" he asked with a frown.

"Livie and Cooper." She shook her head. "They're completely wrong for each other, and the closer the wedding gets, the more they are both going to begin to realize it. That wedding is never going to happen."

"I heard you were back in town," Livie said, the first thing that came to her mind after being startled by Hitch McCray outside her shop.

"I'm not staying, so don't worry."

"I wasn't." She'd forgotten how much she disliked him. For a while, he'd set his sights on her. She'd made it clear she wasn't interested, but that hadn't stopped him until her father had stepped in.

"How have you been?" he asked. "You don't look all that well."

"I'm fine." She started to step past him, but he grabbed her arm.

"I heard you were getting married to some horse wrangler who works for your father," Hitch said with a sneer.

She wasn't about to defend Cooper to this man. She shook herself free of his grasp. "If you'll excuse me . . ." She tried to get around him, but he blocked her way.

"What does he have that I don't?" Hitch demanded, making her wonder if he'd been drinking. Booze had been a problem for him before he'd left town. That and a domineering mother who'd cut him out of her will.

"Manners, for starters," she said, and shoved him aside to get past.

"He's just after your money and your father's ranch," Hitch yelled after her. "You'll be sorry."

She feared he might follow her, but at least he had the good sense not to.

Still she was a little shaken by her encounter with him. Hitch could be unpredictable when he was drinking. What bothered her wasn't what he said but that it wasn't the first time she'd heard it. She was sure Cooper had heard it, as well.

Once on the road, she realized she was hungry. Maybe food would make her feel better, and, anyway, she hadn't eaten since breakfast. With her father out of town, she wasn't up to dining with Angelina and her brother Lane at the ranch.

She drove west toward the Crazies and the small old mining town of Beartooth. It had been a while since she'd gone there. She'd heard that the general store had reopened after a fire had destroyed the original one. But she'd been surprised to find that the new store looked identical to the old one.

Remodeling was still going on at the hotel but it was looking as if it wouldn't be long before it, too, opened.

She parked in front of the Branding Iron Café hoping that Kate had one of her cinnamon rolls from this morning. She'd been craving one for days.

The bell tinkled over the door as she stepped inside. A very pregnant Kate French came out of the kitchen and called, "Sit anywhere you like."

Delia turned and almost collided with Hitch McCray. She heard him groan when he saw her. The two of them had never gotten along. He'd always called her a Hamilton wannabe. Since it was too close to the truth, she'd hated him for it.

But now she needed him.

"I was hoping I might run into you," she said. "I heard you were back."

"Is that right?" Hitch looked more than a little suspicious. He was one of those men who was good-looking until he opened his mouth. "Why?

146

You want to give me a piece of your mind? You sure you can spare it?"

He was making her regret that she'd bothered to talk to him after she'd seen him just minutes before talking to Livie in front of her shop. She reminded herself that she was doing this to keep Cooper from making the biggest mistake of his life.

"I heard you were going to be Olivia Hamilton's maid of honor," Hitch said, sneering. "I also heard she's marrying your boyfriend." He shook his head. "You used to have more pride than that."

The gibe struck its mark, making her sting. It was all she could do not to tell him what she thought of him. "You know Livie and I are old friends."

He laughed. "Since when? I haven't been gone that long. You two haven't been close in years. So why is she really wanting you to stand up with her? Guilt? Or does she just want to lord it over you that she got your man?"

Delia had her own theory as to why Livie had asked her to be her maid of honor. "I think it's her way of telling me hands off. As her maid of honor I'm a coconspirator in this wedding. But don't worry yourself over it. The wedding is never going to happen."

Hitch let out a surprised sound. "You know something I don't?"

She laughed. She'd always known more than

Hitch McCray. "Let's just say I'm not going to let it happen."

His demeanor changed. "Are you serious?"

"Like a heart attack."

He laughed and for a moment he looked handsome again. Maybe she could pull this off, she thought.

"I'm intrigued," he said. "Why don't we go have a drink and you can tell me what I can do to help."

"I have a better idea," she said as she closed the distance between them. "Let's go back to my place."

The smell of food made Livie's stomach growl, but her gaze had gone to the pregnant woman's baby bump as she'd entered the café. Kate looked radiant. Livie had heard that the baby she was carrying was a girl. Her hand went to her own stomach. She felt a twinge of regret. This should have been the happiest time of her life, getting married to the man she loved and pregnant with his child.

She removed her hand, thinking of the man who might have fathered this baby. Was he out there now, watching and waiting? She shuddered at the thought and assured herself that the sheriff would find him and put an end to his threats.

"When are you due?" Livie asked after she and Kate had visited for a few moments.

"Any day," Kate said with a chuckle. "Can't you tell?"

"I am so happy for you. Congratulations."

"Same to you. Jack and I are looking forward to the wedding. Jack said he's never seen a man who has such a way with horses as Cooper Barnett."

Livie nodded. Cooper gave the horses a kind of unconditional love that seemed to make them want to do anything he asked of them. She swore she'd seen the horses look at him with adoration. She chuckled at the thought since she was sure she looked at him the same way.

"Is there any chance you have one of your cinnamon rolls from this morning?" Livie asked after she'd devoured the blue-plate special of meat loaf, mashed potatoes and gravy, green beans and a side of corn bread.

Kate laughed at her request. "Sorry. But I just saw a strawberry rhubarb pie come out of the oven. I could get Callie to put a scoop of ice cream on it for you."

"That sounds wonderful."

When Callie brought it out, Livie thought she would never be able to eat it all, but she did.

The café was filling up for the dinner crowd as she left. In the shadow of the Crazy Mountains, darkness came quickly to Beartooth. A cold breeze stirred the pines as she climbed behind the wheel of her SUV. She sat for a moment, not wanting to go home, but not knowing where else to go.

She wanted to go to Cooper's, to have him take her in his arms, to spend the night next to him in his too-small bed. The thought made her smile before her eyes filled with tears.

Please let this be over. She'd never felt so powerless. What if the blackmailer was never caught? If they continued to ignore his threats, would he just stop?

How long could she and Cooper continue like this? If there was some way to find out if this baby she carried was his, then maybe . . . She would call a doctor tomorrow.

Finding out whose baby it was was a start. But it wouldn't solve everything. It wasn't that simple and she knew it. She and Cooper had problems they couldn't seem to overcome before all of this. If it was his baby, he would insist on getting married, but that wasn't the kind of marriage she wanted.

Livie had always felt in control of her life. She'd never had a problem making a decision. As Cooper had said, she was her father's daughter. She might be impulsive, but she wasn't immobile no matter the problem.

If she waited to cancel the wedding, it would only make it worse because by then she would be showing and everyone would know about the pregnancy.

Taking a breath, she made her decision. She would cancel the wedding tomorrow, call everyone. She couldn't marry Cooper. Not like this. All they did was butt heads over everything.

But it broke her heart. She loved Cooper. How would he take her canceling the wedding? She would have to tell him tonight.

She took the gravel two-lane road that skirted the edge of the Crazies on her way to the Hamilton Ranch. The pines and aspens cast long black shadows across the road. She passed only one other vehicle, an SUV headed into town.

That was why she was surprised when as she came over a rise, a set of bright headlights suddenly illuminated her vehicle from behind. Where had this one come from?

In her rearview mirror, she watched with growing concern as what appeared to be a pickup raced up behind her. The truck was traveling much too fast on the narrow gravel road, its lights blinding.

She touched her brakes, afraid the driver hadn't seen her. As she did the truck began to pass her on the right in a hail of gravel.

Livie hit her brakes, thinking the driver must be drunk. Or crazy. Or—

That thought didn't get a chance to form before the pickup slammed into the side of her SUV, forcing her over into the loose gravel.

She fought to gain control, but before she could, the pickup slammed into her again. Her SUV fishtailed. She saw the pines only an instant before she crashed into them.

Chapter TEN

Sheriff Frank Curry had felt uneasy since talking to both Hitch McCray and Delia Rollins. Over the years he'd seen the resentment a lot of locals had for the Hamiltons. It was the general opinion that the girls were spoiled rotten and that was why none of them had tied the knot yet. No man could meet their high demands. Or was it their father's?

Before leaving his office earlier, Frank had run a background check on Cooper Barnett. The cowboy was definitely an unlikely prospect for a groom for one of the Hamilton girls. He came from the so-called wrong side of the tracks. His mother had run off, his father was a drunk and one of his uncles was doing time at Montana State Prison. He was the kind of cowboy who ended up in trouble.

Which was why Frank hadn't been too surprised to find out that Cooper had a sealed juvenile record. He wondered if Livie knew who she was marrying. Or if Buckmaster did.

Cooper Barnett was now about to marry into a very wealthy and powerful family. That alone might be cause for concern given these blackmail threats. Add to that the fact that the senator had his sights on the White House.

Was it possible Cooper had gotten cold feet and

decided to take what he could and run before the wedding? It wasn't unheard of.

But it made more sense to go through with the wedding and be in line to inherit a percentage of Buckmaster Hamilton's wealth along with a portion of the ranch. That was no small potatoes. Frank knew a lot of cowboys who'd give their left arm to be in Cooper's position.

What had Cooper done to have a juvenile record? Frank knew he had to find out. He picked up the phone and called a judge. "I'm going to need a warrant to open a sealed juvenile record."

He'd just hung up when he got a call from the hospital.

Livie was still shaken after giving her statement to the sheriff about the hit-and-run.

"Would you like me to call the ranch?" the emergency room doctor asked as he finished strapping the temporary splint around her left ankle.

"It's only a bad sprain, but I'd like to see you stay off this ankle as much as you can for a few days. I can give you something for the pain."

She'd had to explain that she was pregnant and have the doctor congratulate her. This was definitely not what she'd imagined for her first pregnancy.

Livie considered having him call Ainsley or her father. Both would have been preferable over calling Cooper. He would be furious that she hadn't gone straight back to the ranch. But if she didn't call him . . .

"No, please call my fiancé, Cooper Barnett."

Livie closed her eyes and lay back against the gurney in the ER as the doctor left to make the call. She couldn't believe what had happened.

The sheriff had asked her if she'd seen the driver. No, she couldn't even be sure it was a man driving the truck.

"What about the color of the pickup?" he'd asked.

"Brown, I think. It was dark. I'm sorry. It happened so fast . . ."

"It's all right. I would imagine there will be some of the pickup's paint on your rig," the sheriff had said. "The driver didn't flash his lights or honk as he tried to pass you?"

"No, he came out of nowhere and . . . he tried to run me off the road."

Now as much as she didn't want to believe it, she knew it hadn't been an accident. Whoever had been driving that pickup had purposely forced her off the road.

Had it been her blackmailer? She shuddered at the thought, reminded that he'd said he could get to her if they didn't pay the latest blackmail demand. But that deadline hadn't passed yet.

She thought of Delia, her once best friend. Surely the woman wasn't crazy enough to run

154

her off the road. Delia probably knew her better than anyone. She cringed at all the things she'd shared with her—including Cooper. Her sisters had thought her crazy to have Delia as her maid of honor at the wedding.

"If your plan is to keep your friends close and your enemies closer," Ainsley had said with a laugh, "well, I fear it might come back to bite you in the behind."

"She's right. Forget about some old promise," Kat had said. "That woman has her sights on your man."

"If Cooper and Livie are supposed to be together, they will be no matter what anyone does," Bo had said, only to have her sisters look at her as if she was so naive they couldn't believe it.

"I know what I'm doing," Livie had told them.

But now she wondered about that. Delia had an assortment of old pickups on her folks' place.

"Your fiancé is on his way," the doctor said. "I'll see about getting you some crutches. I really do want you to stay off that ankle for a while."

She laid back and closed her eyes. Between the pregnancy and the nasty scare she felt exhausted. She must have slept because the next thing she knew Cooper was there.

He took her hand, worry in his expression. "Are you all right? What happened?"

"I had a wreck on the way to the ranch. Someone in a pickup forced me off the road into the trees." She saw at once that Cooper had jumped to the same conclusion she had—that the man was her blackmailer.

"What color was the pickup?"

"Brown, I think. I've already told the sheriff. He's got his men out looking for the truck."

"You're sure it wasn't blue?"

She frowned. "Pretty sure, why?"

"A cowboy in a blue pickup with Montana plates followed you when you left the sheriff's department," Cooper said.

"It can't be the same person," she said with a shudder. "You're sure he was following me?"

"When he spotted me, he took off. I tried to catch him but he got away."

The doctor entered the emergency room with a set of crutches. "She just needs to stay off that ankle for at least forty-eight hours."

Cooper glanced at the splint and said, "Is it broken?"

"Hairline fracture. The sprain is of more concern. Don't worry, she'll be back on her feet way before the wedding," the doctor said, and looked to Livie. "You'll get the hang of the crutches in no time."

"You're coming home with me." Cooper didn't sound happy about that. "It's the only way I'll know that you're safe."

"I don't want to inconvenience you. I can stay in the main house—"

He bristled. "Inconvenience the man you're engaged to marry by moving in with him when you've been hurt?" He softened his tone. "Livie, you were planning to move into my cabin after the wedding, anyway."

She wanted to point out that they didn't know if there was even going to be a wedding. It certainly didn't look promising. Also earlier, she'd decided to cancel it. But right now didn't seem the time to tell him that.

"I just thought because of the way things are between us right now . . ." She let the words die off.

This was the man she loved, but she couldn't think of anything worse right now than moving in with him. With her morning sickness, he would have a constant reminder of the baby she was carrying.

His brow furrowed. "If you'd rather not, I'm not going to force you to."

She saw how much this meant to him. "I would love to stay with you. Thank you. I promise it won't be for long. I'll be back on my feet in forty-eight hours."

Cooper nodded and she could tell that she'd put her foot into it again. He looked as miserable as she felt. "Right. I'll take you to the cabin. You can call your sister. I'm sure Ainsley will pack up whatever you need since, like you said, it won't be for long."

With him already angry with her for not jumping at the idea of staying with him, telling him about her decision to cancel the wedding seemed a very bad idea right now. When she was back on her feet . . . She closed her eyes. Her life was spiraling out of her control.

The next morning when the sheriff reached his office, he was told that Dr. Farnsworth and a woman who didn't give her name were waiting for him.

Nothing had prepared him for when he walked in. He stopped in his office doorway at the sight of the woman waiting for him.

Dr. Farnsworth got to his feet. "I believe you know my patient?" The doctor had only been in the valley for ten years so he wouldn't have recognized Sarah Hamilton.

All Frank could do was nod as he closed his office door behind him. "Sarah?" he asked, his rational mind arguing that it couldn't be her. But after hearing Lester Halverson's confession, he knew she'd survived that winter night her SUV had gone into the Yellowstone River. So where had she been the past twenty-two years and why was she back now?

She rose from her chair to extend her hand. "I just want to see my babies, Frank. Can you help me?"

He looked to the doctor. "I brought her to you

because she seems to be suffering from some sort of memory loss," Dr. Farnsworth said. "The last thing she recalls is giving birth to twins."

His gaze shot to Sarah, who'd lowered herself gingerly back into her chair. He could see that she was scraped and scratched up. She had several bruises on her face. She brushed a lock of blond hair back from her forehead as if embarrassed by her battered appearance. In spite of it, the fifty-eight-year-old woman seemed to have taken great pains with her appearance this morning. He wondered if that was the doctor's wife's doing?

Now she sat across from his desk, nervously picking at a loose thread on her slacks.

"You have no memory of the past twenty-two years?" he asked as he walked around to take his chair behind his desk.

Her eyes filled with tears. She looked confused as she shook her head. Dr. Farnsworth filled him in.

"She doesn't remember how she got to Beartooth or what she was doing in the woods before she stumbled out on the road in front of Russell Murdock's pickup not far from our house."

What had she been doing in such an isolated place? Had someone dropped her off? How else could she have gotten there?

"Russell brought her to me because I was closer than town," the doctor was explaining. "I saw no reason to call you at the time. Her injuries didn't seem to be from making contact with the pickup. They appear to have been made prior to that." The doctor shook his head. "I think her memory loss is fairly complicated and beyond my medical expertise."

"Have you called her husband?" Frank asked.

"She wanted to see you first. She wants you to contact her husband for her, to break the news. I understand he thinks she's been dead all this time?"

Frank nodded. "She was . . . is Senator Buckmaster Hamilton's wife."

The doctor lifted a brow. "I see."

Cooper felt a stab of guilt at the sight of Livie on crutches as he helped her out of his pickup and into his cabin. He'd been angry with her for not going straight back to the ranch where she would have been safe. Or at least safer than on the road from Beartooth to the ranch.

When he'd gotten the call about Livie being at the emergency room, he'd panicked, thinking at first it was the baby. Then he'd realized that the blackmailer could have gotten to her and had rushed to the hospital, terrified it was more serious than the doctor was telling him.

"The baby okay?" he asked now, realizing it was a question he should have asked earlier.

"Fine."

Had he hoped it was gone? Not if it was his. And if it was that other man's?

As he led her into his cabin, he suddenly saw it through her eyes. The space felt cramped. Nor was it ready for her. But what struck him was that as much as he liked the cabin and thought it adequate, it now looked sadly lacking. What had ever made him think she could live here with him after they were married?

"I'm sorry," he said.

She looked over at him. "Why would you be—"

"I haven't given a thought to how you were feeling in all this."

She said nothing as he quickly helped her into a chair and stood her crutches against the wall near her.

"What can I get you?" he asked. "I need to get back." He motioned toward the skeleton of the house he was building for the two of them. There was no hurry on that now and they both knew it.

"Here," he said, and grabbed a small footstool for her to rest her injured ankle on. He saw immediately how touched she was by his simple gesture and felt even worse.

"Go," she said, her voice breaking with emotion. "I'll be fine. I'll yell if I need you."

"Your sister should be here soon." Ainsley had tried to argue with him when he'd called to tell her about Livie's accident and inform her that his fiancée would be staying with him.

"She's going to be my wife," Cooper had finally snapped.

"Is she?" Ainsley had snapped back.

Now he met Livie's clear blue gaze and felt his heart melt at the sight of her. He couldn't bear the thought of her being hurt or in pain. His anger had shoved his love for her into a tight corner. But at times like this there was no holding it back. No matter what had happened last winter, he loved this woman and still wanted her desperately. "I'm glad you called me."

As Cooper left, Livie felt an ache that brought tears to her eyes. It was his sudden gentleness before he left that reminded her of the first time they'd made love.

She'd been out by the corrals after watching Cooper work with one of the wild mustangs. It was his hands and the way he touched the frightened huge horses that made her open up to him.

He'd climbed up on the corral fence with her as they talked under Montana's big night sky. It was the night Cooper had told her about growing up so poor that he was often hungry. She knew he hadn't told her everything, but he'd shared enough to make her understand his need to succeed on his own.

Later they'd made love in the barn loft. She often thought of that night and his tenderness. She'd already been in love with him and thought she couldn't fall any further, but she had. That night, she'd promised her heart to Cooper Barnett.

At the sound of a vehicle, Livie looked out to see her sister Ainsley drive up, followed by Ka in one of the ranch pickups. She saw Cooper call out to them from the skeletal frame of the house where he was working. Ainsley said something back and mugged a face, making it clear that the two had argued. Nothing new there, Livie thought as the door opened and her sisters walked in.

"How could he think that you staying here was a good idea?" Kat demanded, looking around. "Don't tell me this was your idea?"

Livie shook her head.

Her sister stared at her for a moment. "He's afraid he's losing you."

She almost laughed, but she knew if she did it would turn to tears. "Like I said, it's complicated."

Kat pulled up a chair next to her while Ainsley took the items she'd brought from Livie's apartment into the bedroom. "What's this about someone running you off the road?"

She lied because she didn't want another lecture from her sisters. Ainsley would throw a fit and insist that they tell Daddy everything. She wasn't ready for everyone to know, maybe especially Angelina, who was convinced Buckmaster's daughters were all trying to sabotage his chances of becoming the next president. Her stepmother lived in fear of even a whiff of scandal in the family.

"It was an accident. I think the driver might have been drunk."

"You were probably distracted with everything that's been going on," Ainsley said, coming back into the room. She asked Kat to get something out of her car for her. "We brought you a ranch pickup to drive in case you need to get out of here."

"That isn't necessary," Livie said. "I can't drive for forty-eight hours and Cooper can take me anywhere I need to go."

"Still, I want you to be able to leave if you need to, sprained ankle or not. You told Cooper about the baby. I know he's not happy about it. I've seen the way he's moping around."

She wanted to tell her that she was wrong, but when she opened her mouth, Ainsley cut her off.

"I know," her sister said. "It's *complicated*." She eyed her. "You don't have to marry him." Ainsley held up her hand. "Let me finish before Kat gets back. He isn't going to change. He is always going to be stubborn and have to do everything himself and the way he is acting now is just a prime example of—"

"The baby might not be his."

Ainsley stopped on a caught breath. "No." She shook her head. "I don't believe it."

"Like I said, it's complicated."

"Who?"

"That's the complicated part. I have no idea. So

given that, I'd say Cooper is handling things pretty well, wouldn't you?"

After the day he'd had, Frank was glad when he found his wife sitting on the front porch at their ranch. He gave her a kiss and joined her to watch the sun set behind the Crazies.

"How was your day?" he asked, smiling as she made room next to her on the porch swing. He was glad she'd taken the part-time job at the Beartooth General Store because he knew it made her happy working there again after all the years that she'd owned it. He'd had his misgivings, though, about her going back after the original store had burned and she'd almost died in the fire.

"My day was fine. I sense yours was . . . interesting," she said, studying him. "And troubling."

He laughed. "You know me so well."

"Was it your visit to see Tiffany?" Lynette never called Tiffany his daughter. He knew she wanted to believe the child was no relation. He had moments when he wished the same thing.

"She's hired a lawyer who is trying to get her out," he said with a sigh. He didn't mention that she'd asked for his help. He didn't want to spoil the evening by discussing it because he knew how Lynette felt on the subject. Tiffany wanted him to plead for leniency on her behalf. It would go a long way in helping her seek freedom if the father she tried to kill thought she deserved to be released without going to prison.

Like Lynette, Frank feared that neither of them would be safe if Tiffany was free, no matter what she said. But it wasn't a decision he wanted to make tonight. He told himself he'd cross that bridge if and when . . .

"I have a couple of cases I'm involved in that are . . . like you said, troubling."

"Can you talk about them?" asked the former reigning queen of gossip.

He smiled and shook his head. Lynette would hear soon enough about someone having run Olivia Hamilton off the road earlier—just as she would hear that Sarah Hamilton had returned from the grave.

But when she found out that he'd known and not told her . . . He might weaken on the Sarah Hamilton part.

"You have a suspect in one of your cases," she said, studying him again. "One you hope isn't guilty."

He shook his head in astonishment at her. "You're an amazing woman."

"We already know that," she said, and swatted playfully at him. "I suppose you aren't going to tell me who, though."

Frank looked up to where his crows were lined up along the telephone line out to the barn. The one he called Uncle cawed down a greeting. He loved his crow family and had been heartbroken when Tiffany had killed one of the birds out of spite. The other crows had left and, for months, the telephone line had remained empty—just like his life.

"I'm trying to narrow down the field of suspects in the case." His instincts told him that whoever was behind this was closer to Olivia Hamilton than she knew and that Delia Rollins was right about one thing. There was never going to be a wedding. He just hoped there wasn't a funeral.

Meanwhile, there was Sarah Hamilton. He hoped it was a coincidence her showing up so soon after her husband announced his candidacy for president of the United States.

Delia wasn't surprised when she got the call later that night. She smiled at the sound of his voice. Hadn't she known he would call?

"I didn't wake you, did I?"

It would have been all right if he had. "No, Hitch. I was having trouble sleeping."

"Thinking of me?"

She laughed. "You're awfully sure of yourself."

"Not really. You're the first woman who's intrigued me in a long time. I want to see you again."

She smiled but said nothing.

"Since you can't sleep and neither can I, I was thinking . . ."

"Tell me what you're thinking." She lay back on her bed and listened as he described what he wanted to do to her. He had no idea what she planned to do to him.

"That's all?" she asked when he'd finished.

He laughed. "You're incorrigible."

"You have no idea."

Silence followed and she could almost hear the wheels turning in Hitch's head. "This isn't just about getting back at Livie, is it?"

"You know better than that. If you're not here in thirty minutes—"

"I'm already on my way."

I'll bet you are, she thought as she disconnected. "The things I do for you, Cooper Barnett."

Chapter ELEVEN

When Buckmaster Hamilton opened the door to the sheriff the next morning, his first thought was that something had happened to one of his daughters.

"Frank?" he asked, needing to know right away what was wrong.

The sheriff removed his hat, holding the brim of the Stetson in his long fingers. "I need to have a word with you, Mr. Hamilton."

Mr. Hamilton? "If it's one of my girls—"

"It's not," the sheriff said quickly.

168

Buckmaster shrank back from the door in relief. He'd spent half his life worrying about his six daughters. Their mother had missed those nights sitting up with them when they were sick. Just as she'd missed all the other nights waiting for them to come home from dates, fearing the kind of trouble they might have gotten into.

As the sheriff stepped into the entryway, Buckmaster tried to relax. It wasn't the girls and yet the expression on the sheriff's face . . . "What is this about?" His wife, Angelina, came into the room, no doubt having seen the sheriff's patrol SUV drive up. Angelina hated to miss anything.

"What's wrong?" she asked as if, like him, she'd suspected it would involve one of his daughters. Usually she asked, "Which one is it this time?" whenever there was a problem. Even after fifteen years, his wife and his daughters couldn't have been less close. Not that either seemed upset by the state of things. He hadn't tried to get them to come together. Sometimes the best thing he could do was just try to keep peace between them.

"Could we step into your den?" Frank asked him. "It's a private matter."

Angelina raised a brow, but took the hint. "I'll be in the kitchen with the cook discussing this week's meals if you need me."

As she left, Buckmaster led the sheriff down to his den. It wasn't until he'd closed the door and

169

motioned Frank into one of the leather chairs that the sheriff finally spoke again.

"I have some news that might come as a shock," Frank said. "You might want to sit down."

The sheriff didn't have to tell him twice. He dropped into an adjacent chair and braced himself for the worst, even though he thought if it didn't involve his girls, then it couldn't be the worst.

"I tried to reach you yesterday."

"I was out of town. I'm sure the housekeeper told you that. Please, just tell me."

"It's about Sarah."

Buckmaster blinked. *"Sarah?"* His wife had been dead for twenty-two years. "Sarah?" he repeated. For a moment he thought Frank was referring to the foundation that he'd started in her name. His daughter Bo was in charge of it. He had a fleeting image of Bo throwing back champagne at Livie's engagement party. Was there a problem at the charity?

"Sarah survived the night her car went into the river."

At first the words made no sense. *"Survived? What are you talking about?"

"Sarah is alive."

He shook his head. "That's not possible. If she was alive . . ." He met the sheriff's gaze. "She's been alive all these years?"

Frank nodded.

Buckmaster struggled to his feet to step to the bar. His hand shook as he poured himself a drink. He'd never been a drinker. He liked a Scotch to help him relax in the evening. But while it wasn't even ten in the morning, he needed a drink if for nothing else to give him a moment to take in this news.

"You're saying she got out of the river somehow." He listened as the sheriff told him what Lester Halverson had told him on his deathbed.

For a long moment, he couldn't speak. "You and I know that she purposely drove into the river that night. She was *trying* to kill herself."

The sheriff said nothing as Buckmaster returned with his drink. He stood merely staring at the amber liquid, trying hard to make sense of this.

"So she couldn't even get that right," he said with a bitter laugh, and took a sip. The alcohol burned all the way down. He could never forgive her for what she'd done. "So if this is true, where has she been all these years?"

"I don't have all the details," Frank said. "I've only spoken with Sarah for a few moments when she stopped by my office."

Buckmaster looked up aghast. "She's in town? She contacted you, instead of me?"

The sheriff looked down at his hat in his hand for a moment. "She was afraid the shock might be too much for you if she suddenly appeared at your door. Also she was worried about how her daughters—"

"They aren't her daughters," he snapped. "Sarah gave up any rights to them when she abandoned them the way she did."

The sheriff pulled out a small piece of paper. "I have a cell phone number you can call. It belongs to Russell Murdock. He lent her his phone temporarily."

"Russell Murdock?"

"He's the one who found her. I'm sure she'll explain everything when you see her."

Buckmaster shook his head, refusing to reach for the slip of paper. Frank finally put the note on the coffee table. "Is there anything you'd like me to tell her?"

"Tell her to go to hell and this time stay there."

Cooper was already gone when Livie woke the next morning. Finding herself alone in his bed, she felt miserable. She couldn't bear this. Why had she agreed to come here? Had she thought things would be different if they were together? And why had Cooper insisted on putting himself through it?

Last night had been pure hell. Cooper had fixed them both something to eat and then had gone back out to work on the house. She hadn't even heard him come in it was so late. But when she'd gotten up to go to the bathroom as she now had to do so often because of the pregnancy, she found he'd made himself a bed on the couch.

Earlier in the evening she'd tried to talk to him.

"This is going to be tough enough," he'd said, cutting her off. "Let's not belabor it, okay?"

Now, she used the crutches to go to the front window and look out. She thought he must be exhausted, working at the ranch for her father during the day and then on the house into the wee hours of the night. Since today was Saturday, apparently he planned to work all day on the house that the two of them would probably never live in.

She watched him work. He had his shirt off, his muscled back and arms tanned from working like that in the spring sunshine. The cowboy was the sexiest man she'd ever known. Long-legged, slim hipped with broad, strong shoulders. She closed her eyes, recalling the feel of being in those arms, then quickly turned away from the window.

She couldn't do this. She thought about driving the pickup her sister had left her, but it hurt to put any weight on her ankle. She'd give it another day. She could always come back for the pickup tomorrow.

Pulling out her phone, she called her sister Ainsley. "Come pick me up. I can't stay here," she said, fighting tears.

"I'll be right there."

It wasn't until she'd hung up that she saw something in the kitchen that made her heart break even more. Cooper had picked wildflowers and put them in a water glass on the table. It was such a simple, unexpected touching gesture and one she knew was his way of bridging the gap a little between them.

She stumbled on her crutches to the table, pulled out a chair and sat down. Wiping her eyes, she knew she couldn't leave him. Going back to her father's ranch would seem like another betrayal to him. Maybe he couldn't love her and no longer wanted to marry her, but she couldn't hurt him any more than she already had.

She called Ainsley only to get voice mail. She didn't leave a message. Putting her phone away, she took one last look at the wildflowers her fiancé had picked that morning and waited for her sister so she could tell her she'd changed her mind.

"She wants to see her children," Buckmaster raved as he paced the living room floor at the ranch. "Her children. She doesn't even seem to realize that after twenty-two years her children are grown women."

Angelina was rubbing her temples. She'd taken several pain pills and looked as if she needed more. "You can't keep her from seeing them," she said, making him stop in his tracks. "Let her see them, if that's all she wants, and then she'll leave before the media gets hold of this."

"I damn sure can keep her from them! The

woman tried to kill herself to get away from them. She has no right to come back here now and demand—"

"Why has she come back now?" Angelina asked. "You're sure all she wants is to see the girls?"

"How the hell should I know?"

"Well, we need to tell Lane so he can get out in front of this if the media hears about it, and how can they not?" Angelina let out a cry as if this news was finally settling in. "Is our marriage even legal with her alive?"

He waved that off. It was the least of his problems. "I know why she went to the sheriff instead of coming straight to me. She doesn't have the guts to face me on her own. Sarah wanted to commit suicide? I'd have seen that she got her wish. After all these years, she wants to see the children she abandoned? Over my dead—" He stopped in midbreath as he saw Ainsley standing in the living room doorway.

He hadn't heard her come into the house. She had her keys in her hand, her purse over her shoulder and was wearing a jacket as if headed somewhere. *"Mother committed suicide?"* Ainsley took a step into the room, frowning as she did.

Buckmaster couldn't speak for a moment. He'd spent the past twenty-two years keeping the secret of Sarah's death from his daughters as well as the general public. The sheriff suspected and so did others who'd investigated the so-called accident. But he'd managed to keep a lid on the truth.

But as he looked at Ainsley, he knew everything would come out now—including the fact that Sarah had bungled her death and for some damned reason had come back from the grave.

"There's something I have to tell you," he began.

"Your mother is alive," Angelina said, getting to her feet. "She's come back to Beartooth to see you and your sisters."

He looked at his wife and swore.

"Buckmaster, sometimes it's best just to rip off the bandage," Angelina said. "I will let your father tell you what he knows. It isn't much since he hasn't talked to your mother—or to our lawyer." She looked pointedly at him before walking out.

He watched her go. Just what he needed—two wives who gave him grief. Wait until the press got hold of this. They would have a field day.

"Where are your sisters? I think you'd better get them over here now. I don't want to have to say this more than once. But for heaven's sake, don't tell Harper and Cassidy. It's finals week. I won't have them flunking out of college because of their . . . mother."

Back at the sheriff's department, Sarah Hamilton looked nervous as Frank motioned her into the chair across from his desk. It was the same chair she'd occupied the day before. He'd been relieved when the woman had decided to stay in a motel in town until things could be sorted out with her husband. Going out to the ranch would be the worst thing she could do right now given the way Buckmaster felt.

He knew she was anxious to see her children, but all six of her daughters were grown women now. Sarah still thought of them as the way they'd been the night her SUV had gone into the river.

"You saw him?" Her voice was soft, little more than a whisper.

"I did. I gave Buckmaster your number."

"I suppose he was surprised." She nodded as if it had been a ridiculous thing to even ask. "Of course he's angry," she said, still nodding. "Rightly so. Did he give you any indication as to whether or not he might call?"

Frank was saved by the sound of her cell phone ringing. She seemed surprised as she dug it out of her pocket.

"I'm not used to having a phone," she said and fumbled with it as if she really hadn't used a smartphone before.

"I should answer it," she said, and left his office.

Frank watched her as she headed toward the front door of the sheriff's department. Her steps faltered before she could reach it. He heard her say, "Yes, I'm listening, Angelina," as she seemed to brace herself.

After a few minutes, her whole body seemed to deflate. "Yes, I understand," she said, and dropped the phone back in her pocket as she continued on out the door.

Cooper knew he shouldn't have been surprised when he saw Ainsley drive up and quickly race away with Livie. Hadn't he known his fiancée would hightail it back to the ranch after just one night at the cabin? Still he couldn't help feeling disappointed. More than likely Livie had confessed everything to Ainsley, who in turn insisted they go to the all-powerful Buckmaster Hamilton.

He tried to make it hurt less by telling himself that he'd dodged a bullet. Did he really think anything would be different if he and Livie were married?

Disgusted with the way he was feeling, he went into the cabin for a drink of water. He spotted the flowers he'd left her on the table, picked up the glass and dumped them into the trash, angry with himself. It had been a silly sentimental gesture.

As he started to get a drink of water, he saw the envelope Delia had given him at the lumberyard. It was where he'd tossed it on the kitchen counter. He was glad Livie hadn't seen it or, worse, opened it since he had no idea what Delia had put inside.

For a moment, he thought about not opening it. He was so frustrated, so worn out and worried.

When he'd asked Olivia to marry him, he'd thought he had their life planned. He'd known it wouldn't be easy, but he'd believed that because they loved each other, they could work through any problems.

How foolish that seemed now. Olivia was pregnant and he couldn't even be sure he was the father of her baby. That weighed on him, but not as much as the fact that someone was threatening her if he didn't pay seventy-five thousand dollars. There was only one way that was going to happen —if the money came from Buckmaster Hamilton.

"And the damned fool would probably pay it and his daughter would be fine with it," he said under his breath as he ripped open the envelope.

But blackmailers didn't stop once they realized you would keep paying, he told himself.

It was the alternative that bothered him. What if it was the blackmailer who'd run her off the road and not some drunk rancher? If so, he would have expected another note from the blackmailer, another threat. But since there hadn't been one and now that the sheriff was involved, maybe there would be an end to this.

Something metallic fell out and hit the floor. He looked down to see what appeared to be a house key.

"Oh, Delia," he said, closing his eyes for a moment. She was making it so easy for him, offering him a place away from all this.

He knelt down and picked up the key. It looked new, which made him feel even worse. As he pulled an invoice of his latest purchases from the envelope, he saw that she'd also written him a note.

I'm here if you need a place to think or just a cold beer and a friend to talk to.

He swore and tossed everything on the kitchen counter as he heard someone drive up. When he opened the door, he'd hoped to find Livie standing there.

"Delia? What are you doing here?" he asked, sounding as exasperated as he felt.

"Your fiancée called the sheriff on me," she said, and angrily pushed past him into the cabin.

"She's not here, if she's the one you're looking for," he said, closing the door and leaning against it.

"Where is she?"

"Home, I would assume."

Delia studied him for a moment. "She called off the wedding?"

"What?"

"Well, if she hasn't yet, she will. I'm sorry."

"Are you?"

"I want you to be happy, Cooper," she said, stepping toward him. "Olivia Hamilton wasn't the right woman for you."

"But you are?"

Her eyes locked with his. "Yes, I am and you

know it. I understand you because we're the same."

"Delia."

She took another step toward him, but he stopped her with one raised hand.

"I don't want to talk to you about this."

"About your breakup?" she asked.

"About Livie. She could come back at any moment. I don't want her to find you here."

"Maybe that is the best thing that could happen."

He shook his head. "I'm not giving up on her." It surprised him to hear himself say it.

Delia looked at him as if she felt sorry for him. "It's only a matter of time. Things will get better once you get her out of your life."

He scoffed at that as she left. Why was Delia so sure that Livie would call off the wedding even though she might be carrying his baby? What made it all so confusing was that he was still angry with her for taking off that night and ending up in some other man's bed. That the man might really have drugged and raped her only made it worse.

But what really bothered him was that they might never know the truth. Could he live with that?

Could he live without Livie? He loved the damned woman. And the baby . . . What was he going to do?

He turned and went back outside. He knew it was foolish to keep working on the house. If he didn't live there with Livie, then he didn't want to live there at all. But he had to believe that all his work wasn't for naught. Just as he had to believe that he and Livie would get past this somehow once the blackmailer was caught and they knew the truth.

Buckmaster saw that Ainsley had gathered Livie, Kat and Bo in the ranch den. The only one sitting down was Livie. She looked sick to her stomach and she was wearing a splint on one ankle and there was a set of crutches next to her. What was that about?

He couldn't worry about it now, he thought as he looked into their anxious faces. Clearly, Ainsley hadn't told them anything.

Bracing himself, he faced them. He knew which daughter would blame him and he wasn't surprised after he told them about their mother.

"How could you have not told us that our mother's death wasn't an accident?" Kat demanded.

Still it hurt to have Kat instantly blame him. "It isn't something you tell your daughters. 'Oh, by the way, your crazy mother plunged her car into the frozen river because . . .' Hell, I don't know why she did it."

Livie still hadn't said a word, but she looked pale, as if she had taken the blow harder than the others. Or maybe it was the wedding, Cooper and now one more thing. Of his daughters, he feared it might hit her the hardest because she was so much like her mother.

"Where is she?" Kat asked. "I want to see her."

Buckmaster let out a groan. "You really want to see the woman who abandoned all of you?"

"Don't *you* want to see her?" Bo asked.

He recoiled at the idea. "No. I wish she'd stayed dead."

"She's our *mother*." Ainsley sighed as she dropped into a chair.

"She might have given birth to all of you, but she wasn't a mother," he snapped. "A mother doesn't do this to her children."

"Or to her *husband?*" Kat said. "Do you really have no idea why she did what she did?"

"You want to blame me? Fine. But remember, I was the one who raised all of you. Where was your mother?"

"Exactly. Where *was* she?" Kat asked. "You seriously want us to believe you didn't know she was alive?"

He let out a bitter laugh. "I was caught flat-footed by this, trust me. I had no idea." He itched for a drink, but he feared he wouldn't be able to stop once he started. "Your mother put her car in the river and then when she survived that, she just . . . disappeared, letting us all believe she was dead. Letting me mourn her death for years. Letting me blame myself because, honest to God, I don't know why she did it." His voice broke.

Kat crossed her arms over her chest. "Well, I for one am not going to condemn her until I give her a chance to explain. You said she left you her number?"

He nodded and pointed to the note the sheriff had left on the table. He'd seen Angelina with it earlier and was a little surprised she hadn't destroyed it. "Be my guest."

"Dad, wanting to see our mother doesn't in any way discount everything you've done for us our whole lives," Ainsley tried to assure him. "We love you and appreciate the sacrifices you've made."

He could see that Kat and possibly Bo would have argued that he hadn't really sacrificed. He'd gone on with his life, remarried, left for months to chase a political career—and they would be right.

"I did the best I could," he said, hating that he sounded defensive.

"No one is arguing that," Kat said, picking up the number from the coffee table. "Is there any-thing you want me to tell her?"

Buckmaster shook his head. "All I want to know is when she's leaving again," he said, and walked out of the room.

Livie felt shell-shocked as she got to her feet and followed her father out of the room on her crutches. When her sister had arrived at Cooper's cabin and told her their father wanted to see them, Livie just assumed that he'd heard about the blackmail threats, the pregnancy, the car wreck, the pretty much broken engagement . . . Why else would everyone be gathered in the den when she came in?

Her father had been visibly upset. Also Angelina wasn't anywhere in sight. The woman seldom left their father's side.

"Is it about me?" Livie had wanted to know.

"Not exactly," her sister had said mysteriously.

"What is it? Daddy isn't dying, is he?"

Exasperated, Ainsley had snapped, "Oh, for cryin' out loud, Livie. Of course he isn't."

"Then what was so important that—"

"He'll tell you. Have some patience." Ainsley had ushered her into the den where she'd found her two other sisters waiting, both looking as anxious as she'd felt.

Now she caught up with her father at the bottom of the stairs. "I'm so sorry," she said, touching his arm.

He stopped, and when he turned to her, she leaned her crutches against the banister and threw her arms around him. She'd never seen him so unhappy. He seemed smaller, as if he'd diminished in both size and stature.

Livie had always believed that her father could fix anything. But he couldn't fix this. He looked like a broken man. She'd seen what betrayal had done to Cooper and now her father. It pained her to see how badly he was hurting, even after all these years. "I wish there was something I could do."

He smiled. "I'm so sorry this had to happen now, especially with your wedding . . ."

"Cooper and I are thinking about postponing it."

"No." He looked stricken. "You love Cooper. He loves you. I know the two of you have your problems and I'm probably one of them, but don't let anything stand between you."

His words broke her heart. She hugged him tighter and fought tears. There were some things that couldn't be fixed. She feared she and Cooper were one of them.

"What did you do to your ankle?" he asked, concerned as he handed her the crutches.

"It's nothing to worry about. I'm fine. Dad, I think you should see Mother," she said as she stepped back. She'd called him Daddy since she was a child. But she wasn't a child anymore and lately she'd realized it was high time she grew up. "You might always regret it if you don't."

He shook his head. "When it comes to your mother, I have nothing *but* regrets. What about you?"

It took her a moment to realize he wasn't talking about her mother anymore. "Regrets?" She nodded, but lifted her chin. "It's what we do now that decides our future, though, right? Isn't that what you always say?"

He smiled at that and touched her cheek. "If you let Cooper go—"

"I won't. I can't." She studied him for a moment. "You still love her," she said, recognizing the real source of his pain.

He started to argue that she was wrong but gave up. "Your mother broke my heart. She's the only woman I've ever truly loved."

"If you still love her, you have to go see her." At a sound, they both looked up to see Angelina standing on the second-floor landing above them, listening to everything they'd said.

Chapter TWELVE

"Let's not let this divide our family," Ainsley was saying when Livie returned to the living room.

"He just wants to punish Mother for what she did," Kat argued. "He's not using me to do it." She glanced at the splint on Livie's ankle as if registering it and the crutches for the first time. "What happened to you?"

"Car accident." She dropped into a chair and leaned the crutches against the arm. She'd never felt so tired. "Think about how Daddy feels. He loved her. He just told me that she was the only woman he's ever loved. Unfortunately, Angelina overheard us talking."

The room fell silent for a moment.

Bo stepped to the bar and poured herself a drink. "I wonder what this means for the Sarah Hamilton Foundation."

"I'm sure your job is secure," Kat said.

"I wasn't worried about my job," Bo snapped back. "The foundation actually helps people. I have employees . . ."

"This is what I'm talking about," Ainsley cut in. "Let's not start fighting among ourselves."

"Everyone is going to be talking about us," Bo said. "It will affect the foundation. So what do I tell my employees, my donors?"

"To mind their own business," Kat said as she stepped to the bar and took the bottle away from her sister. "I'm going to call our mother. I want to see her. Anyone going with me?"

"Could this get any worse?" Bo lamented.

Livie sighed. "I'm pregnant and I'm not sure it is Cooper's. I have to call off the wedding and, oh, yeah, I'm being blackmailed by the possible father of the baby and I have no idea who he is or where he is. And my car accident? It wasn't. Someone tried to run me off the road."

Her three sisters stared at her, openmouthed.

"You aren't serious," Bo said.

"How could you not know who the man is?" Kat demanded.

"It's a long story. He was pretending to be someone he wasn't." She didn't add that so was she.

"If you're trying to make us feel better about our

mother coming back from the dead . . ." Bo said.

"Also I have morning sickness off and on all day," Livie added, feeling closer to her sisters than she had in a long time. "And Cooper . . ." Her voice broke.

"Okay, you win," Bo said, and put down the drink she'd poured before Kat had taken the bottle from her.

"If Cooper doesn't get on board with this, then too bad for him," Ainsley said. "I don't want you to go through with something you don't want to."

"If you mean the baby . . ."

Her sister cut her off. "The baby stays. Dad will be tickled to have a grandchild no matter how he gets one. What is that old saying? It takes a ranch to raise a baby?"

Livie smiled through her tears as each of her sisters came over to hug her.

"Does Dad know yet?" Kat asked.

She shook her head.

"What about the dragon lady?"

"Are you kidding?" Bo made a disparaging sound. "Angelina pretends none of us even exist. She certainly isn't going to notice there is anything wrong."

"I wonder how she's taking all this," Ainsley said. "I know she's putting on a good front, but . . ."

"They aren't legally married, are they?" Kat said. "So does that make Dad a bigamist? If so, it could really hurt his run for president."

They all laughed, though weakly.

"Seriously?" Kat said. "A suicidal wife back from the dead? The scandal could be bad for him. If we're speculating on what drove her to do it—excuse the pun—then can you imagine what the press will make of it?"

"Don't," Livie said, feeling nauseous again. "Daddy's hurting enough right now. Do you really think this could cost him the White House?"

"When you said it was complicated . . . Are you really being blackmailed?" Ainsley asked, looking worried.

Livie smiled and reached over to take her big sister's hand. "Not to worry. The sheriff is trying to find the man. So is Cooper." She couldn't help glancing toward the window. Where was her blackmailer now? She feared closer than she wanted to believe.

Russell was surprised to open his door and find Sarah Hamilton standing there. She was half turned, her face tilted up to the sun, her eyes closed.

"Hello," he said, surprised even more at how glad he was to see her.

She seemed to start as she opened her eyes and smiled at him. "I was just enjoying the day. I always loved this time of year."

He smiled back at her, wondering what she was doing here, but glad nonetheless.

"I hope I didn't catch you at a bad time. The sheriff was kind enough to give me a ride out." Her voice broke and he realized she'd come here because she had nowhere else to go.

"No, not at all." He quickly stepped back to invite her in. "I just made iced tea. Would you like some?"

"I would love a glass." She stepped in, blinking as her eyes adjusted to the dimness inside the house. "Frank said he'd pick me up in an hour or so."

"I'll call him to tell him it isn't necessary. I can take you wherever you would like to go. Please," he said before she could object. "I would like to."

She smiled and glanced around. "You have a nice place here."

"Thank you. Come on in the kitchen. It's bright and sunny in here so we can enjoy this spring day." His wife had always complained that the living room was too dark. She, too, had liked sunshine.

"I wanted to thank you," she said as she took a seat at the kitchen table by the window.

He got their tea and sat down across from her. "Thank me? I almost killed you."

"Not true, but still, I do feel like a cat with nine lives."

"Do you want to talk about it?" he asked after a moment.

Her eyes filled with tears, but she shook her

head. "Everyone has so many questions." She met his gaze across the table. Her face seemed to soften. "They don't seem to realize that I am as much in the dark as they are."

"Which is a good reason to enjoy each day and not delve too deeply in the past, I would think."

She smiled at that and took a sip of her tea. "You make a very nice glass of tea, Mr. Murdock."

"Wait until you try the tuna sandwich I'm going to make us for lunch." When she started to decline, he added, "Eating alone is one of the worse things about losing my wife. We were married more than forty years."

"I'm sorry, I hear you lost her recently. I can't remember the last time I had a tuna sandwich," she said with a small self-deprecating smile. "Then again, I can't remember anything, can I? I'd love one."

They drank their tea in a companionable silence, the sun shining in the kitchen window, dust motes dancing in the golden light.

This was what Russell realized he really missed the most since his wife died. For a while, he didn't feel as lonely.

"Sarah, I don't know if you've noticed the small guesthouse I have out back, but I was thinking . . ." He met her gaze and hesitated. "It's probably not—"

"Russell, I would love to stay in your guest-house, if you're sure it isn't an imposition. I feel so . . . exposed staying at the motel in town and so far away from my children."

He smiled, happier than he had been in a very long time. "Then it's settled. We'll move you in today."

She laughed. "Everything I own is on me. There is nothing to move. Thank you. I really don't know what I would have done without your help."

When Livie limped into the cabin after her sister dropped her off, she found Cooper standing in the small kitchen.

"I should have known you would hightail it the first chance you got," he said. "Did you forget something? Is that why you came back?"

She stared at him for a moment confused before she realized why he was angry. "I didn't leave. I mean, yes, I had to go to my father's. But not for the reason you think." With regret, she saw that the glass of wildflowers that had been on the table was gone. "My mother is alive and in Beartooth."

"*What?* How is that possible?"

She shrugged as she sat down and he took the crutches from her. "That's just it. No one knows, including my mother. Apparently she's suffering from some form of amnesia."

"That actually happens?" he asked as he dropped into a chair next to her.

She felt weak and exhausted from all of it. "I suspect she is a special case since apparently the last thing she remembers is giving birth to Harper and Cassidy." A wave of nausea hit her. Her stomach roiled. "I . . ." She couldn't get the words out, just pushed herself up and limped as quickly as she could into the bathroom. She didn't have time to slam the door, barely making it to the toilet, where she dropped to her knees.

As she finished heaving, Cooper's hand appeared holding a wet washcloth. She took it, mumbled thanks and wiped her face.

"Better?" he asked.

She nodded. "I didn't want you to see me like this," she said as he helped her to her feet. "It was the main reason I hesitated moving in with you."

"How often does this happen?"

"Too often," she said with a groan.

His gaze was sheepish. "I'm sorry. I didn't know how sick you've been."

"Thank you."

"Is there anything I can do, anything I can get you?"

Livie couldn't help but be heartened. "No, it should be getting better now that I'm almost three months in." She wanted to bite her tongue. Had she really ruined the moment by reminding him what had happened three months ago?

"It's okay," he said, seeing her cringe. He cupped her cheek and she leaned into his warm hand and closed her eyes. Tears leaked from under her eyelashes. She breathed in his familiar scent as if taking her last breath. "Oh, Coop."

To her surprise, he pulled her into his arms and held her. "It's okay," he whispered into her hair. "Trust me, somehow it's going to be all right."

Nettie was working at the Beartooth General Store when Mabel Murphy came in to tell her the news.

"Sarah Hamilton is alive!" Mabel practically crowed. "And that's not all. I heard it wasn't an accident her driving into the river. She was really trying to kill herself." Mabel nodded as if it was all now perfectly obvious. "Or was she just trying to escape those six children and Buckmaster Hamilton?"

Frank had broken the news to Nettie before she'd left for work.

"I know how you hate to be the last one to hear," he'd said, and grinned at her. "Sarah Hamilton has returned from the dead."

She'd listened in shock to his story. "What does she look like after twenty-two years?" Nettie had wanted to know.

Frank had shrugged. "She looks fine."

"I mean, is she old and haggard?"

"No, she's aged, but haven't we all."

Nettie had been frustrated as she'd tried to get more information out of her husband. "So does Buckmaster know? Is he going to see her? What about her daughters?"

Frank hadn't been able to answer more than, "Buckmaster knows. I told him."

"How did he take it?"

"How do you think? Lynette, that's all you get, so thank me for that. At least Mabel Murphy won't be catching you flat-footed with the news."

She'd groaned at the time, but could laugh now. Frank had known Mabel would be the one to stop by the store. *Who's the worst gossip in Beartooth* now? Nettie had wanted to demand. Since she'd given up the role, Mabel had gladly stepped in. Mabel was married to one of the men on the Beartooth volunteer fire department who had been at the river the night Sarah allegedly died. He would have known it had looked like a suicide, but the speculation had been squashed at the time to protect Buckmaster and his girls.

"I heard Buckmaster is fit to be tied," Mabel was saying. "Not to mention his . . . wife, Angelina." She mugged a face. No one liked Angelina. "Bet she had a conniption fit. Is their marriage even legal?"

"I would imagine Buckmaster had Sarah declared legally dead seven years after her car went in the river," Nettie said. "Though I believe in a case where it appeared obvious that she probably didn't survive, he could have had it done sooner. As for the marriages, a judge will probably have to sort all that out."

"What a fine kettle of fish this is," Mabel said

contentedly. "I do feel for the daughters, though. Twenty-two years of believing your mother dead. Not to mention finding out that she tried to kill herself. You don't think Buckmaster would have told them that, do you?"

No, Nettie didn't. "Still, they should be happy to see their mother, don't you think?"

Mabel raised a brow. "Would you, knowing that she abandoned you? What would make a woman do that? I just wonder what brought her back now after all this time."

Nettie did, too. She had the feeling that her husband suspected something, but he wasn't telling. "I wonder where she's been all this time. She could have another family."

Apparently that hadn't dawned on Mabel. Her eyes glittered at the prospect. "Wouldn't that be interesting . . ."

After Cooper left to go to the Hamilton Ranch to check on a horse, Livie changed clothes and got ready for her appointment. She felt guilty for not telling him about it. Or for driving herself rather than asking Ainsley.

But she was getting around well on the walking splint and her ankle felt better this morning. This was also something she needed to do on her own. Ainsley had been nagging her about telling their father not only about the blackmailer, but also about the pregnancy.

"You *have* to tell Dad," Ainsley had said earlier on the drive back to the cabin.

"Now just doesn't seem—"

"You're three months pregnant already. You can't keep this a secret much longer, and if you're really planning to cancel the wedding . . . Have you told Cooper?"

"Not yet." She had tried to concentrate on the Montana landscape blurring past. Her love for the land was almost as much a part of her as her love for Cooper.

"Dad is strong. He can take it."

"But can Angelina?" Livie had joked, trying to lighten the mood. "Seriously, Dad will want to do something and that will only set off Cooper. But I will talk to him. I promise," she'd said, but her mind had been on her doctor's appointment.

She'd made the appointment several days ago. She had to know who the father of her baby was. The drive didn't take long. She did her best to enjoy the beautiful spring day, but it was useless. Her thoughts were on Cooper and his sudden tenderness earlier.

He loved her. And she loved him. Was it possible they could get through this?

Fortunately, she didn't have to wait long at the doctor's office. After he examined her, he asked her to get dressed and meet him in his office.

"You're about thirteen weeks along," he said

once she was seated. "I understand you're interested in paternity testing?"

To his credit, the doctor hadn't blinked when she'd told him. She listened as he explained about two tests, amniocentesis and CVS. "Both are invasive procedures that pose a risk of miscarriage."

She knew this but was hoping there was some way. "There isn't anything else?"

"There is one noninvasive test that can be done after the fourteenth week. It uses the mother's and the alleged father's blood. By the fourteenth week, the mother carries enough of the baby's DNA to give a result with a ninety-nine percent accuracy."

"After fourteen weeks?" That would mean waiting another week. Right now that seemed like a lifetime. A lot could happen in a week, she thought as she left the doctor's office. But what if it wasn't Cooper's baby? In that case, she could definitely wait to hear the results.

What would Cooper say when she told him about the test? She had no idea. Right now she got the impression he was trying to forget there even was a baby.

Since she was out, she decided to pick up a few things in Big Timber. But as she drove down the main street, she noticed a blue pickup turn into the diagonal parking in front of the Grand Hotel. She recalled what Cooper had said about a blue pickup following her.

Was this the same pickup?

Slowing as if looking for a place to park, she watched as the man behind the wheel climbed out. From the back, he looked like any other cowboy from the area. But as he started to close his door, he turned to toss something into the cab.

Livie's pulse jumped. It was him! The man who'd rescued her at the end of January, miles from here.

As he started to turn in her direction as if suddenly aware of her stopped behind his truck, she quickly hit the gas and turned away. The last thing she needed was for him to recognize her and take off. But when she dared glance back, she saw him head into the Grand's bar.

Driving up the street, she found a parking place and pulled in. She was shaking so hard she had trouble dialing the number. "I need to speak with Sheriff Curry. It's an emergency.

"I just saw the man who's blackmailing me," she cried when the sheriff came on the line. "He's driving a blue pickup. He's parked in front of the Grand Hotel."

"Have you mentioned this to anyone else?" Frank asked.

"No."

"Good. Don't. Especially your fiancé. I'll handle this."

Cooper was in the corral with one of the mustangs when Rylan West drove up. He knew he'd been

200

avoiding his friend since the night of the engagement party, but right now he was glad to see him.

"What's going on? Last time I saw you, you were on cloud nine," Rylan said after the two of them walked around to a shady part of the barn to sit down.

"I didn't want to bother you with my problems. You've had your own."

Rylan nodded as he looked out across the pasture where the mustangs were running in the wind, manes and tails flying. "It's been tough. First Carson's death, then losing the baby."

"How is Destry?"

Rylan smiled. "She's strong, probably stronger than me most days. So what's going on with you? The wedding is still on, right? I mean, I am still your best man."

Cooper filled him in. He trusted his best friend with the news. When he'd first met Rylan, they'd become fast friends. Rylan had told him about his sister's murder and how it had driven him and Destry apart for years, but how they had found their way back together.

"Coop, what are you going to do?" his friend asked when he finished.

He shook his head. "I'm angry with Livie for taking off in the middle of a storm, for putting herself in a position where something like this could happen. I'm mad at myself for always fighting her. She'd accused me of having a chip on my shoulder." He let out a self-deprecating laugh. "I've always said she was wrong, but damned if she isn't right. It's made me take a good hard look at myself and the part I played in all this. But I'm furious with this man for taking advantage of her and I want to do something about it."

"And the baby?" Rylan asked.

Cooper looked away. "There are moments when I look at Livie and . . ." His voice broke. "I love her so much that I don't care whose baby she's carrying because it's hers and that is all that matters, but then in the next moment I think about the man . . ."

"Have you told her this?"

He shook his head. "What if I always look at that child and see that other man?"

"If you love her . . ."

"I wish it was that simple."

Rylan laughed. "It is. But believe me, I know how tough it is to forgive and forget. If there's anything I can do . . ."

"It's just good to see you."

"Did you ever find the horse that followed her up into the mountains?" Rylan asked after a moment.

"It's one of ours from the ranch. Ainsley checked the names of those who are currently employed there. Unfortunately, Livie is the only one who can recognize him. But we believe his initials are D.C., first name Drake. There was no

Drake. No cowboy with the initials D.C. Maybe Livie is right and it was just some random cowboy who'd followed her up the mountain and it means nothing."

After Rylan left, Cooper walked up to the main house. Now that Buckmaster was home, he wanted to ask him about that day. He found him in the sunroom, and while he didn't want to disturb him after the news, he didn't want to put this off any longer.

"Sorry to bother you," he said.

Buckmaster looked up, his expression brightening. "You're not bothering me. Join me. I was just having a glass of lemonade. I can get—"

"I'm fine," he said, motioning the older man back into the chair he'd been occupying. "I just need to ask you a quick question. The day after the party when you saw Livie before she went on her ride, did you happen to notice if anyone else rode out after that?"

He frowned thoughtfully. "I remember watching her. You know, you're right. It wasn't long after that I saw someone head in the same direction."

"Do you know who it was?"

"Lane. Is there a problem?"

Lane Broadwater, Angelina's brother? "Did you ask him to look after her?"

"No, come to think of it, I was surprised to see him on a horse. Like his sister, he seldom rides. Why are you asking about this?"

Cooper shook his head. "I saw tracks when I went after her. I was afraid someone had followed her up into the mountains. I'm sure it was just a coincidence that their paths crossed." How else could he explain it?

Word of Sarah Hamilton's return from the dead spread like a wildfire through the county. Speculation ran rampant at the Branding Iron Café.

"Where's she been all these years? Must have had amnesia. Hit her head and couldn't remember who she was, bet that was it."

"And now, twenty-two years later, she suddenly remembers? Not likely. No, I think we all know why she did what she did."

Nettie had a habit of stopping in at the café even on the mornings when she didn't work at the general store. She loved Kate's cinnamon rolls and loved listening to the gossip, even if she was no longer spreading it.

She'd heard the rumors twenty-two years ago that Sarah Hamilton hadn't hit her brakes. The rumors had died down pretty quickly back then. But now they ran rampant. Word was that Sarah had sped up as she neared the river and went off the road in one of the only spots where there wasn't any guardrail. Her SUV was moving so fast, she'd ended up in the middle of the river before it had broken through the ice.

The word *suicide* had been whispered about all those years ago, but Buckmaster Hamilton claimed she'd fallen asleep at the wheel. At four in the morning in the middle of winter? And what had she been doing on that road to begin with, miles from her husband and six children?

"Maybe she planned the whole thing," Kate said, keeping her voice down now as she joined Nettie at the table. Kate wasn't one for gossiping but even she was curious about Sarah's return. "Maybe she wasn't even in the car when it left the road. Didn't I hear that she wasn't wearing her seat belt? But who leaves behind six children?"

"A woman faced with *raising* six children," Nettie said. "If she'd stuck around, she might have had a whole lot more. Who knew Buckmaster was so randy."

Kate laughed and put a hand over the baby growing inside her. "No, I can't imagine a mother doing that even with six children."

"Not everyone is like you, Kate," Nettie said. "I do wonder why she's back."

"This has got to be an incredible shock for her daughters."

"And for Buckmaster, and what about his current *wife?* I doubt anyone is that sympathetic when it comes to Angelina, though. Bet she's putting the senator through hell."

"Can you imagine when he opened the door to

find his dead wife standing there," Kate said. "I'm surprised it didn't give him a heart attack."

"As far as I know, he hasn't laid eyes on her yet," Nettie said.

Chapter THIRTEEN

Unable to stand another minute in the house with Angelina, the disapproving looks of his daughters and the chance that his dead first wife might show up at his door, Buckmaster drove into Beartooth to the Range Rider.

The bar was empty this time of day, which suited him just fine.

Clete poured him a Scotch and said, "Haven't seen you for a while."

He figured everyone in town already knew about Sarah. "I've never needed a drink more badly than I do right now. I'm sure you heard I now have two wives."

"I wouldn't wish that on any man."

"You have no idea," he said, and took a drink. Angelina had been so strong and capable before this. Now, she was acting jealous and possessive and downright paranoid. It didn't help that she'd overheard him say Sarah was the only woman he'd ever loved.

"Women," he said, drained his glass and slid it

back to Clete. "Right now, I don't want either of them."

"Careful, you might get your wish."

"Can you believe my daughters are angry with me over all this?" he asked as Clete placed another Scotch on the cocktail napkin in front of him.

The bar was cool and dark. He hoped it stayed empty because he didn't want to leave.

"I've never understood women," Clete said. "If you find out what they want, let me know."

Buckmaster shook his head. "My daughters don't understand why I don't want to see her. My first wife, the one back from the dead. Why would I want to after everything she's put me through?"

"You must be curious, though, right?"

He hated to admit it. "I'm too angry with her. How could she abandon her own children?"

"She must not have been in her right mind. All she had was the clothes on her back, right?"

Buckmaster frowned as he realized Clete had a point. "Her purse was found in her car so she didn't even have any money. At least, none that I knew of."

"If she had a credit card and used it . . ."

"I would have known she was alive." He looked down at the amber of the Scotch, the first drink warming him inside, but also making him think clearer than he had since hearing the news.

"So how *did* she survive?"

"That old hermit, what's his name?"

"Lester Halverson?"

Buckmaster knew there was no keeping a lid on any of this. The press would get the whole story and he was almost looking forward to it. At least he would know the truth. He sure as hell couldn't depend on Sarah to tell him the truth.

"He found her, dried her clothes, kept her from dying of hypothermia, but then she got dressed and took off with someone in the middle of the night. At least, that's his story, according to the sheriff."

"So someone picked her up from Halverson's house?"

Another man. Buckmaster hadn't considered this and wondered why it had taken him so long to put the pieces together.

He pushed the Scotch away as he dug out his cell phone. Was it possible she'd been having an affair the whole time they were married? There was only one way to find out.

Although he'd sworn he would never call her, he'd taken down the cell phone number the sheriff had given him. Just in case.

He braced himself and punched in the number, half expecting Russell Murdock to answer.

"Hello?"

Sarah's voice was the same and for a moment Buckmaster almost hung up.

"Hello?"

"It's me."

"Buck?" The way she said it brought back too many memories of summer nights tangled in the sheets of their big bed.

He swore under his breath. "I need to see you."

Silence, then, "We should meet somewhere public."

"I don't plan to kill you, Sarah."

"I only thought it might be easier after all this time."

"Nothing about this is easy, *especially* after all this time," he snapped. "Everyone in the county is already talking. I prefer not to have everyone watching us. Remember the creek where we used to go as kids?"

"Of course."

"Let's meet there. Unless after we talk there is a good reason I'm going to want to kill you."

"Give me thirty minutes."

When the sheriff walked into the Grand Hotel's bar, he saw a man fitting the description Olivia Hamilton had given him.

The cowboy had a beer in front of him and he was flirting with the female bartender. That the bartender was responding matched Olivia's story. The cowboy was good-looking and a charmer.

"Excuse me," the sheriff said. "Are you driving that blue pickup outside?"

The man shot a wink at the bartender before

smiling over at Frank. "I sure am, Sheriff. Is something wrong?"

He'd run across his share of cocky cowboys in his day. This one was no different. "I'd like to see some identification, please."

The cowboy dug out his wallet. It was tooled leather. As the man removed his driver's license from it, Frank couldn't help but notice the initials carved into the leather on the front: D.C.

He glanced at the Wyoming driver's license. Drake Connors out of Laramie, Wyoming. The address was a post office box.

Frank handed the license back. "Your truck outside has Montana plates on it."

"Yep, just bought it."

"What brings you to this area?"

"I'm looking for a job and if I can find one around here, I'll be sure to get a Montana driver's license to go with the truck." He chuckled as if he was a pretty funny guy.

"I'm going to have to ask you to come down to the sheriff's department."

"You're joking? What for?"

"Right now I just want to ask you a few questions."

"If I refuse?" Drake Connors asked, more wary.

"Then I will arrest you on suspicion of attempted murder and blackmail."

The cowboy didn't look so cocky now. "You've got the wrong man."

"Well, I think we can find that out quickly enough. Are you going to come willingly?"

Drake Connors pushed his beer away and held up his hands. "I have nothing to hide."

Frank wouldn't have bet on that.

Buckmaster pulled in next to the creek and cut his engine. He could see the clear sparkling water through the pines and cottonwoods. This had been their favorite spot, an oxbow in the creek. The water rushed over a colorful array of rocks in one spot but pooled into a deep green pond in another as it made the corner. Kids still came here during the hot summer months to swing from the rope tied to one of the larger cottonwood limbs that hung out over the deepest part.

This was where he'd asked Sarah to marry him.

At the sound of a vehicle he got out and walked on down to the edge of the water to sit on one of the large boulders. It was almost smooth on top from all the bare feet that had climbed it to dive into the rambling creek.

He heard the vehicle engine die, then the sound of a truck door opening, then another door.

Turning in surprise, he saw that Sarah hadn't come alone. Why was that? Didn't she have her own vehicle? It hadn't crossed his mind that she might not. Just as she hadn't had her own cell phone. He reminded himself that she'd left without a dime. How had she lived all these years?

He wasn't happy to see that a man had brought her.

"Russell?" Russell Murdock, the W Bar G Ranch manager, the man the sheriff said had found her. Found her where?

On the passenger's side of the truck, he caught movement through the pines.

"Sarah asked me to come along," Russell said before looking across the pickup's hood to where Sarah must have been standing. "I'll be here if you need me."

Buckmaster felt his stomach churn, emotions running wild. Sarah had brought along a . . . what . . . a bodyguard? Did she think that little of him? Or did she have real reason to fear him? Was Russell Murdock the man she'd run off with twenty-two years ago? The moment he thought it, he knew that couldn't have been the case since Russell hadn't left back then. He'd been married all these years and only recently had buried his wife.

But that didn't mean he hadn't been the man who'd picked her up at Lester Halverson's.

When Sarah stepped from behind the trees, he felt a start. At first, because of the bright spring sunlight, all he saw was her silhouette. But it was so much as it had been all those years ago that he felt an old stirring and swore under his breath.

She moved out of the shadows, down the hill toward him and the creek.

At first he thought she looked exactly as she had the last time he saw her. But as she came closer, he saw that, like him, she'd aged. But she was still beautiful, still made his heart race at just the sight of her.

The weight of all those wasted years struck him hard, making it almost impossible to take a breath as she stopped a few feet from him.

He stood staring at her in amazement. Until that moment he hadn't accepted that she really was alive. It had seemed like a dream or a nightmare, but now it was all too real.

"Sarah." He hated that his voice cracked. He fought for his next breath, fought to maintain some kind of control over his raging emotions.

"Maybe we could sit down by the creek," she suggested, her voice as cool as the breeze coming off the water. If she felt anything, her voice didn't give it away.

He followed her a few yards farther along the bank until they came to a series of rocks. She took a seat on one, leaving him several to choose from a few feet from her.

"I don't know what to say." This was certainly not the way he'd planned it in his head on the drive out here. He'd seen himself demanding answers, voice raised, his tone filled with righteous indignation.

"I know this all seems surreal to you," she said. "It does to me, too."

"Does it?" He hated the edge to his voice.

"Buck, my last memory was of giving birth to our twins."

He stared at her. "What are you saying? That you don't remember *anything?*"

"I remember us, our daughters . . ."

He shot to his feet. "You don't remember driving into the river or taking off with someone and staying hidden for twenty-two years?" His voice had risen enough that he heard Russell open his door and step out.

"No, Buck, I don't. When Russell found me . . ."

"The night you went in the river?"

"No, a few days ago he found me as I came out of the woods outside of Beartooth. Russell was coming down the road when I stumbled out of the trees and in front of his pickup. I had no memory of where I'd been or that twenty-two years had passed. I just wanted to see you and my daughters."

"That's real damned convenient, Sarah."

"No, Buck, it's not. You should know how hard this is on me. To realize that my daughters are all grown now and I missed . . ." Her voice broke.

He sat back down, lowered his voice. "What about me, Sarah? What about how hard it has been for me?"

She met his gaze. He'd forgotten how blue her eyes were. "I'm so sorry."

He turned away as he fought the pain and anger.

"What now, Sarah?" he demanded, turning back to her.

"Russell told me that you'd married. Also that you're a candidate for president. I'm so happy for you. I don't want to cause you any trouble. I only want to see my daughters, then . . ." She shook her head. "Then I don't know." Again her voice broke. "I'll leave, if that's what you all want."

"Have you seen a doctor? Does he think your memory will come back?"

"I've only seen a retired doctor outside of Beartooth, Dr. Farnsworth. He's given me the name of several neurologists in Bozeman. I haven't made an appointment yet. I wasn't sure how long I would be staying."

"Where *are* you staying?"

"I was at a motel in Big Timber, but Russell was kind enough to offer me his guesthouse."

"I'll just bet he was," Buckmaster said under his breath.

"It isn't like that, Buck," she said, sounding tired as she got to her feet. "Have you told the girls?"

He nodded, realizing there was little more to say. They had shared so much, including six daughters, and yet he felt as if he was looking at a stranger.

This wasn't the woman he'd fallen in love with. He didn't know this woman. And yet, he felt a pull toward her stronger than gravity.

"We can talk again, if you want," she said. "I'm sorry I can't tell you what happened that night or anything about all these years since. It feels as if no time has passed, until I look in the mirror." She sighed. "I get so tired. I should go." She started up the hill.

He said nothing as he watched her. Russell went around the truck to open her door and help her in. She seemed small and as broken as he felt.

He stayed by the creek until he didn't hear anything but the burble of the water against the bank.

At his office, the sheriff texted a mug shot of Drake Connors to Olivia. Within minutes she texted back that he had the right man.

"You don't mind if I record our conversation, do you?" he asked Drake.

"I'm thinking I might need a lawyer."

"You'd be the best judge of that. Let me ask you this. Do you know Olivia Hamilton?"

The man's expression gave him away. He started to shake his head.

Frank said, "You met her up by Monarch last January, rescued her after her car went off the road in a snowstorm. Starting to ring any bells?"

Drake sighed. "Okay, I met her, but nothing happened that night and I never saw her again."

"You didn't drug her?"

Again he hesitated. "I gave her a little something to help her sleep."

"You didn't then have intercourse with her?"

"No, I did not." He sighed. "I was upset because I'd been stood up that night. So I put Olivia Hamilton in the master bedroom bed just to take a photograph of the two of us. I was trying to get back at someone."

"The woman who actually owned the house, Amelia Wellesley?"

He nodded. "But I swear nothing happened. I put her in the bed, took a photo of the two of us and then I left."

"How did you leave? Before that you were driving the homeowner's vehicle, right?"

Drake seemed surprised at how much Frank knew. "I had a friend from Monarch pick me up. Did Olivia tell you that I had her car towed for her? It should have been there when she woke up. Does that sound like a guy who would take advantage of her?"

"You drugged her."

"It wasn't like that. We had some wine. She was still upset about going off the road. I think she might have had a fight with her boyfriend. I saw her looking at her ring finger a few times."

"You're a very observant guy," he said.

"I pay attention," Drake said with a shrug. "I gave her one of Amelia's sleeping pills, and then later I was worried about her. I was thinking since she hit her head in the crash, maybe I shouldn't have given her anything, so I went in to check on her. She was out like a light, but fine. That's when I got the idea of the photo."

Frank actually believed that Drake Connors was telling the truth.

"When did you get the idea to start blackmailing her?"

"What?"

"You're saying you aren't blackmailing her?"

"Hell, no. Look, I don't know what she told you—"

"How long have you been in town, Mr. Connors?"

He blinked at the quick change of subject. "I got here yesterday. I'm here looking for work, like I told you."

"Can anyone substantiate where you were yesterday afternoon and evening?"

"You mean like an alibi?" He raked a hand through his hair. "Sure, I got into town and drove up the West Boulder. I was at the Road Kill bar most of the afternoon and evening. You can ask the bartender or just about anyone who was there."

Frank would bet this was the man Cooper Barnett had chased out of town yesterday. But if Drake Connors's alibi checked out, then he wasn't the one who'd run Olivia off the road last night.

"How did you buy the new truck if you are out of work?"

Drake looked away for a moment before he said, "It was a gift."

"From . . ."

"Howard Wellesley. And there was no black-mail involved."

"He paid you not to see his wife anymore? You don't consider that blackmail?" Frank asked.

Drake shrugged, but couldn't hide the grin.

Despicable, he thought, but in his line of work he ran across all kinds.

"Do you have a bank account?"

"Nope, never needed one." He sounded proud of the fact.

"You're sure you didn't get into town, steal a pickup and run Olivia Hamilton off the road?"

"Hell, no. Did she say it was me?"

Frank thought of the typed blackmail notes. "Do you own a computer?"

"No, why? Look, I really don't know what this is all about. I told you, I never saw her again after that night."

"But you recognized her name."

Drake gave him a sheepish look. "Okay, yes, I knew her name but only because I didn't believe the fake one she gave me so I checked her driver's license."

"You gave her a fake name, as well, I understand."

Again the cowboy looked sheepish. "It was kind of a joke between me and Amelia." He shrugged.

"I'd like to take a look in your truck. I can get a warrant . . ."

"Take a look. Like I said, I have nothing to hide."

Frank wasn't that surprised to find nothing of interest in the man's pickup. He found a lot of nice clothing, some expensive cowboy boots and hats, but nothing that would connect him to either the blackmail or the hit-and-run.

"Is everything you own in your truck?" There hadn't been a computer or any paper or envelopes, but Drake was the kind of guy who could find a computer and paper when he needed it.

"I don't like staying in one place very long."

"I can imagine. You say you're looking for work locally?"

"I heard the Knight Ranch might be hiring."

"Does your being in town have anything to do with Olivia Hamilton?"

"Truthfully, I'd completely forgotten about her."

Chapter FOURTEEN

Cooper had been out working on the house when the sheriff drove up. Livie hadn't said anything to him, just as Frank had advised. She'd been a nervous wreck waiting for the sheriff to call.

Once seated in the cabin, the two listened to what Frank had to tell her about Drake Connors, torn between desperately wanting to believe the man and afraid to.

"And you *believed* him?" Cooper demanded.

"I think some of what he told me was truthful," the sheriff said. "He swears nothing happened that night and I tend to believe him. As far as the blackmail threats . . . there is no evidence to refute what he claims."

"But he admitted plying her with wine and giving her a sleeping pill," Cooper argued.

The sheriff nodded. "However, there is no way to prove that he did anything more than that without physical proof."

Cooper glanced over at her. "You're saying that if she had gone to the sheriff up in Monarch at the time—"

"But I didn't," Livie said, cutting her fiancé off.

Cooper swore. "So the only proof will be if she's carrying his child."

"Even then, you would have to prove that sexual intercourse hadn't been consensual," Frank said.

Livie groaned inwardly. "What about the black-mail?"

"He swears he knows nothing about it."

"Can't you check his bank account?" Cooper asked.

"He says he doesn't have a bank account nor has he ever had one. Given what we know about him, I would imagine it's true. The man is driving a truck that he says was purchased for him. I'm trying to verify that. He says he's here looking for work. If he got the ten thousand, then it's gone. But like I said, there is nothing at this point to tie him to the threats."

"What about forcing Livie off the road last night?"

"He has an alibi that checks out. Numerous people saw him at a bar from early afternoon until it closed. He wasn't the one who ran you off the road."

Cooper raked a hand through his hair in frustration. "So he's going to get away with this."

"We don't know that it didn't happen just as he said," the sheriff pointed out.

Livie prayed it was true and that this baby was Cooper's, not that it might be enough to save their relationship at this point.

Frank looked to Cooper. "I'm going to give you some good advice. Let me handle this. Don't go after this man."

"Wouldn't you under the circumstances?"

"I'd be tempted," the sheriff admitted. "But it would be a mistake. You could end up behind bars for assault and what would you have accomplished?"

"Maybe just a little satisfaction in that I'd kicked the crap out of him," Cooper said.

Frank picked up his hat. "Sorry I couldn't be of more help. But if he was behind the blackmail threats, I doubt you'll be getting any more."

"Yeah, we've thought that before," Cooper said. "And we were wrong." As he stormed out to the house he was building, Livie waited until the sheriff left before joining him.

"Coop, I thought you'd be relieved."

He swung his hammer, slamming a nail into a pine two-by-four before snatching up another one and doing the same.

"Could you please stop that," Livie cried. "I didn't *sleep* with him. That is, he didn't sleep with me. He was having an affair with Amelia Wellesley. I was just in the wrong place at the wrong time and he used me to make her jealous."

She could see that Cooper was having a hard time swallowing this story.

"I didn't believe it at first, either. But I do now. He didn't even sleep in the same bed. It was Amelia he wanted. That's why he took the photo of the two of us and sent it to her."

Cooper let out a low growl and put down his hammer. "If not him, then who is behind the blackmail? Or are you going to tell me that Amelia Wellesley is behind the blackmail? Maybe he sent your photo to someone else."

She hadn't thought of that. She hadn't thought of a lot of things lately, she realized. "Coop, this baby—"

He cut her off. "Sorry, but there isn't a man alive who, finding you naked in his bed, isn't going to make love to you."

Before she could argue the point, he stormed over to his pickup.

"Where are you going?" she demanded of his retreating backside.

"Anywhere but here right now," he said over his shoulder as he climbed into the truck. The engine rumbled to life and he left in a cloud of dust.

Russell was surprised when he got the call from the sheriff. It was late afternoon and thunderheads were forming over the Crazies.

"Could you show me the exact spot where you found Sarah Hamilton?"

"Of course."

"I'll pick you up in ten minutes if that's all right."

It was less than ten minutes, but Russell was ready. He'd walked out to the guesthouse to tell Sarah where he was going. She'd said she would be fine. She was going to take a nap.

Once on the road, the sheriff asked him how Sarah was doing. "I understand she's staying with you."

"In my guesthouse," Russell said. The small guesthouse had come with the ranch he'd purchased years ago.

Frank looked over at him. "And how is she doing?"

"It's hard to say. She's frustrated by her lack of memory. She's seeing a neurologist soon. I'm sure she hopes he can help." Russell felt a strange loyalty to Sarah that had nothing to do with guilt over nearly killing her.

But at the same time, he was worried about her.

"I think she's starting to remember something," he said, and looked out the side window. The sun slanted down through the pines to make patterns on the narrow dirt road. "It's right up here past the cemetery."

"What makes you think she's starting to remember?"

"The memories are . . . scaring her." Russell looked down the road, recalling how she had suddenly stumbled out of the pines and into his path. "Here," he said.

The sheriff braked to a stop. *"Here?"*

Russell understood his surprise. There was nothing close around here—no houses, no other roads, nothing.

"What kind of shape was she in when you found her?" Frank asked.

"Not good. Scraped up, her hair a mess, clothes soiled. Dr. Farnsworth's wife fixed her up before you saw her."

The sheriff was looking around. "So how did she get here?"

Russell had asked himself the same question. "I thought for sure I would find her car broken down up the road. But she didn't have a purse or car keys or anything except the clothes on her back." He shook his head. "It was as if she'd been dropped here by aliens."

Frank looked over at him as he pulled the patrol SUV off the road and killed the engine. "I hope you don't mention that to anyone. You know how rumors are in these parts."

Russell laughed, but realized the sheriff was serious as they both got out.

They walked a few yards up the road until Russell came to the place where he saw her footprints in the shallow barrow pit.

"This is it." He glanced into the dark of the pines. "She came out of there."

Buckmaster walked into his house to see his attorney waiting for him with Angelina and her brother. He cursed silently. The woman just couldn't wait for him to take care of this, could she?

"Patrick was kind enough to come by, but he insisted we wait until you got here," Angelina said, sounding put out.

"Well, he is *my* attorney." Buckmaster walked to the bar and poured himself a drink.

"And I'm your *wife*. At least, one of them. I was just filling Patrick in on what has happened. As *your* lawyer, he needs to know."

"I told her I prefer to hear it from you," Patrick said diplomatically.

He took a swig of the Scotch before turning to

the man. "Sarah is alive. She tried to take her life twenty-two years ago, failed and now claims she doesn't remember anything at all from that time. Her last memory is of giving birth to our now college-age twins."

"How do you know that?" Angelina demanded. "You *spoke* with her?"

"At length," he said without looking at her. "I assume what Angelina is so desperate to know is whether or not this marriage is valid," he said to the lawyer.

"There are some legal matters we should discuss," Patrick said, and glanced at Angelina and her brother, Lane, pointedly. Lane didn't seem to be paying any attention, his mind elsewhere. He was probably mentally writing up a press release for damage control since it wouldn't be long before the press got hold of this.

Buckmaster waved a hand through the air. "Whatever you have to say, you can say it in front of Angelina and Lane. They're more worried about all this than I am." He saw his wife's face darken with anger and looked away. "This was something I didn't want to deal with right now, but since you're here, lay it on me."

Patrick cleared his voice. "I'm afraid there could be a substantial amount of paperwork involved. You had an insurance policy on your first wife that you cashed following her death. The insurance company might now sue you for reimbursement. Or they might go after your first wife for fraud. If it can be proved that her alleged death was a suicide and the policy shouldn't have been paid . . ."

He nodded, seeing dollar signs. "I get it. In other words, this is going to cost me since Sarah doesn't seem to have a pot to pee in."

"Also your first wife might ask for compensation. Legally, she would have a right to fifty percent of your assets under Montana marriage law since you didn't have a prenuptial agreement at the time of your marriage."

Angelina swung around to stare at him. "You had me sign a prenup but not Sarah?"

"I was twenty-five. Sarah was twenty-four. We were kids so madly in love that the last thing we were thinking about was a prenup," Buckmaster snapped. He recalled, though, that his father had suggested it, afraid he might endanger the ranch. Now long passed, the old man must be rolling in his grave, Buckmaster thought.

"What about the marriages? Am I a bigamist now?"

The lawyer shook his head. "Because of the element of peril rule, the presumption of death was accelerated. Which means that it was assumed after her car accident that she was dead so you could have had her declared legally dead probably much sooner than you did."

"He didn't have any reason until he met me,"

Angelina said. "So is our marriage legal or not?"

Buckmaster nodded at the attorney to tell her.

"It is valid."

"I suppose I should be relieved," Angelina said. "But it sounds as if Sarah can clean him out now."

"I have plenty of money, dear. You really don't need to worry."

"It is going to take more than plenty of money for your run for president," she said just as sweetly.

"Since the estate is large and complex, the paperwork, as I said, could be sizable. Has Sarah mentioned any kind of financial arrangement?" Patrick asked.

"No, she said she just wants to see her daughters."

Angelina made a disbelieving sound. "How can she ask for anything after leaving us to raise her daughters all these years?"

"She *hasn't* asked for anything," he reminded her.

"Well, her timing is definitely suspect. It's as if she wants to destroy your political career," his wife said.

"That isn't important right now," he said through gritted teeth.

"How can you say that? People are already talking. You'll need more staff to handle the backlash of all this."

Buckmaster finished his drink. "Lane can take care of whatever needs to be done for now."

Her brother looked up. "I'm on top of it."

"Then everything is great." The Scotch settled him. He waited until Patrick packed up his briefcase and left before he turned to his wife. Drawing on the last of his patience, he said, "I know this is hard on you, but give me a chance to figure out some things before you throw any more at me. Can you do that?"

Tears welled in her eyes as she rose with her usual dignity and left the room without a word. Lane got a call and quickly left, as well.

Outside, thunder rumbled and an arrow of lightning splintered the sky. Buckmaster glanced to the window. He was more worried about the storm that had hit his family.

Over the thunder and lightning, Sarah heard the sound of a vehicle pull up in front of the house. She assumed it was Russell returning. He'd left earlier with the sheriff.

"He merely wants to see where I found you," Russell had told her. "Nothing to worry about. Will you be all right until we get back?"

"I'll be fine. I'm going to take a nap." She hadn't been able to sleep, though. When she'd closed her eyes, she kept seeing disturbing images that made no sense to her. Also she had to wonder why the sheriff was interested in where Russell had found her.

So she was glad when she heard Russell returning. She wanted to know what the sheriff had found. Also she didn't want to be alone right now. It was one reason she'd taken him up on his offer of the guesthouse. Being out here was enough like being on the Hamilton Ranch that she felt as if she had come home. Once she'd understood that twenty-two years had passed, she had known Buckmaster would have probably remarried.

Still it hurt. In her heart, she believed that he had been the only man for her. But she couldn't even be sure about that. Maybe she had married again, had another family. No, she thought as she went to the door. She didn't believe that.

So what had she been doing the past twenty-two years? As she started out of the guesthouse, she almost collided with a tall blonde. She had heard about Buck's new wife and talked to her on the phone briefly, so the moment she saw the woman's angry expression, she knew who she must be. She felt a shocking instant hatred even before Angelina Broadwater Hamilton opened her mouth.

"We need to talk," the woman said.

"I thought we already did the other day when you called me to tell me to leave town or I would regret it. If you had wanted to talk, I would have

231

thought you wouldn't have hung up on me." Sarah had been expecting a face-to-face run-in with Angelina—just not out here at Russell's guest-house with no one else around.

What she barely could admit to herself is that those lost twenty-two years scared her. Who was she? Given the disturbing images she had begun seeing, she feared there might be something wrong with her.

"I know what you're up to," Angelina said.

"I'm not up to anything," she said as lightning lit the darkened sky. Where was Russell? Why wasn't he back yet? "I really think you should leave."

Angelina let out a bark of a laugh. "I really think you should have stayed away." She pushed past Sarah into the guesthouse. "I don't think you want Russell Murdock to hear this."

So Angelina didn't know that Russell wasn't over at the house. Still, she would have liked to have this discussion somewhere else. Out here on Russell's ranch, she had felt at peace.

Angelina Hamilton was interrupting that peace and causing her to have disturbing feelings. She stood outside for a moment trying to harness her dark emotions. The coming storm boomed and crackled around her. She could smell rain but it hadn't started to fall yet. She realized she'd balled her hands into tight fists.

Forcing herself to straighten her fingers, she turned and stepped into the small guesthouse.

Angelina was looking around impatiently. "Do you have anything to drink?"

"Water?"

"Seriously, that's all you have?"

"I don't drink alcohol." As she said it though, she had a flash of herself drinking Russian vodka. She could almost feel the cold sharpness on her tongue.

"Of course *you* don't drink." Angelina tossed her purse on a chair and crossed her arms over her chest. "I forget that you were the perfect wife. It was bad enough when I had to live in your dead-wife shadow. Now to have you back in the flesh . . . When are you leaving?"

"I don't know."

The blonde nodded as if she'd expected as much. "What do you want?"

The same thing Buck had asked. "Nothing. As I told Buck—"

"Right, you just want to see your children. He might have bought that, but I don't. How much money will it take to get rid of you?"

"I don't—"

"Don't tell me again that you don't want anything. Do you have any idea what you've done?" Angelina demanded angrily. "You couldn't stand the thought that Buckmaster was headed for the White House and you weren't going with him. Is that it? Well, you've screwed up his chances with this scandal. Everyone is going to think he did something to make you *want* to kill yourself. They won't realize that you're just some crazy bitch."

Sarah took a step toward her, thinking Angelina might be right about the crazy bitch part. "What makes you think you can talk to me like that?"

The woman looked a little alarmed, as she should have. "I want you gone," she said with less force than she had earlier.

Sarah took another step toward her. She could feel the cold hatred she'd experienced the moment she recognized the woman. It seemed to consume her as if it had a force of its own. "What if I want *you* gone?"

Angelina looked astonished. "*I'm* Buckmaster's wife."

Sarah's laugh felt brittle as old glass. "So am I apparently."

"Only until he gets this straightened out legally, then you're just a bad memory. Not even your daughters want anything to do with you."

She felt something deadly coil inside her. It came with a flash of memory. Like her tongue had remembered the vodka, her right hand remembered the feel of a lethal knife clutched in it.

"You should leave now or I won't be responsible for what I might do."

Angelina looked at her as if she thought she was joking. "Are you *threatening* me?" Her gaze met Sarah's and the woman seemed to flinch.

At the sound of a vehicle, Angelina picked up her purse from where she'd thrown it. Her eyes narrowed as she started past Sarah, but she gave her plenty of space. "I don't know who you think you are."

Sarah didn't know who she was, either. But she sensed she was somebody dangerous.

The sheriff looked into the darkness of the trees, already a little spooked. He told himself it was just a coincidence that this is where Sarah had come out of the trees. The spring weeds had grown up in the barrow pit, but not so high that he couldn't see the top of the weathered wooden cross on up the road a dozen yards.

The cross marked the spot where Jenny West had been murdered.

He'd never come out here that he hadn't felt the eeriness of this lonesome spot. Even now he felt a chill. Behind him he heard a rumble of thunder and felt the wind pick up as the thunder-storm moved in. But right now the approaching thunder-storm was the least of Frank's concern.

What had Sarah Hamilton been doing out here in the woods in the middle of nowhere? Russell said she'd come out of the pines. They were miles from anything. The next ranch was Dr. Farnsworth's up the road four miles or so. Behind them was the cemetery, and three miles from there the town of Beartooth.

Someone must have dropped her off out here. But why leave her so far from anything? And what was she doing in the trees?

"I need to take a look," he told Russell. "Would you mind waiting in the patrol car?"

"No problem."

Following the tracks, he started into the pines. Sunlight fingered its way through the branches. The air smelled damp and sweet inside the shelter of the trees. But the wind rocked the tops of the pines and, off in the distance, lightning flickered.

Frank hadn't gone far when he lost the tracks and then picked them up again, drawing him deeper into the woods. He could feel the storm coming in. When he'd first stepped into the woods, he'd expected the footprints to stop a few yards in. He'd tried to picture a scenario that would land her here.

Maybe she'd hitchhiked back to town, gotten in trouble with whoever was driving, possibly fearing for her safety or her life, had jumped out when the vehicle stopped and run into the woods to hide. It could explain what she'd been doing out here. At the sound of a different vehicle she would have hurried out and stumbled in front of Russell's pickup.

But how far would she have gone to hide in the woods? As he looked ahead, he saw her tracks continuing deeper and deeper into the trees. The pines became more dense. The wind howled in the branches overhead. This time the thunder and lightning were closer. He felt the hair rise on his neck as a bolt of lightning ricocheted over the tops of the pines.

In the growing darkness from the storm, he lost her trail, but then spotted where a small limb had been broken off. As he ducked through the bough, he found her trail again in the soft dirt.

What had she been doing this far back off the road? He could understand if she'd run back here out of fear. But this far? It made no sense. There was nothing but more trees for miles and no other roads. What could she possibly have been doing this far back in here?

He thought about her lack of memory. He was skeptical because it came with the job. Who forgot twenty-two years? Also who suddenly "awakened" deep in the woods outside of the town where she had lived all those years earlier? According to her, she remembered nothing before running in front of Russell Murdock's pickup.

But if true, that shot the hell out of his scenario, didn't it? She couldn't have hitchhiked back here unless she'd known where she was going.

Frank couldn't help but think about what Russell had said about her being dropped by aliens.

He stopped for a moment. The dark woods had taken on an eerie quality. The dense trees didn't allow him to see but only a few yards ahead of him. Maybe it was the approaching storm. Or maybe it was all his years of being a lawman, but he had a spooked feeling even before he heard the soft rustling sound ahead in the trees.

He'd often listened to other lawmen talk about the things that had spooked them. Being spooked was different from being scared. Scared was healthy since lawmen were often putting themselves into the path of danger with people who were violent.

"I think evil stays in places where something horrible has happened," he recalled a deputy sheriff saying one time. "I've felt it. It takes on a life of its own. That's why when you return to a place where something horrendous has happened, you get goose bumps. I've felt it and it spooked the hell out of me."

Reaching for his weapon, he moved toward the sound as the first drops of rain began to fall. He hadn't gone far when he caught a flash of movement out of the corner of his eye. He spun to his right, his heart drumming and weapon drawn.

The dark nylon of the empty parachute fluttered in the wind high above the ground where it had gotten caught in the towering pine tree.

Chapter FIFTEEN

The wind had picked up. It thrashed the limbs of the trees next to the cabin and howled across the eaves. Livie looked out, hugging herself as she saw that the thunderhead over the Crazies was quickly moving in her direction. She hated storms and had as far back as she could remember.

Ainsley said her fear began when she was three—not long after their mother had died. Or at least they thought it had. She couldn't remember her mother so she couldn't believe that had anything to do with it. Ainsley had always come into her room and sat with her during the storms. She wished she was here now.

Thunder rumbled in the distance. Lightning flashed over the mountains, splintering down into the foothills. The lights flickered, went out for a few moments and then came back on. Even though it was still early, the storm had darkened the sky outside, forcing her to turn on the lights inside the cabin.

When her phone rang, she was relieved to see it was Cooper. "I'm at the ranch. One of the horses got into some barbed wire. I'm waiting for the vet to arrive. Are you all right?"

"Fine," she lied. This one had her more on edge than any had before. She'd been running scared as it was, knowing that Drake Connors was still out there somewhere. The lights flickered again as the wind slammed a tree limb against the side of the cabin.

"I should be home soon," he said. "I know how you feel about thunderstorms."

She smiled to herself. He did know and he did care. "I'll be fine until you get here." She'd barely gotten the words out before the lights flashed off. Holding her breath, she waited for the electricity to come back on. Seconds passed, then minutes.

The cabin was as dark as the inside of a boot. She tried to remember if she'd seen any candles around as she made her way into the kitchen. In a flash of lightning that lit the cabin, she opened the top drawer and found a flashlight. Turning it on, she discovered several utility-type candles and some matches.

She put the candles on a dish on the table and lit them. They did little to chase away the darkness. A crack of lightning made her jump. She glanced toward the window a moment before the thunder boomed overhead, making her shudder.

In that instant, she saw lights coming up the road. Cooper. Thank God. He'd got someone else to wait for the vet and had come home to her. She moved toward the door, the flashlight still in her hand. To her surprise, it hadn't started to rain yet. The air felt electrified, though, as she opened the door. Outside, the sky was so dark it was like night.

The wind whipped her long hair into her face as the pickup stopped by the new house structure. He must have something he needed to drop off at the house. Surely he wasn't thinking of working tonight. She needed him. He knew how she hated storms. Wasn't that why he'd come right home?

She couldn't bear another moment in the cabin alone. She limped toward him, hurrying as fast as she could. She could smell the rain and feel the cold in the wind. Another bolt of lightning sliced across the dark sky, momentarily blinding her.

Livie stumbled and almost fell as thunder boomed overhead. She was already halfway across the drive when she realized the pickup's engine had been wrong. She shone the flashlight at the pickup. This wasn't Cooper's truck in the yard and the man who emerged wasn't her fiancé. She dropped the flashlight to dig her cell phone from her pocket and dial 9-1-1 as she recognized Drake Connors. When she looked up, he was running toward her.

Nettie had been washing the dishes at the kitchen sink when she looked out and saw the crows. She would have sworn they were watching her. She laughed and called to the one Frank had named Uncle.

"Best get out of the coming storm."

The bird cawed back and she laughed. The day she'd moved into Frank's house on his small ranch, the crows had swooped down on her, yelling and carrying on something awful.

"They hate me," she'd told Frank.

He'd hugged her and tried to reassure her. "They aren't sure about you yet. Don't worry, you'll make friends. I'll show you how. They get to know people as individuals. Right now, you're a stranger."

"They do seem to recognize you," she admitted. Frank had shared his fascination for crows with her over the years. She'd seen the way the young ones played tag and teased one another, and had come to understand that they were indeed intelligent creatures.

"Here," he'd said, and had given her a bag of unsalted peanuts. "Toss some to the crows each day. You wait. You'll have them eating out of your hand."

"I hope not literally," she'd said, and he'd laughed.

It had taken a few days, but he'd been right. Now they greeted her each time she came home as if they'd been waiting for her. Sometimes they followed her to see if she had more peanuts.

When she came outside, they would caw down at her from the telephone line as if to say hello. She always called hello back, feeling like less of a fool as time went on.

"They feel safe again here," Frank had said. "I leave the barn light on. Keeps the owls away at night. Makes it easier for the crows to spot trouble."

Yes, she thought now, the crows had become his children.

Drying her hands, she went into the living room to Frank's small desk. The envelope was in the top drawer. She'd tried to reseal it after steaming it open, but the glue wasn't holding.

Opening it, she looked at the DNA test that had been done on Tiffany Chandler.

"Lynette?"

She hadn't heard her husband come into the house because she'd been so lost in thought.

Frank looked from her to the open manila envelope in her hands. When his gaze returned to hers, he made a sound as if in pain. *"Lynette."* Her name came out a plea.

"I'm sorry," she said. "I found it and . . ."

He nodded as if he understood only too well.

"I had to know."

Again he nodded. "But I don't *have* to know." He started to turn.

"I think you do," she said. "Frank, what if she isn't yours?" She studied his face, not sure what to expect. His expression didn't change as he took off his hat and walked over to hang it up.

His back to her, he raked a hand through his thick graying blond hair. She noticed how much it had grayed recently and felt a stab of shock. Sometimes she forgot how old they were since he would always be that young man she'd fallen in love with.

Nettie waited, biting her tongue since she had never been good at quiet and was nervous to fill the void.

"Do you really think it would make that much difference to me?" Frank asked without turning around.

"I don't know. I hope it would. Pam lied about everything else."

He swung around. "Tiffany *believes* I'm her father. She was raised to hate me so I feel responsible. That's why I never opened the DNA test results, Lynette. It doesn't matter."

"So you don't care who her real father is? If Pam really was pregnant before she left Beartooth? Or if Tiffany's father is someone from around here?"

She saw that he hadn't let himself think of that. His expression soured and she knew he was finally considering it.

"Don't you want to know the truth finally?" she asked.

His cell phone rang. He let out a curse as he drew it from his pocket and said, "Sheriff Curry."

She watched him listen for a moment before he said, "I'll be right there," and reached for his Stetson.

"Frank—"

"We'll discuss this later," he said and, without looking at her, turned and walked out the door.

Livie shouted into the phone over the thunder as she stumbled back. Drake was running at her. She started to turn toward the cabin, but when he saw what she intended to do, he cut off her escape.

Somewhere to hide. The ebony skeleton of the new house was etched against the night, but she didn't dare run that way. Cooper had told her just yesterday to stay away as the subflooring wasn't on part of the house. He didn't want her falling into the basement.

Lightning zigzagged across the sky, illuminating the land before her for a moment. Her only other option was the barn, but before she could reach it, the corral loomed up in front of her as the storm dropped like a shroud over her again. The thunder that followed was like a gunshot next to her. She shuddered and told herself to move!

She hobbled toward the barn and corrals, moving as quickly as she could with the splint. She'd tried taking it off earlier, but her ankle was still too weak. The storm had pitched the ranch into a black hole of wind and noise. Only an occasional flash of lightning lit her way.

Glancing back, she saw that Drake was having trouble following her. He couldn't see the unfamiliar ground any better than she could him—except when lightning lit the sky.

She heard the mustangs before she saw them.

They snorted and stomped in the corral, several rearing as she hurried toward them. As she reached the corral and slipped through the rails, the horses shied away. She stopped in the stormy darkness as rain began to fall in huge hard drops that pounded down, splattering around her.

Livie could see nothing. For a moment, all she could hear were the mustangs in the corral and the pounding of her heart. Then she heard Drake swear as he must have collided with a rusty piece of farm equipment in the tall grass between the corral and the new construction of the house.

In a burst of lightning, she saw him bent over rubbing his leg. He hadn't seen her until one of the mustangs let out a bellow. His gaze swung to the corral. Belatedly she realized that the horses had signaled where she'd gone.

"I just want to talk to you," he called through the rain. "I'm not going to hurt you." His voice was the comforting tone she remembered.

She felt anger bubble up inside her. "I called the sheriff when I saw you drive up." She edged along the corral away from the direction he'd headed after hearing her voice.

"Then we don't have much time," he called back, sending a chill through her colder than the soaking rain. She shivered and moved along the corral railing away from him. Behind her the horses stomped and snorted so close she could feel their breath on her neck.

He was feeling his way toward the corral, toward Cooper's mostly wild mustangs.

Futilely she looked around for a weapon. There was nothing she could see in the darkness and rain.

He was closer now. She could hear him breathing hard. Had he hurt himself badly enough that it would slow him down if she had to make a run for it? Not enough since he was still coming in her direction.

"We can settle this easy enough, you and me," he said. Lightning flashed behind him, throwing his large dark shape into silhouette. Had he seen her?

She had no choice. She moved deeper into the corral, into the herd of wild horses. They shifted and jumped away, several rearing much too close.

Some of the mustangs shied away from her, but even in the blackness she could make out the shape of the lead mustang. He stomped and snorted and chuffed, dancing toward her.

This is suicide, she thought as she began to move cautiously away from him, but deeper into the herd of horses.

"Livie, that's what everyone calls you, right?" Drake's voice sounded as if he'd stopped at the edge of the corral. He would have heard the horses, seen them through the rain and the dark. He wasn't stupid enough to get into the large corral. Or was he?

Cooper kept a shotgun just inside the door of the barn. If she could reach it . . . "Easy," she whispered as she moved among the wild horses as she'd seen Cooper do. They knew her scent because of all the time she'd spent out here watching him work with them. That was the only thing that gave her hope that she could cross through them to the barn door—and the shotgun inside it.

Drake Connors had stopped talking. She knew he was trying to figure out where she was. Would he dare try to follow her? She'd seen him limping. But he'd no doubt seen her limping, as well. She prayed for the sound of a sheriff's patrol car siren. Had the dispatcher heard her over the storm when she'd answered the 9-1-1 call?

Drake could try to run around the corral and cut her off on the other side before she reached the barn door. But after his earlier accident in the tall grass, she didn't think he would chance it in the dark.

"You're going to get yourself killed," he called from the corral fence. "And for what? Let's talk. Aren't you curious about what happened that night?"

She shuddered at the thought of his hands on her. "You drugged me," she said, and kept moving slowly through the herd.

"I saved your life that night. You would have frozen to death in that ditch if it wasn't for me."

She could hear him moving back and forth at the edge of the corral. He didn't want to get in with the mustangs. She couldn't blame him. At least the horses had seen her before and, while they didn't like her being among them, none of them had attacked her. Yet.

She ached to know the truth about that night, but wasn't sure Drake Connors would tell her. "You took advantage of me."

"Not in the way you think," he said. "I just put a little something in your wine to help you sleep. When Amelia stood me up, I moved you into the master bedroom and took a photo to send to her and then I left. Your car was waiting for you the next morning when you woke up, right? See, I rescued you."

She rolled her eyes. "I woke up naked in your bed."

"Technically, it wasn't my bed."

"Nor your house."

"*Nothing* happened."

It was the same story he'd told the sheriff. If he was telling the truth, then the baby was Cooper's, had always been Cooper's. But what was he doing here now? "Why should I believe you?"

"Because it's true. I might have been interested if you had initiated something. But the way you kept fiddling with a spot on your ring finger, I figured you were either married or engaged, probably had a fight with your husband or boyfriend."

It surprised her how he'd hit on the truth, but apparently the man made his living by taking advantage of women just like her.

"That's why I'm here. I'm willing to settle for fifty thousand and you'll never see me again."

So it *had* been him blackmailing her. "You're not getting another dime. I shouldn't have paid you the ten thousand." In the distance she thought she heard a siren. She wondered if he heard it, as well.

"I'm afraid I can't let you off that easily." He'd stopped just yards away. She could see him at the edge of the corral. "I know you don't want me to tell your fiancé that you came on to me that night, do you? Or I could go to the press. Your father would hate that kind of bad publicity especially now that he'd announced he's running for president."

She felt the heat of his gaze even through the darkness and the rain. How could she have felt safe with this man? Because that night he was playing a different role. Just as she had been.

"If my fiancé gets his hands on you . . ."

"Come on, let's get out of this rain," he said. "Fifty thousand and I'm out of your life and your father's and your fiancé's."

"That's the sheriff," she said as the siren sound grew louder in the distance. The lightning and thunder had moved to the east. Only the rain stayed, splattering on the wet earth around her.

"I'm not paying you another dime and neither is anyone else. It's over."

"Maybe not," he said. She saw him hesitate and look back toward his pickup. Water ran off the brim of his cowboy hat as he turned to look at her again. He smiled through the rain. "If you won't give it to me . . . well, there are other fish to fry."

"If you go to my father, he's more apt to shoot you than give you a cent."

He tipped his hat, rain pouring off it. Then shooting her a grin, he turned and limped back through the drowning rain to his truck.

As Cooper was coming down the road, a dark blue pickup came barreling out of his ranch. He didn't get a good look at the driver, but he saw it was a man wearing a cowboy hat as he swerved to miss getting hit.

"What the hell?" he said, and looked toward the cabin, his heart suddenly in his throat. Had that been Drake Connors?

Livie? He raced up the road, windshield wipers flapping as the rain pinged off his old pickup hood, terrified to think what the man was doing at the cabin. As he came to a stop in front of the cabin, Livie came hobbling from the direction of the corral. He threw open his pickup door and leaped out, terrified by the expression on her face. It *had* been Drake Connors!

He ran to her, grabbed her and dragged her into his arms, hugging her too tightly, but needing to feel the life in her, needing her more than his next breath.

"Livie. Livie." She trembled against him. He swore he could feel her pounding heart in sync with his as she clung to him, emitting a heart-breaking sound that tore at his soul.

"You're all right," he whispered against her wet hair as he bent over her. "You're all right." He realized that she was soaked to the skin. What had she been doing out in the pouring rain?

Lightning etched a jagged line in the sky to the east. Thunder rumbled deep in his chest as he brushed her wet hair back, cupping her face in his hands. She closed her eyes and pressed her cheek against his hand. A soft moan escaped her lips that he heard even over the rain as he kissed her.

"Did he hurt you?" he asked her as he drew back from the kiss.

She shook her head, her gaze meeting his.

He felt his heart swell. "I love you, Livie." The words rose up in his throat straight from his heart. "I love you." Her searching gaze probed his, looking for what he knew she needed more than her next breath.

"Don't you know I would die for you—or kill if I had to?" Sweeping her up into his arms, he carried her back to the cabin to the shower. He would have climbed in with her, but he wouldn't be staying for long. Once he had her warm and dry, wrapped in an old quilt, she told him what had happened.

"Did you call the sheriff?" he asked.

She nodded. "I called but the dispatcher must not have been able to hear me. I heard a siren . . ."

"There was a wreck down by the bridge. I saw the sheriff down there as I drove home. You must have heard one of the deputies headed for it. I passed him just before I reached the turnoff here."

"I'm so sorry for all of this," she said, looking away guiltily.

He turned her to face him so their eyes met. "We're way beyond that. We're in this together." As he looked toward the rainy darkness, he made a silent promise to her. He would put an end to this. Tonight.

"Where are you going?" Livie asked as Cooper pulled on a dry coat to go back out. The thunderstorm had moved on, the rain finally going with it. She could hear water dripping off the eaves and smell the fresh dampness coming in through a partially open window in the kitchen.

"There's something I have to do," he said without turning around.

Her heart lodged in her throat. "Tell me you're not going to—"

"Trust me. In the meantime, keep the door locked." He stepped to a gun cabinet, opened it and pulled out a shotgun and a box of shells. "You know how to shoot. On the off chance that the bastard should come back here, use it." He stood the shotgun against the wall by the door, the box of shells next to it.

She studied his face and looked into his dark eyes. "You're scaring me, Coop."

He shook his head. "I'll be back." With that he was gone out the door. She listened to the sound of his old pickup engine until it died away, then she got up and, locking the door, leaned against it.

For a few moments earlier, she'd thought he might make love to her. She ached for that intimacy between them. Closing her eyes, she thought about being in his arms and his words spoken out in the rain. He loved her. She'd seen his need for her. He wanted her as desperately as she wanted him, needed him.

But that January night still hung between them. She put a hand on her stomach. Drake had lied about not being the person blackmailing her. Had he also lied about what had happened that night?

Her cell phone rang, making her jump. "Hello?" For just a moment, she thought it might be Drake calling. He'd left so suddenly . . .

She was relieved to hear a familiar voice.

"Are you all right?" Ainsley asked. "I know how you hate storms."

"Fine."

"You don't sound fine. I saw Cooper's truck here earlier so I was afraid you were alone."

"He came home just in time, so I'm fine."

"Good." Ainsley still sounded worried. "Have you thought any more about telling Dad what's going on with you?"

"I'll talk to him tomorrow," she promised. "But I think the matter is all taken care of." She told her sister what had happened with the sheriff, leaving out Drake Connors's earlier visit and his demand for fifty thousand dollars. What had he meant about other fish to fry? She didn't think he would risk going to her father. Was there another woman he was blackmailing?

"You must be so relieved. That should be the end of it," Ainsley said. "But more important, the baby."

"If he's telling the truth, then I'm carrying Cooper's baby," she said, thinking about the test that would prove it soon. She prayed that this was one thing Drake hadn't lied about.

"What about Cooper?" her sister asked.

Yes, what about Cooper, she thought, glancing out into the darkness.

"Is he relieved?"

"He doesn't really believe the man. Maybe he's afraid to believe it's true."

She could practically hear Ainsley shaking her head in frustration. "Your fiancé is so stubborn."

"Yes, he is. But he's also sweet." She thought again of the way he'd held her earlier. "He loves me."

But later, after hanging up with her sister, she had a hard time getting to sleep. The more time that passed, the more she worried about Cooper. She knew where he'd gone—after Drake Connors. All she could hope was that he didn't find him.

Chapter SIXTEEN

When Livie found her father the next morning, he was with Angelina in the big ranch kitchen. She stopped in the doorway. It was clear that the two of them had been arguing. According to Ainsley, they'd been at it ever since the news of Sarah Hamilton's return from the grave.

She had enough going on in her own life that she didn't want to get in the middle of their problems. Cooper had come home very late last night. She'd awakened and rushed out of the bedroom to find him undressing. Clearly he was planning to sleep on the couch again. She'd so hoped he would come to bed with her. Even if they didn't make love, she'd thought he might hold her.

Her heart had dropped further when she saw the blood on his torn shirt.

"What happened?" she'd cried as she noticed that his knuckles were also scraped and bloody.

"Nothing to concern yourself about. Go back to bed."

"Oh, Coop." He'd stepped closer to her as she began to cry.

"Come on, let me take you back to bed. Everything is all right now."

She had desperately wanted to believe that. When he'd lain down next to her last night in the bed and held her, she'd prayed it was true.

This morning, though, she'd awakened to find his side of the bed empty and Cooper long gone.

As she started to turn away from her father and Angelina, the movement caught Angelina's eye. She stopped talking in midsentence to glare at her.

"Sorry to interrupt," Livie said as her father also turned in her direction.

"Well, since you have, you might as well come on in," Angelina said, turning away from Buckmaster to pour herself a cup of coffee.

"What is it, sweetheart?" her father asked.

"There is something I need to tell you, Daddy."

"Whatever it is, you can tell us both. I am still your father's wife."

Buckmaster looked as if he might argue, but let out a sigh and said, "What is it, Livie?"

She quickly filled him in, leaving out nothing. At one point, he pulled out a chair at the table and dropped into it. Angelina remained standing, her face a stone mask.

"Livie, what were you thinking?" her father

demanded when she got to the part about the blackmail. "Why didn't you come to me?"

"I wanted to handle it myself and now Cooper . . ."

"Cooper doesn't have that kind of money."

"We aren't *paying* the blackmailer. The sheriff . . ."

"Do you think that's wise, involving the sheriff?" Angelina said. "If this gets out along with everything else . . ."

"Angelina, the last thing I'm worried about is my political career right now," he snapped as he shoved to his feet. "This man has to be caught and stopped."

Livie saw for the first time how much he and Cooper were alike. "I talked to the sheriff this morning. Half the state will be looking for Drake Connors. In the meantime, I'm staying with Cooper."

Angelina made a sound, turning away to pop a piece of bread into the toaster.

"Does that mean the wedding is still on?" her father asked.

She nodded. For now.

"Oh, Livie, I'm so sorry for what you've been through," he said, coming around the table to hug her.

Past him, she saw Angelina's hands shaking as she buttered her toast. Her stepmother was clearly furious with her for causing even more problems.

"Cooper will take good care of you," her father said, surprising her.

"Yes, he will. I guess you heard. My sisters and I are going to meet Mother at the Branding Iron later."

Angelina let out a disgusted sound, dropped her toast and left the room. A few moments later, Livie heard her on her cell phone talking to her brother, Lane.

"I'm glad you girls are seeing your mother," her father said, surprising her.

As she left, she passed a very pale Angelina. She heard her father tell her, "Stop looking like the world is coming to an end."

"How little you know," she snapped back.

Frank had called in the state crime lab techs when he'd found the parachute in the tree last night before the storm. He'd had several of his deputies secure the scene until they arrived. It had been a long night with car accidents, domestic disputes. He hadn't gotten home until late, and not wanting to disturb—or deal with—Lynette when he was that exhausted, he'd slept in the spare room. He'd left before she'd gotten up this morning.

Right now, he didn't want to think about her or the DNA report she'd opened. He was angry and upset, more with himself than her. He should have opened it when it came, but he kept telling himself it didn't matter.

He was anxious to hear what the crime team had found on and near the parachute. Surely that wasn't how Sarah Hamilton had come back to Beartooth. And yet her tracks had led him right to the spot. With her reappearance apparently as much a mystery to her as the rest of them, he wasn't taking any chances.

If he was right and someone had literally dropped her off . . . His mind reeled with the possibilities. That's why he'd decided to secure the scene and let the state techs get the answers.

Meanwhile, he'd put a BOLO out on Drake Connors after Olivia Hamilton's call this morning. He made a note to talk to Olivia about a restraining order when he saw that he had another message from the doctor at the state mental hospital. He almost ignored it. He really didn't want to deal with what he assumed the doctor wanted to talk to him about. He had enough on his plate right now.

Tiffany had told him she was depending on him to help her lawyer get her freedom. Frank figured the doctor would want to verify that.

But the reason he hadn't returned the call was because he couldn't in good conscience trust Tiffany Chandler to be loose. Not to mention trust his own safety and that of Lynette—even his crows.

Tiffany had killed one of his crows before she'd tried to kill him because he'd made the mistake of telling her how much his family of crows meant to him. He'd been studying them since he was a boy and was fascinated by their intelligence. He'd also found some of them to be capable of joking along with all their other skills.

She'd killed the crow to hurt him. When she'd turned the gun on him, one of the crows had swooped down and distracted her, saving his life. But after that, the crows had felt threatened and had left. He'd thought they might never come back, having read about instances like that. Crows had some way of telling other crows about food—as well as danger.

But they *had* come back, making him feel as if life was going to get better.

He couldn't do what Tiffany was asking him to. Which meant he had to tell her—and her doctor and her lawyer.

Picking up the phone, he called Lynette to tell her where he was going. There wasn't much he could do at his office but wait, anyway. He would drive up to the state mental hospital and get this over with.

"You don't usually go back this soon," Lynette said when he told her. "If this is because of—"

"It isn't. I'm sorry I got upset. It's all fine." He disconnected. He dreaded the drive to the hospital this soon after the last one.

But more than anything he dreaded telling Tiffany he couldn't help her secure her freedom. He had no idea what she would do.

● ● ●

Sarah couldn't help being nervous. Intellectually, she knew that her daughters were adults now, but in her mind they were still children.

The twins were just babies twenty-two years ago. Ainsley had only recently turned ten. Kat, dear Kat, with her father's frown was eight. Bo, the sweet, adorable apple of her father's eye, was five, and Livie was the image of Sarah at three.

She couldn't believe Livie was now planning to get married this summer. All those lost years, her daughters had grown into young women.

She'd been so glad when she'd gotten the call from Kat that they wanted to see her. Now, as she looked toward the café door, she realized she might not even recognize her own daughters. Tears burned her eyes. Hastily she wiped at them, warning herself that she would be a stranger to them.

She wouldn't cry. She wouldn't force herself on them. She would be patient. She'd waited too long to see her children. That thought struck her as odd and she questioned, like most of her other thoughts, if it was even true. Had she been waiting twenty-two years?

The door to the café opened. She shot to her feet and tried not to wring her hands as a blonde woman came in. She caught her breath, shocked at how much Ainsley looked like her at that age. How that must have hurt Buck, she thought, her meeting with her husband still on her mind.

It had been so much harder to see him than she had thought it would be. She had expected his anger. She just hadn't expected what she'd glimpsed in his eyes—behind the pain, she'd seen a love that she'd thought as dead as he'd believed her.

"Ainsley," she said, then looked to the next woman coming through the back door. "Bo." Her gaze shifted. "Kat," she said, and smiled even broader. She swore she wouldn't cry but seeing them all grown up . . .

When Livie appeared, she had to fight tears even harder. Livie, all grown up, and getting married soon.

"Please, come in. Let me look at all of you." Her gaze went to the door.

"Harper and Cassidy haven't been told yet," Ainsley said.

Sarah tried to hide her disappointment. "They're away at college?"

Her oldest daughter nodded.

"Well, I'm glad you are all here," she said, wanting to hug each of them. But she stood where she was, seeing that they weren't ready. She'd known this would be excruciating, but not to this extent. They were her daughters, her flesh and blood. She'd given birth to them, nurtured them for the years she'd been with them, and yet, they didn't know her. Worse, they didn't trust her.

"We should sit down." She motioned to the large table. "Kate was kind enough to leave us a pitcher of iced tea and some treats." They'd picked the café on the one day of the week it was closed so they would have privacy.

"We have questions, as you might imagine," Kat said.

"Of course you do. I will try to answer them the best I can," she promised, knowing that they would go away as frustrated by her answers as she was.

Her daughters seemed to relax a little as they each took a seat.

She poured them all tea and passed around the plate of cookies. All the time, she could feel them staring at her—just as she wanted to do with each of them. She kept seeing them as children.

"Is it true that you tried to commit suicide the night your car went into the river?" Kat asked. Her sister Ainsley shot her a warning look.

"It's all right," Sarah said, and took a sip of her tea. "I'm told that I did." She shook her head. "I have no memory of it and I can't imagine doing such a thing. The thought of leaving my children . . ." Her voice broke and she fought the tears that burned her eyes.

"So you really can't remember any of it?" Bo asked.

"No, and believe me, I've tried."

"Then you don't know where you've been the past twenty-two years?" Ainsley asked.

She shook her head. "I know it sounds crazy."

"It sounds unbelievable," Kat said.

Sarah noticed that Kat hadn't touched her tea or taken one of the cookies. She remembered her as a child. She'd been obstinate and headstrong. Sarah and Buck had joked that she was just like her father.

"I'm hoping my memory returns, but what I do remember is each of you. You all were my first thought when I found myself back here."

"We heard that you stumbled out of the trees and Russell Murdock hit you with his pickup," Livie said.

"It was more like he knocked me over. I wasn't injured. He took me to a doctor he knew. At first they thought I had hit the truck hard enough to give me memory loss, but that wasn't the case."

"So no one knows what has caused your . . . amnesia?" Kat asked suspiciously.

Sarah smiled. Kat had always been the inquisitive one when they were children. She was also the one who asked "Why?" about everything. She shared this with her, hoping Kat would appreciate her memory.

"And you, Ainsley, you were like a little mother to the others," she said. "I can see that you still are." She turned to Bo. "You were the one who gave your father and me the most trouble because you were so smart. One time you cut Olivia's hair." Sarah laughed at the memory. "You did a good job for your age actually. But you said to me, 'Her bangs were in her eyes.' I laughed so hard because your tone made it clear that you weren't impressed with my mothering skills."

The room fell silent at her words. Again she had to fight tears. "I was a loving mother, though. I adored each of you." Another long silence fell, this one heavier. If she'd loved them, then why would she have tried to kill herself?

She looked away, wiping at errant tears, and saw a large dark SUV go by. She caught a glimpse of the woman behind the wheel. Angelina Broadwater Hamilton glared back at her for a few moments before driving on past. Sarah doubted it was the first time she'd driven by.

"I suppose you have some memory of me?" she asked to fill the unbearable silence. She swallowed, her mouth suddenly dry as she looked around the table at her daughters. Somehow she'd survived all these years. She would get through this, as well.

Ainsley nodded, so did Kat. "I remember you," Bo said. But Olivia shook her head.

"You were only three," Sarah said. "I'm not surprised you don't remember me." Again her voice broke and this time the tears came of their own accord. "I've missed so much. I would give anything to have those years back." She swallowed and pulled a tissue from her purse to wipe her eyes.

"What now?" Kat asked. "Are you going to stick around this time?"

"I don't know why I left before or if there is anything that could keep me from staying. I've made an appointment to see a neurologist in Bozeman in hopes of recovering some memory of the time I've been gone." She didn't tell them how frightened she was of what might be lurking in her past. "I want to stay, but it will depend on if you want me here. If your father does, as well. I don't want to hurt his future plans. He's a good man. He'll make a wonderful president."

She didn't tell them, but she feared that whatever secrets lurked in those twenty-two lost years might not let her stay. In fact, she feared her past might come looking for her.

At the hospital, Frank was told that Tiffany didn't want to see him.

"It's important that I talk to her."

"I'm sorry."

He raked a hand through his hair in frustration. "Well, can I at least see her doctor?"

The doctor made him wait five minutes before he was led down the hall to his office. The conversation was short and sweet.

"Tiffany tells me that you think she isn't dangerous to society and should be released."

"I'm afraid because of doctor-patient confidentiality—"

"You're wrong. Tiffany is dangerous. I know her. I knew her mother. It would be a mistake to let her out. If there is a hearing, that's what I will tell the board."

The doctor seemed surprised. "Tiffany will be sorry to hear that," he said.

"I had hoped to tell her myself."

"I don't believe that would be a good idea."

He lifted an eyebrow. "So you aren't convinced Tiffany should be released any more than I am," he said with a shake of his head. Why did it continue to shock him that Tiffany lied? She'd been raised by a professional liar.

As he was leaving, he passed a man in the hallway. Recognizing him, he nodded. It wasn't until Frank reached his pickup that he realized he'd seen the man there at the mental hospital in passing before on several occasions. He'd always been so upset after his visits with Tiffany that it had never registered before that the man was from the Beartooth area.

Now that it did, Frank sat behind the wheel of his pickup feeling stupid. The man, Lloyd Jones, had been a wrangler on Judge Bull Westfall's ranch back when Frank's ex, Pam, used to spend a lot of time visiting there.

He let out a bitter laugh as he thought about what Lynette had been trying to tell him last night. As he climbed back out of the truck and went inside the hospital, he knew he shouldn't have been so gullible. Pam had lied to him at every turn. He'd assured himself that the dead and gone Pam not only couldn't surprise him anymore, she couldn't hurt him.

And yet when he reached the doorway of the visiting room, he felt such a stab of pain that it almost doubled him over.

Lloyd, now probably in his early fifties, had his back to Frank and his arms around his daughter. Tiffany, who was facing the doorway, had been smiling. Until she saw Frank. He watched a variety of emotions move quickly across her expression. Surprise. Anger. Then grudging acceptance. She smiled that smile that had sent chills through him since the first day he'd met her.

He'd suspected from the beginning that Tiffany wasn't his. Had he wanted a child so badly that he'd let himself be deceived by his ex-wife yet again? Apparently so. He'd told himself that it hadn't mattered, just as it hadn't mattered what Nettie had found in the DNA report. He'd felt responsible for Tiffany because he'd believed that Pam had deceived her daughter, as well.

Looking into Tiffany's eyes now, though, he saw that he was the only one who was deceived. Tiffany knew that Lloyd Jones was her father—not Sheriff Frank Curry. How long had she known? From the beginning?

Long enough, he thought. She'd been playing him. He thought of all the trips to the hospital, all the times he'd tried to help her. He'd wanted to love her, to heal her, to make things right with his crazy ex-wife and this frail child.

But it had never been possible because he had never had the power to do any of that. He'd been only a target of Pam's hatred for him. And Tiffany had been part of it. He'd hoped that he was some-where in that child's genes that he could reach, and all the while, it had been a lie.

He stumbled back from the sight of Tiffany hugging her father to lean against the wall. He'd been so torn between wanting a daughter and yet not wanting a daughter who hated him enough to try to kill him. For a moment he had trouble catching his breath. Pam had set him up from the start, pouring hate into the girl against the man she believed hadn't loved her enough.

He closed his eyes, surprised by the well of emotions that threatened to drown him. He knew he should be relieved. A part of him was and that made him feel guilty. But the bottom line was that he'd let both Pam and Tiffany—a girl who had no connection to him—play him out of guilt.

He waited for the inevitable anger, the blind fury, he'd felt when he'd once turned in his badge and gone looking for Pam, planning to kill her. He'd never know if he would have since some-one else got to her first.

Opening his eyes, he was surprised how quickly the anger had passed. Pam and Tiffany's reign of tyranny over him was done. He felt as if a weight had been lifted off his shoulders. Relief surged through him. He was finally more clear-headed than he'd been in a long time.

Now all he needed to do was make sure that Tiffany was never unleashed on the public. The only emotion he felt as he left the hospital was sadness and even that didn't last as he headed home to the woman he loved.

Chapter SEVENTEEN

Frank had just returned to Beartooth when he got the call from his deputy that they'd found Drake Connors.

"His body is lying next to his pickup beside the road not far from the Hamilton Ranch," Deputy Sheriff Bentley Jamison said. "It looks as if someone ran him off the road, beat him up and then put two bullets in his back."

"Have you called the coroner?"

"I called you first."

"I'll call Charlie. I'm on my way."

When Frank arrived at the scene some miles outside of Beartooth, he saw that coroner Charlie Brooks was already there. It didn't surprise him to see that Jamison had everything under control.

A former homicide detective from New York, Jamison had been an asset to the local sheriff department's shortage of manpower. His training in New York was invaluable for a small department like theirs.

"What have we got?" he asked Charlie as he took in the scene.

"One of the two slugs in the back killed him. Looks like .45 caliber," the coroner said. "I can tell you more after the autopsy."

Frank hoped he was wrong about who had done this. He walked over to where Jamison was inspecting the vehicle.

"Some recent dents in the victim's pickup," the deputy said. "Looks as if whoever ran him off the road was driving an oxidized red vehicle."

Frank thought of Cooper's old red pickup and groaned silently. "Anything else?" Frank asked.

"This was next to the victim." Jamison showed him an evidence bag with a scrap of fabric. "Possibly from the assailant's clothing?"

Frank recognized the fabric. It was the same light blue check fabric as the shirt Cooper Barnett was wearing yesterday.

"Also it appears that some of the blood on the victim might belong to his killer."

"Let me know as soon as the lab has some results," Frank said. "In the meantime, I have a suspect I'm going to talk to." As he got into his patrol SUV, he realized the body had been found on the road not far from the Hamilton Ranch as well as Cooper Barnett's.

He found Cooper at the Hamilton Ranch working with the mustangs. Frank could understand the young man's fascination with the wild horses. He thought of his crows. Maybe we all wanted to take the wild out of animals—and other humans, he thought, thinking of his job. Since the wolf reintroduc-tion into Yellowstone Park, there were more people determined to adopt a wolf pup and turn it into a dog. It wasn't that easy to take the wild out of them, though, he thought. Just as it wasn't that easy eradicating the wild in people.

One look at Cooper Barnett's bruised face and Frank feared he had his man.

"I wondered how long it would be before you showed up," Cooper said when he saw him.

"Guilty conscience?"

"He had it coming and you know it."

Frank shook his head. "I asked you not to take the law into your own hands. You're going to have to come with me."

"The bastard filed charges against me?" Cooper demanded, sounding shocked. "He knew he had it coming. I thought he'd take his medicine without running to the sheriff."

"You admit to beating him up?"

"Hell, yes, I do. I'd do it again."

Frank rubbed the back of his neck. He'd tried

to warn Cooper. The young man reminded him of himself when he was his age. It was one of the reasons Lynette had decided to marry Bob Benton instead of him. She'd thought him too wild to make a good husband.

"How was he when you left him?" he asked.

Cooper frowned. "None the worse for wear. What's he saying? If he's thinking of suing me, he's in for a surprise. I don't have any money. Hell, I'm flat broke."

"Do you own a .45 pistol?"

The cowboy stilled. "I keep it under the seat of my truck. I didn't threaten him with it, if that's what he's saying. Or are you going to write me up for not having a concealed weapon permit?"

"Let's see the gun."

Cooper climbed out of the corral and walked with the sheriff to his old faded red pickup. Frank noticed that the cowboy was limping and that his knuckles were scraped and bruised. Also his left eye was badly bruised and there were several cuts on his jaw. He recalled the way the victim had looked. Apparently the two had fought for some time before the shooting.

Now that he got a good look at the pickup, it was clear that Cooper had run Drake off the road. Some of Drake Connors's blue pickup paint was visible on the old pickup where it was freshly dented.

"I keep it right here wrapped up in . . ." Cooper

pulled out an old towel but there was nothing in it. He felt around under the pickup's seat.

"Where's your gun?" Frank asked.

"I don't know. It's always been right here." He looked at the sheriff, fear narrowing his dark eyes. "What's going on?"

Frank reached for his handcuffs. "I'm sorry, son, but I'm going to have to take you in."

"What for?" Cooper demanded.

"The murder of Drake Connors."

Chapter EIGHTEEN

"Well, that was torture," Bo said as the four of them left the café after seeing their mother. They piled back into Ainsley's SUV. Across the street, Russell Murdock picked up their mother and drove away.

"Do you believe her?" Livie asked as she buckled up her seat belt.

"It doesn't matter if we do or not. Can't you see the implications?" Kat demanded as they headed back to the ranch. "She has no visible means of support. The only way she is going to be able to stay is if our father supports her."

"I hadn't thought of that," Bo said.

"Well, he *should* give her money. She's his wife and our mother," Ainsley said.

Kat made a rude sound. "Can you imagine

how Angelina is going to take that, though? When he's spent money on us, she always acts as if he's just throwing it away and ruining their future."

"I interrupted one of their arguments this morning," Livie said with a sigh. "I assume it was over Mother. Angelina was shaking she was so mad when she heard about my problems."

"She is so self-centered. I'm sure she is furious that this thing with Mother might hurt Dad's run for presidency," Bo said. "She was planning to be living in the White House soon. Can something like this keep him from winning?"

"I wouldn't think so," Ainsley said.

"But we don't know where Mother has been," Kat said. "What if she has another family and those kids are criminals or something?"

"This isn't going to hurt his ability to run," Livie said. "What could have changed is his desire. It's almost as if politics was all he had after Mother died and now that she's back—"

"Excuse me?" Kat interrupted. "Mother didn't die. She tried to kill herself and our father had more than politics. He had six daughters to raise."

Livie sighed. "You know what I mean. He's different now."

They all fell silent as the ranch came into view and they saw the sheriff's patrol SUV parked out front.

"Oh, no," Livie said, her heart dropping as she

saw the sheriff bring Cooper from around the back of the house in handcuffs.

"How did it go?" Russell asked Sarah on the drive back to his place.

She tried to put on a bright face, but inside she was brokenhearted. "They had a lot of questions I couldn't answer."

"But it was good to see them?"

She turned to him. "It was wonderful. They have grown into such beautiful, successful, independent women. I couldn't be prouder. The two younger ones, Harper and Cassidy, couldn't make it. They're in college. I'm not sure they've been told yet."

"I know it must have been difficult."

"It was, but it was interesting to see their personalities from when they were children. Those personalities are only stronger now. Buckmaster did a good job of raising them."

When Russell said nothing, she looked over at him. "What is it?"

"If you want to thank someone for raising them, you should thank Ainsley. She was the one who raised them while Buckmaster chased his political dreams."

"That's not fair," she said, surprised she was defending Buck. "He had a right to chase his dreams. He would have even if I had been around."

Russell looked over at her. "You mean while you were at home raising six children."

She let out a laugh. "Is that what people think? That I tried to kill myself because I wanted more to life? Or that I had to escape because Buckmaster had saddled me with six daughters?" She shook her head. "All I ever wanted was a house full of children. Buck knew that. He supported me and I supported him in his political dreams."

"Sounds like a perfect marriage."

She cringed at his sarcasm. "If I had everything I wanted or needed, why would I drive into the river? Isn't that what you're asking?"

"I'm sorry, forget I—"

"No, it's all right. Don't you think I've asked myself the same thing? What would make me leave my beautiful children?" She shuddered. "It haunts me. But it wasn't Buck's doing. That much I know."

They drove in silence for a few miles. She could see that he didn't believe that. Everyone wanted to blame Buck. She hated that and wished she could set them all straight. "You don't like him much. Why is that?"

"A mother who loved her life must have had some powerful reason to want to end it, that's all. You don't remember anything after you had the twins. What if something happened that made it impossible for you to live with Buck any longer, something so bad that you would leave your children behind? Are you telling me that Buckmaster Hamilton isn't capable of sending you into that river?"

His words stirred a dark and ominous image. She felt a shudder of fear as she tried to see what lurked in the darkest recesses of her memory, but it quickly slipped away.

"Are you cold?" Russell asked, noticing her shiver.

She hugged herself. "I feel as if someone just walked across my grave."

Livie jumped out of the SUV and ran to Cooper, but the sheriff held her back. "What's going on?" she cried, all her fears from last night seeming to have come true. "Why are you arresting him?"

The sheriff didn't answer as he put Cooper into the back of the car and slid behind the wheel. As he started the patrol SUV, her father came out of the house to pull her back.

"Did he tell you what's going on?" she cried.

"I was in calling my lawyer," her father said. "Cooper's apparently been arrested for the murder of Drake Connors. Isn't that the man you told me about this morning?"

"Drake?" Her world dropped out from under her.

"Let's get Livie in the house," Buckmaster said to her sisters as she slumped against him.

She felt like a rag doll as they half carried her

into the house and set her down on the couch. "Tell me this isn't happening."

"Who is Drake Connors?" Kat asked.

"The man you told us about?" Ainsley asked.

She nodded and closed her eyes.

"You don't seem surprised that your fiancé has been arrested," Angelina said as she came into the room. "Blackmail wasn't bad enough. Now murder?" She shook her head. "Are you all out to get your father?"

"For once, Angelina, could you not make this about you," Buckmaster asked pointedly, and let out a deep sigh.

"Cooper didn't kill anyone. I know him, he couldn't," Livie said, praying she was right. She kept thinking about the way he'd looked when he'd come home last night. The blood. The torn shirt. The scrapes and bruises on him.

"Why don't you tell her," Angelina said as if she hadn't heard either her husband or Livie.

She opened her eyes and looked up at her stepmother, hearing something in Angelina's voice. "Tell me what?"

"This isn't Cooper's first time behind bars," Angelina said before Buckmaster could speak.

"Angelina," her father admonished.

Livie sat up straighter on the couch, her fear growing. "What is she talking about?"

Her father looked as if he wanted to throttle his wife. "Cooper has a juvenile record."

She couldn't believe this. "For what? And how do you—"

"I don't know what it was for because the records were sealed," her father said, shocking Livie. Her father had Cooper investigated before all of this? Of course he had. She knew the sheriff wouldn't have given him this information.

"So it could be anything, even murder," Angelina added.

Buckmaster shot her an exasperated look.

Her father had known about this probably from the first. Why was she surprised that he'd done some checking on Cooper? "You didn't think he was good enough for me?"

"Livie—"

"No, all this time, Cooper has had this chip on his shoulder. He was right about you all judging him."

"Livie, we just wanted you to be happy," Ainsley said.

"Sweetheart, I would have had any man my daughter fell in love with checked out no matter his pedigree," her father said. "I wasn't worried about some juvenile record. I'm still not. I've already spoken to my lawyer. Patrick is contacting the best criminal attorneys in the nation. Of course I'll put up bail, whatever it costs."

She felt her heart go out to her father. He'd always looked after her. He liked Cooper, she was sure of it. He believed that he was innocent, just as she did. "Thank you."

"Are you sure posting his bail is what Cooper would want?" Angelina asked snidely. "He's always said he wouldn't take a dime from you."

"Enough, Angelina," her father snapped. "You are only making matters worse."

She gave him a deadly look. "Clearly Olivia doesn't know the man she was about to marry. First blackmail, now murder. Why hasn't someone considered Cooper himself might be behind the blackmail threats?"

At Buckmaster's glare, Angelina turned and, back ramrod straight, left the room. As she did, she pulled out her cell phone and made a call. "I apologize for my . . . wife," her father said. "She is under a lot of stress with everything that is going on with Sarah."

"Don't make excuses for her," Kat said. "I think we are finally seeing the real woman behind the plastic face."

Ainsley sat down on the couch next to Livie and hugged her. "Are you all right? I'm sure this is just a misunderstanding." She lowered her voice. "Cooper was with you last night, right?"

Sadly Livie shook her head. "He left right after Drake Connors was at the house. When he came back—" her voice broke "—his knuckles were scraped and bloody as if he'd been in a fight and there was blood . . ." Tears choked her. "Quite a bit of blood on his shirt and it was torn, a piece missing."

Her father swore.

"He couldn't kill anyone." But then again Livie hadn't known anything about a juvenile record that had been sealed. Why hadn't Cooper mentioned that? Probably because he'd told her little about his life before he'd arrived on the ranch looking for a job. Did she really know what he was capable of doing?

Yes, she thought. She knew him. He was stubborn and impossible. He dug in his heels and he was his own man. But he wasn't a killer.

"I need to see him," she said, looking to her father. Everyone had grown quiet and she could see from the faces that they all had their doubts about Cooper's innocence now.

"I doubt you'll be able to see him until the bail hearing," her father said. "But he'll get to make a call after he's booked. I'm betting he'll call you instead of a lawyer. When he does, tell him I'm doing everything I can for him."

Chapter NINETEEN

"We need to talk," Buckmaster said when he found Angelina in the office she shared with her brother at the far end of the house. She seemed surprised to see him and put what she'd been reading away in her desk drawer.

"I know you're upset, but the way you're behaving . . . It isn't like you."

She laughed at that. "How would you like me to behave? The world we built is falling apart and you don't seem to care. Hasn't Sarah and your children taken enough from you?"

"I'm sorry you see it that way. I love my daughters. They've enriched my life. I'm sorry they haven't yours."

She said nothing, lips drawn into a tight line of anger.

"None of this is the end of the world, especially our world. I think you're overreacting," he said as he pulled up a chair and sat down. "Angelina, nothing has changed."

"Hasn't it, Buckmaster?" She'd always called him by his full name, unlike Sarah. Just the thought of his first wife gave life to an old ache inside him that warred between blazing anger and long-smothered desire for the woman who'd deserted him.

"I spoke with the Republican Committee chairman this morning," Angelina said, turning to face him. Her voice was again the calm, conciliatory and reasonable one he'd known for fifteen years. "The party wants you. They *need* you. You can win and they know it. I didn't give him any specifics, but the chairman said that you need to get back on the road campaigning and distance yourself from—"

"Angelina, this isn't the time. With Sarah back and Livie's fiancé under arrest for murder—"

"Exactly, if we can get ahead of the—"

"*Stop.* I'm only in my fifties. There's time. But right now—"

"You didn't feel that way before you heard that Sarah was alive. You were committed. So many people are backing you. The campaign is just beginning. Now isn't the time to back off." She crossed her arms over her chest, her blue eyes like lasers.

"Maybe my priorities have changed. I'm worried about my daughters and what all this is going to do to them."

She shook her head. "You're still in love with her."

"I don't have the time or the energy for this," he said, pushing to his feet. "Can't you please just give me some time to digest all of this? There is too much going on right now to leave. There is plenty of time to hit the campaign trail before the primaries."

"This what we've been working for all these years," she cried. "Building a platform, getting you in a position that the presidency was the next step. You know that. You said it was what you wanted. Your numbers are good. You can *have* this."

"Don't you mean *you* can?"

"Yes, damn it. I have been at your side working

for this for fifteen years," she said, sounding close to tears again, the reasonable voice gone. "I can't let you throw it all away because your brood-mare of a wife suddenly turns up or one of your daughters picks the wrong man."

He blinked, surprised at her anger. Angelina had never showed any emotion—not even in bed. He knew his girls called her the Ice Queen behind her back.

"I'm not throwing anything away," he said reasonably. "Just don't push me right now." Walking to the door, he turned to look back at her. She was angrily wiping at her tears. "Like I told you before, everything is going to be all right."

"Not as long as Sarah is in our lives."

"She isn't *in* our lives," he said.

"Just as she isn't in your thoughts?" she demanded with a sneer.

As he left the room, he realized that maybe Angelina knew him better than he'd thought.

"With Cooper in jail, Livie, you can't go back to that cabin," Ainsley said.

Her sisters had gathered around her in the ranch living room, assuring her that their father would take care of everything.

"Dad said he should have Cooper out on bail by tomorrow afternoon at the latest," she said. "I want to be waiting for him at the cabin." She saw her sisters exchange looks.

"Cooper never mentioned being arrested when he was a juvenile?" Kat asked.

"I'm sure it was just some stupid thing that kids do," Livie said, hoping that's all it was. "Just think, if we hadn't been the Hamilton girls, we could all have gotten thrown into jail at certain times growing up. Dad kept each of us from a scrape or two here and there."

"Or at least his name and his lawyer did," Kat said.

"You can't think Cooper would hurt anyone," Livie said, needing them to believe it as much as she did. "You all know how he is with the mustangs. Is that a man who can kill?"

"I think we're all capable—under the right or wrong circumstances," Kat said.

"What if he did kill this man?" Bo asked, and quickly held up her hands when they all turned on her. "I'm just saying. The guy possibly drugged you and raped you. Personally, I wanted to find him and take a baseball bat to him."

"But you didn't want to kill him," Ainsley pointed out.

"I'm not Cooper, though," Bo said. "We all know how he is."

"He's stubborn, he's mule-headed, independent and he has a lot of pride," Livie said. "And occasionally he's a hothead. But he's not a murderer." She stood. "I'm going back to the cabin."

"I think that's a good idea," Angelina said as she walked in the room. Their stepmother stopped in the middle of the room, arms folded over her chest, and gave them an impatient, angry look. "I think you all should get back to your lives. This household has been disrupted enough. Your father and I are doing our best, but we don't need any more distractions."

"Livie's fiancé was just arrested for murder," Kat said. "Are you calling that a distraction? Or my mother's returning from the dead?"

"You know perfectly well what I mean. Your father is upset enough. He doesn't need all of you hanging around stirring things up."

"We get it," Bo said, and stood. "We're leaving."

"Can you believe her?" Kat said when the four of them were outside.

"She's right." Bo pushed a lock of hair back from her face. "I for one need to get back to work and don't you have a big art exhibit coming up?"

They all turned to look at Kat. "You're going to be part of an exhibit?" Ainsley asked. "Kat, that's wonderful."

"Not part of, it's her own exhibit in a gallery in Bozeman," Bo said even though Kat was giving her the shut-up look.

"I didn't want anyone to know until I had all the photographs ready," Kat said. "I'm not satisfied with what I have so I need to shoot a lot more." Kat, the perfectionist, Livie thought.

"So do it," she said. "I agree with Bo. We all need to get on with our lives. I will be fine. The man who was blackmailing me isn't going to be a problem. Cooper will be fine, too. The sheriff will catch the person who really did kill Drake Connors." Her sisters looked skeptical.

"Didn't you say you were working for some television series?" Bo asked Ainsley.

"I was hoping you had all forgotten about that," her sister said. "I am. I took the job as a favor for a friend. I'm going to be traveling around the state scouting locations for a while, but I hate to leave yet, not with everything—"

"Go," Livie said. "I will keep you up-to-date on what's happening with Cooper. As for Mother . . ."

Bo sighed. "Right, only time will tell. She could have already disappeared again and we won't see her for another twenty-two years."

Livie hugged each of her sisters.

"Eventually, we'll have to tell Harper and Cassidy," Ainsley said. "But they'll be home soon."

"What about the wedding?" Kat asked.

The mention of the wedding made the three sisters look to Livie again.

"There *will* be a wedding," she said with more conviction that she actually felt. She had to believe in a happy ending for her and Cooper. And the baby.

● ● ●

To Livie's surprise, Sheriff Frank Curry and a deputy she didn't recognize were waiting for her when she returned to the cabin. Had they realized their mistake and released Cooper? Is that why they were here, to tell her?

But as she climbed out of her SUV and saw Frank's solemn face, she knew better. "Sheriff?"

"I have a warrant to search the property including the cabin," he said, holding the papers out to her.

She thought of Cooper's torn and bloody shirt he'd come home in last night. She'd planned to wash out the blood, but once she'd seen how badly it was torn, she'd tossed the shirt in the trash. But she hadn't taken it and the rest of the trash out to the burn barrel. Had Cooper come home and burned the shirt?

The thought did nothing to steady her. What would it say if Cooper had done that? That he was guilty? That he was destroying evidence?

"When can I see Cooper?"

"He's being booked now." Frank glanced at his watch. "You won't be able to see him until his bail hearing."

All she could do was take the warrant and lead the way into the cabin. She glanced toward the trash in the kitchen. The sleeve of Cooper's ruined shirt hung over the side of the can.

She closed her eyes, fighting nausea.

"I'd appreciate it if you wouldn't touch anything," Frank said, and then must have seen how pale she was. "It might be better if you took a seat." He steered her to the kitchen table and got her a glass of water.

"Thank you." She took a sip and watched as they quickly searched the cabin. It didn't take them any time at all to find Cooper's shirt. "I was the one who threw it away," she said as if that mattered.

"We're going to take a look around the property now," the sheriff said.

She'd seen that he'd bagged Cooper's jeans, as well as his socks and boots that he'd been wearing last night. There was blood on the jeans and a dark spot on the toe of one boot. More blood? Her stomach roiled at the sight.

Standing up, she moved to the window to watch the two law officers looking around the yard. Her heart dropped when they saw the shooting range Cooper had set up for her when they'd first started dating.

She had told him that her father had taught her to shoot. He'd challenged her to a shoot off. While he'd gone to get his pistol from under the seat of his old pickup, she'd set up some old cans along the fence.

The deputy had one of the cans now. She watched him rattle it and then give a thumbs-up to the sheriff as he bagged it as evidence. He bagged several more cans as she watched.

She hadn't bothered to ask how Drake Connors had been killed. She'd just assumed that he'd died because of the fight. Now she suspected he'd been shot. Her heart thrummed. Why else would the sheriff and deputy be looking for slugs from Cooper's gun?

She jumped when the sheriff knocked on the door. Before she could get to it, he stuck his head in. "Mind if I have a few words with you?"

Livie hesitated. Should she ask for a lawyer first? She decided it would depend on what Frank asked her.

"Do you know where Cooper's pistol is, the one he keeps under the seat of his pickup?"

She shook her head, realizing she shouldn't have been surprised it was missing. "Anyone could have taken it. We all knew he kept it there. Whoever killed Drake must have taken it to frame my fiancé."

"Do you know of anyone who might have reason to kill Drake Connors?"

He didn't say it, but she knew he meant "anyone other than Cooper."

"No, but the man had to have enemies. I'm sure I'm not the first person he's blackmailed."

"We haven't been able to prove that he was responsible for your blackmail threats," Frank said. It was only her word against the now-deceased Drake that he'd demanded fifty-thousand dollars when he came out to the cabin yesterday.

"Have you talked to Amelia Wellesley?" Livie asked. "She can tell you what he was like."

"I haven't been able to reach her."

Livie groaned inwardly. Even if the Wellesleys hadn't taken off for Europe, she doubted Amelia would have admitted the truth.

"If you think of anything we should know . . ." The sheriff seemed to hesitate. "Are you going to be all right?"

Her hand went to her stomach. All she could do was nod.

He tipped his hat and walked out to the patrol SUV where his deputy was waiting.

As they drove away, she rushed to the bathroom and threw up.

Nettie was about to close up the Beartooth General Store for the day when Mabel Murphy came in like a whirlwind.

"I'm sure you've heard," Mabel said, her tone hopeful that Nettie hadn't. "Some man has been murdered and Olivia Hamilton's fiancé has been arrested for it!

"Murder," Mabel continued. "As if things couldn't get any worse at the Hamilton Ranch with Buckmaster's wife just showing up out of the blue, now the groom is locked up for *murder!*"

"Deliberate homicide," Nettie said. "That's what it's called in Montana and the man is innocent until proven guilty."

Mabel snorted. "Shot some cowboy twice in the back—after he beat him senseless. Doesn't take much to figure out what it was about." She lifted her eyebrows. "Jealousy," she said, if Nettie wasn't following along.

"What can I get you today, Mabel?" Nettie asked, and looked pointedly at the clock on the wall. "I was just about to close up for the day."

Mabel mumbled under her breath as she looked around, clearly not needing anything but another ear to bend. "I heard they haven't found the murder weapon."

Nettie didn't take the bait. She'd heard Frank on the phone with his deputies. They were still looking for the gun, mostly along the road from the murder scene to Cooper Barnett's place. The assumption was that he threw it out after the shooting, but she wasn't about to tell Mabel that.

"Let me see what I need," Mabel said, clearly disgruntled that Nettie had seen through her ruse as she picked up a few unnecessary items and put them on the counter.

"Six dollars and twenty-nine cents," Nettie said, telling herself she was never as bad a gossip as Mabel, but fearing that she was.

The bell over the front door jangled and they both turned to see Lane Broadwater come in. He was blond and blue-eyed like his sister and not bad looking in a pretty-boy kind of way. Nettie couldn't remember the man ever shopping at the

Beartooth General Store or his sister either for that matter.

"I should look around and see if there is anything else I need," Mabel said, and quickly went around one of the aisles just far enough that she wouldn't miss anything.

Lane looked around for a moment, before heading to the cooler. He pulled out a cola and made a beeline for Nettie. "Hot out this afternoon," he said as if that explained his visit.

Nettie might have believed that except for the fact it was anything but hot. After that thunderstorm yesterday, it had remained cool and a little overcast.

She'd never officially met Lane Broadwater. They didn't travel in the same circles. Also Nettie had little interest in politics and neither did Frank.

Lane shot her a smile that made Nettie wonder if the man was running for election himself or something. "You're the sheriff's wife." He held out one freshly manicured hand. "I don't believe we've met. I'm—"

"Buckmaster's campaign manager." Nettie shook the man's hand. "He already has my vote. Is that going to do it?" she asked, motioning to the cola.

He looked around. "I might get some gum, as well." He added a pack to his order. His smile had slipped. He seemed to be stalling.

"That will be two dollars and eleven cents."

Lane nodded distractedly as he dug out the exact change. "I understand your husband is heading up the murder investigation."

Mabel unsettled a stack of canned goods on the other side of the aisle, sending them crashing to the floor.

"Is he?" Nettie said. "I hadn't heard." She realized that Lane must have heard that she was the biggest gossip in the county. Unfortunately, that would now be Mabel, who was busy picking up the canned goods she'd dislodged.

"Then you wouldn't know how the case is going." Lane made a face as if this trip had been a complete waste of time.

Nettie could almost hear Mabel straining to hear.

"I hate to see that young man go to prison, or worse, be put to death for something he didn't do."

"What makes you think he didn't do it?" Nettie asked, and then bit her tongue since this was exactly what the man wanted her to ask.

"I shouldn't say this. In fact . . ."

"Oh, please do," Mabel said as she came around the end of the aisle, clearly unable to contain herself any longer.

"I should probably talk to the sheriff about what I saw."

"What did you see?" Mabel asked.

He looked around the store as if worried about

who might be listening. Nettie almost laughed. "I saw someone take something out of Cooper Barnett's truck two days ago."

"What?" Mabel asked, big-eyed and practically drooling.

"I think it was the murder weapon because apparently Cooper kept it under the seat of his pickup." He looked from Nettie to Mabel and back. "I feel so disloyal. That's why I haven't talked to the sheriff."

"Who did you see?" Mabel cried.

"I can't believe she would kill anyone, but I suppose if someone hurt my sister, I'd want to kill him, too. Ainsley's been more like a mother to Olivia and has always protected her."

"Ainsley Hamilton?" Mabel gasped, then covered her mouth with her hand.

"You didn't hear it from me," Lane said quickly, and turned to leave.

"Don't forget your purchases," Nettie said.

Chapter TWENTY

Cooper was still in a daze by the time they reached the sheriff's department. All of his personal property was confiscated, but he'd only had his keys, wallet and cell phone on him.

Booking was a blur. Since this wasn't his first arrest, he knew the procedure only too well. After having his Miranda rights read to him, he answered questions about himself, stood through the mug shots, was fingerprinted and supplied a sample of his DNA. His clothes were taken and he was given an orange jumpsuit to wear.

"Don't I get to make a call?" he asked when he was told he would be taken to a jail cell. He was led into a small room with nothing but a phone on the wall. A deputy stood outside the door as he made the call to Livie. He couldn't imagine what she was going through or what she might think. She had to know he couldn't kill anyone, right?

His heart in his throat, he listened to her cell phone ring three times before she picked up.

"Coop?"

"Livie." He said it on a relieved breath. "Are you all right?"

"I'm fine. I'm just worried about you."

"You have to believe I didn't kill that man."

"I know, but . . ."

"I can't really talk about it right now, but he was alive when I left him."

"Daddy called a lawyer for you and he'll be at the bail hearing. He said the soonest they can get you out will be tomorrow afternoon."

"Livie, I doubt even your father will be able to get me out. They're talking deliberate homicide."

"If there is a way, he'll find it."

"I appreciate everything your dad is doing. Please tell him that for me." He desperately needed to see her, to touch her. It had been too long. He'd been such a fool. Nothing mattered but the two of them. How had he let anything get in the way of that?

"I hate being locked up in here. I'm worried about you."

"Me? I'm fine. By the way, Rylan West called. He's concerned about you and said if there is anything he can do . . . Oh, and the sheriff stopped by." She didn't tell him everything because she didn't want to upset him. He had to be scared enough.

"Take care of yourself. And the baby."

She sounded close to tears when she spoke. "I'm at the cabin waiting for you."

"I can't wait to get back to you." The deputy tapped on the door. "Listen, I have to go. Livie, I'm sorry about everything. I've been a real jackass. I love you."

"I love *you*."

Livie held the phone to her heart after Cooper hung up. She didn't tell him about the sheriff taking his clothing and bullets from their make-shift old firing range. She hadn't wanted to worry him. She was worried enough for both of them. Her father would do all he could, but even Buckmaster Hamilton couldn't fix everything and she suspected he was just now learning that.

Someone had killed Drake Connors. It had to

be someone else he'd duped. Unfortunately, she knew little about him except that from the moment he stopped last winter to rescue her, he'd put her life in peril.

She had to help Cooper. But how?

Pulling out her cell phone, she put in a call to Amelia Wellesley. The more she'd thought about it, the more convinced she was that the woman had known the man. She thought that maybe Amelia would open up to her, woman to woman—if she could get past Bob.

"Wellesley residence, summer residence," Bob said with the same indifference he'd exhibited two days before.

"I was calling for Amelia Wellesley," she said.

"They aren't here. I'm finishing closing up the cabin. They're spending the summer in Europe and are unavailable." His words were clipped, as if he'd had to say the same words numerous times.

"There must be some way to contact them."

"They will be traveling and left no forwarding number."

She didn't believe that, but he hung up before she could question him further.

The lawyer Buckmaster had sent, a man by the name of Patrick Forrester, arrived shortly after Cooper was taken to his cell.

Forrester was a distinguished gray-haired man

in his sixties with a no-nonsense air about him.

"I didn't kill anyone," Cooper said after they shook hands.

"We aren't concerned with that right now," the attorney said, and waved him into the chair opposite the small table in the room they had been provided.

"I wanted to let you know what happens next," Forrester said. "The information the sheriff's office has gathered will be given to the prosecutor's office. The prosecutor will then review the information before making an independent decision as to what charges should be filed."

"I'm worried about my fiancée." With Drake Connors dead, Livie should be safe but he couldn't shake the feeling that she wasn't. "I didn't kill Drake, but whoever did . . ."

"Wouldn't have any reason to want to hurt your fiancée. I'm sure Mr. Hamilton . . ."

Cooper shook his head. "I just talked to her. She's stubborn like her father. I'm worried what she might do."

"Then I will try to get you out on bail as quickly as possible," Forrester said. "The prosecutor has seventy-two hours to decide what you will be charged with, then you will have to appear in court for an arraignment. At that time you will plead . . ."

"Not guilty. I told you, I didn't kill anyone."

". . . and there will be a bail hearing."

"What if the charge is deliberate homicide? Will a judge agree to bail?"

"Mr. Hamilton is ready to put up any bond necessary to get you out." The lawyer met his gaze. "He is convinced you won't skip."

"He's right."

Forrester closed his briefcase and stood. "Then we are done here."

"Wait, what about taking my statement?"

"Mr. Hamilton has hired me to find you a criminal attorney should one be needed. He or she will be handling that end of it."

When Frank came home that night, he looked exhausted. Nettie had made dinner and kept aside a plate for him.

She met him at the door with a cold beer. "Why don't you have a seat on the porch. It's so nice out and the crows have been waiting for you to come back all day."

He smiled at that and bent to kiss her cheek. Taking the beer, he went outside. She heard the porch swing creak as he lowered himself into it. She got herself a beer and joined him after turning on the oven to reheat his dinner.

"Rough day?" she asked unnecessarily.

"The worst," he said without looking at her. His gaze was on the sunset and the silhouettes of a string of black crows. Uncle called down to him. "Hey, Uncle," he called back.

She was dying to ask about his visit to the state mental hospital and Tiffany, but she was afraid to. So she told him about Lane Broadwater's visit to the store and how he'd tried to incriminate Ainsley Hamilton.

"He said he *saw* her take the gun?" Frank asked, and took a sip of his beer.

"Not exactly. Just saw her taking something out of the pickup."

Her husband nodded.

"Why would he cover for Cooper Barnett?" she asked. "If Cooper Barnett's gun is the murder weapon . . ." She looked at her husband for clarification and got nothing.

He smiled. "Mabel driving you crazy?"

She had to laugh. "I was never that bad."

He grunted in answer, forcing her to elbow him in the ribs.

"I won't be going up to the mental hospital again," he said into the quiet that followed.

She held her breath for a moment. "Does Tiffany know?"

He nodded. "I might get called to testify before the board if they ever decide to release her." He looked over at his wife. "I will fight her getting out until my last breath."

Nettie took a drink of her beer, feeling as if she could breathe for the first time in a long time. She hadn't realized how afraid she'd been that Tiffany would manipulate Frank into helping her seek her freedom. He'd accepted that she wasn't his child and that whatever Pam thought he deserved, he was no longer going to be made to feel guilty.

She put a hand on his leg. "I saved you some dinner, if you're hungry."

"Maybe later."

They finished their beers to the sound of the spring night and the creak of the swing. "I'm thinking it might be time for me to retire."

Nettie looked over at him in surprise. "You're just tired."

He smiled at her.

As she rose, she bent to kiss his cheek. "It will be better tomorrow."

Frank grunted. "I'm not counting on that."

"I know you have a number for Mrs. Wellesley," Livie said when the caretaker answered the phone the second time and she told him who she was. "I have to talk to her. A friend of hers was murdered. She'll want to talk to me."

She suspected Bob wasn't a huge fan of Mrs. Wellesley and that was the only reason he'd handed over the number.

"How did you get my number?" Amelia demanded when she came on the line.

"Drake Connors is dead. Murdered." Silence. "I need to know if you had anything to do with it."

"Are you crazy? Of course not. Why would I kill him?"

"What about your husband?"

Amelia let out a laugh. "If Howard was going to have him killed, he wouldn't have paid him off, now would he?"

It didn't sound likely, Livie thought, remembering Drake's new pickup. "Well, *someone* killed him."

"Let me guess. They've arrested your fiancé."

"So you *have* been following the news."

Again Amelia laughed. "I have better things to do, thank you. It was a simple deduction. Your fiancé is a hothead. Add to that the fact that you browbeat our poor caretaker to get my number, so you must be desperate for a reason."

"Did Drake give you any idea who he was with before you?"

"Right, we talked about his other conquests at length."

"He must have mentioned friends, family, his parents, someone."

There was a sigh on the other end of the line. "I'm not sure his parents are alive and I don't know any of his friends or . . . Wait, there *was* someone. He called a woman once while the two of us were together. I thought it was an old girlfriend, but he said it was his kid sister. He was probably lying. Sorry, but that's all I've got."

"This kid sister, did he say her name?"

Silence, then finally, "Mel. I could hear what sounded like a crowd in the background. Later I checked his phone. He'd called a bar in White Sulphur Springs, so I really doubt it was a kid sister."

Mel. "What bar?"

"The Silver Spur."

"Thanks."

"So he really is dead?"

"Someone shot him twice in the back."

"Had to be a woman. The stupid bastard turned his back on her." She chuckled. "His last mistake. Good luck clearing your fiancé. Hey, and don't call me again." Amelia hung up.

They had finished having breakfast the next morning when Russell saw Sarah wince. "Another headache?"

"It's nothing."

He seriously doubted that. "They seem to be getting worse. When do you see the neurologist?"

"I called. I can't get in for a while. I have to see a regular doctor first and get a referral." She rubbed her temples and he got up to get her some aspirin and a glass of water.

"Any more memories coming back?" he asked after she'd downed a couple.

She shook her head, shifting her gaze away.

It was the first time she'd lied to him. He knew

something was going on, the headaches and the terrified look she would get. She would quickly try to cover so he didn't know. But he did know. "You can trust me."

Sarah reached across the table to take his hand and squeeze it. "You have been so good to me. I really do appreciate everything you've done."

"I'm glad I can help. I don't want you going through this alone. I don't mean to pry."

"You're not," she said, removing her hand. "You're merely concerned and maybe there is good reason. Maybe there is something in my past . . . that I have to fear."

He had no doubt there was definitely something in her past. He couldn't help but wonder if it involved Buckmaster Hamilton or whoever had picked her up that night after she'd gone in the river.

"You're safe here."

"I don't want anything to happen to you."

So he was right about the memories scaring her. "Nothing will."

The cell phone he'd lent her rang. She glanced at it, then at him. "Buck," she said, and rose to take the call. He could hear her out on the porch talking softly.

He caught only a little of the conversation and felt guilty even for that. Getting up from the table, he began to wash up their dishes. For the life of him, he couldn't understand a man who'd had six children with this woman and apparently wanted nothing to do with her. Something had to have happened between them, something that had made Sarah want to kill herself.

"You should have left those for me," Sarah said behind him. "Let me at least try to pay you back for your generosity by helping out around here."

He finished the last dish and turned to shake his head. "You're doing me a favor by being here. After over forty years of marriage, losing my wife left me . . . well, at loose ends. It was lonely out here."

"You don't have any children?"

"One daughter. Judy couldn't conceive. My daughter, Destry—"

"Destry Grant is your daughter?"

He explained how he and Destry's mother had spent one night together that resulted in her conception. "As far as she knew, W. T. Grant was her father. But since I was his ranch manager, I got to watch her grow up. It was a secret I kept for her mother."

"At least you had that."

He nodded. "Destry's married to Rylan West. She and I are getting to know each other as father and daughter, but she has a life of her own with the ranch and the kids. I have two beautiful grandchildren. I try to spend as much time with them as I can." He felt as if he was complaining and quickly changed the subject. "Is everything all right with Buck?"

Sarah gave him a weak smile. "It's hard to say. He wants to see me again."

"When?"

"This morning, if possible. Russell, I can't keep asking you to drive me."

"I'm happy to do it. Unless you prefer I not. You're welcome to take my pickup."

She shook her head. "I don't have a driver's license. At least, I don't think I do. And I appreciate you being close by. Is that selfish of me?"

"Not at all. Like I said, I'm here for you."

"This isn't because of the way we met, is it?"

"No," he said with a laugh. "I don't feel guilty since the doctor said I barely tapped you with my pickup and that I'm not responsible for your memory loss. Maybe I just like you."

Her smile was shy. "I like you, too."

But you still love Buckmaster Hamilton, he thought. He feared the man would only break her heart more than he suspected the senator already had.

Chapter TWENTY-ONE

"I should never have said anything," Lane complained when the sheriff called to say he wanted to see him. "But I was feeling so conflicted."

"What exactly did you see?" he asked once Lane was seated in a chair across from his desk. Lane was pale, too perfectly groomed, and the few times he and Lane had crossed paths, the man had been too slick.

Frank laughed inwardly, thinking what Nettie would say about his evaluation of Lane Broadwater. He imagined that Lane had gotten beaten up a lot at school.

Lane took his time. "I just happened to look out the window. I saw Ainsley. She was acting strange, you know, looking around to make sure no one was watching. She opened the door of Cooper's old pickup and reached under the seat. Whatever she took, she quickly stuffed it under her jacket and returned to the house."

"Did anyone else see her?"

Lane thought for a moment. "I doubt it. Everyone else was gone from the house."

"Why didn't you think to bring this to my attention?" Frank asked.

"I completely forgot about it until I heard that Drake Connors had been shot."

News traveled fast. Gossip even faster.

He nodded but there was no need to encourage Lane to continue.

"I was heading into the store where your wife works when I remembered. I shouldn't have just blurted it out like that, but I was so . . . shocked by the implications."

Frank looked up from his notes. "What implications are those?" he asked innocently.

Lane's blue eyes widened. "Why everyone knows how protective Ainsley is when it comes to her sisters. Once Olivia told everyone about this awful man and what he'd done . . . well, Ainsley was beside herself."

"You believe she killed Drake Connors?"

He looked appalled at the idea. "I'm not saying that. I'm just saying . . ."

"That you saw her take the gun."

"I saw her take *something*."

The sheriff closed his notebook. "I appreciate you coming forward."

"What happens now?" he asked.

"I'll speak to Ainsley."

"Does anyone have to know that I was the one who saw her?" he asked. "As you know, I'm employed by her father."

"Well, it will come down to her word against yours."

He blinked. "But I have no reason to lie."

Frank got to his feet. "If you think of anything else . . ."

• • •

Once Livie heard from her father that Cooper's bail hearing wasn't until late that day, she made the decision to drive up to White Sulphur Springs, Montana. She wanted to talk to the young woman Amelia had said Drake called his little sister.

She found the Silver Spur bar along the main drag of town. It wasn't quite noon so the bar was fairly empty. Four men and one woman who looked like regulars were at the bar. They turned as she walked in. In small-town businesses, everyone always turned, expecting to know the person who'd entered.

Stepping up to the bar, Livie slid onto a stool. The bar was cool and dark, most of the light illuminating the booze bottles in front of the back bar mirror.

The young blonde woman behind the bar didn't look even twenty-one. "I'm looking for Mel."

"I'm Melody," she said hesitantly. "But some people call me Mel."

Now that she was here, Livie realized she didn't know how to approach the subject of Drake Connors. "Are you Drake Connors's younger sister?"

The girl laughed, exposing a charming gap between her teeth. "I'm not really his little sister." She gave a shy look. "You know Drake?"

Livie glanced down the bar. The regulars were

so quiet it was obvious they were all listening. "Is there somewhere we could talk for minute? It's about Drake."

"Look, if he took money from you . . ."

"It's not that." But it was an interesting assumption. "Something has happened to him." She was a little surprised that no one here seemed to know about the murder. Maybe it was because the television was turned to a reality show instead of the news and she didn't see any newspapers lying around. Not that a murder in Beartooth might make the news up this way, anyway.

"I guess we can step into the office." Melody looked down the bar. "I'll be right back."

Livie followed her into a small cluttered room. There wasn't a place to sit down since the chairs all had papers or boxes of liquor on them. But she didn't have much time, anyway. "I assume Drake was your boyfriend?"

"Definitely not. We were just friends. You said something has happened to him?"

"He's been killed."

The young woman's jaw dropped. *"Seriously?"*

"I'm sorry to have to be the one to tell you. Were the two of you close?"

"Naw, not really. He came in a lot, talked a lot." She rolled her eyes. "He always had big plans. Dressed like he had money. Was a good tipper, though," she said, finally showing some regret at his passing.

"I was hoping you could tell me something about him for an article I'm writing about his death. I only met him once. Do you know anything about his past?"

"What did you say your name was?"

"Olivia Hamilton." She said it before she realized she should probably have come up with a name to go with her story about being a journalist.

"I can't believe this. It's so sad. He was actually saying he was making some changes."

"What kind of changes?"

"I got the feeling, even though he pretended to be somebody, that he was pretty poor growing up, you know. I heard around that he preyed on rich women. He was cute enough, so why not, right? He told me he was going to get a real job, maybe even settle down. But first he had to get some money that someone down by Big Timber owed him."

"He didn't mention a name?"

"Naw, but he had that look, you know? It was some rich, married woman. He was driving a brand-new truck." Melody looked pointedly at her. "Aren't you going to write this down?"

"I have a good memory."

"He said it was time he quit living the way he had been," she said thoughtfully. "He laughed and said that one of these days it was going to get him killed. I guess it did."

"He didn't say what kind of changes he had in mind?"

"Naw, I think he was just talking."

Drake Connors was a liar. So what had made Livie think she could get anything helpful by driving up here? Drake had told his "kid sister" that he was going to Big Timber to collect money. No doubt he'd been talking about getting it from her.

"Can you think of anything else?"

"He did hobnob with some interesting people. He got a call right before he left the bar," Melody said. "I tried not to eavesdrop." Sure she did. "He was definitely talking to a woman and being real sweet, you know? I heard him say something about a senator he was going to see while he was down there. I assume he was talking about Big Timber."

Livie did, too. So he was planning to go to her father? Is that what he'd meant about other fish to fry?

"So yeah, it's sad to hear he's dead," Mel was saying. "Sounds like he should have taken the job his mother suggested down that way."

"His mother?" Livie asked.

Frank didn't hold much stock in Lane Broadwater's story. But he had to find out if there was any truth to it nonetheless.

"Ms. Hamilton, thank you for coming in," he said when Ainsley came down to his office.

315

When he'd told her he had some questions, he shouldn't have been surprised to see that Buckmaster had come with her. "Senator. Both of you please have a seat."

"What's this about? And for God's sake, call me Buckmaster. It isn't like we haven't known each other for years."

Frank nodded as the senator settled into a chair next to his oldest daughter.

"If this is about getting Cooper out on bail . . ."

"Actually, I'm following up on a lead. I was hoping Ainsley could help me."

"Any way I can. Just name it," she said.

"Did you know that Cooper Barnett had a .45 pistol?"

Buckmaster frowned. "The one he kept under the front seat of his pickup? Everyone knew about it."

Frank nodded. "How many people knew about the gun?"

He shrugged. "Anyone who worked at the ranch. Cooper had pulled it out several times when we were having that trouble with a den of rattlesnakes near the horses. Are you trying to tell me it's the murder weapon?"

He turned to Ainsley. "Did you ever take the gun out of his pickup?"

"No," Ainsley said.

Buckmaster let out a curse and demanded, "Why would you ask her that?"

"Did you take anything out of the truck a day or two before the murder?"

"No, I never went near his truck. I had no reason to."

Buckmaster was on his feet. "What the hell is this about?"

"I have an eyewitness who claims he saw Ainsley take something out from under the seat of the truck."

The senator's eyes narrowed. "Cooper wouldn't tell you this. That boy is no fool. Who is this eyewitness?"

When Frank said nothing, Buckmaster said, "Your eyewitness is lying to either cover for that young man or . . ." He let out another curse and sat back down more heavily this time. "Or trying to incriminate my daughter." He shook his head, aging right before the sheriff's eyes.

"I had to ask."

Ainsley said, "I will take a lie detector test."

"That won't be necessary." Frank got to his feet. "Thanks for coming in."

Buckmaster nodded and rose again. "You find out who your allies are when something like this happens, don't you."

After they left, Frank sat for a long while trying to understand why Lane Broadwater would lie about seeing Ainsley take the gun. There was no doubt in his mind that Lane had lied and that Ainsley was telling the truth. If Lane was covering for someone, it had to be someone in that house. Buckmaster? Or was Lane covering for himself? That seemed unlikely. Lane didn't seem any closer to the Hamilton girls than his sister was.

Why muddy the water, though, when Cooper Barnett had already been arrested for the crime?

All he could imagine was that Lane was afraid some other evidence was going to come out. Frank had to wonder what it might be. The murder weapon?

"Oh, I know who you are," Drake Connors's mother said before Livie could introduce herself. "Mel called. She did some checking and found out who you really were and what you were really up to." She started to close the door on her.

"Please, I need to talk to you. I'm trying to find out who killed your son."

"We *know* who killed him. Your *boyfriend*."

"Cooper didn't kill him. Wouldn't your son want you to find his real killer?"

Alma Connors peered through the crack in the door. Her eyes suddenly swam with tears. "Drake was a good boy."

Livie doubted that, but nodded. "I'm so sorry for your loss. I saw him that day and he said something that makes me think that, after I talked to him, he went to see the person who killed him. I thought you might know who that person is."

His mother looked skeptical, but stepped aside

reluctantly to let her come in. The house was small and cluttered. It smelled of cooked cabbage and the rugs were threadbare. Was this where Drake was raised? Is this what started his quest for the finer things in life any way he could get them?

Alma stopped in the middle of the living room and crossed her arms, not offering Livie a chair. She realized she'd better make this quick.

"When I accused Drake of blackmailing me—"

"My son would never blackmail anyone."

Did she know her son at all? "When he left, he said he was going to see someone else he knew down by Big Timber." She had the woman's interest now.

"But he didn't say who?"

Livie shook her head. A part of her still feared that Drake had been planning to go to her father.

His mother seemed to consider this.

"That's why I needed to talk to you. Do you know who he might have been planning to visit down there? Melody thought you might know. She said you'd suggested someone he should contact for a job?"

Alma looked surprised. "I mentioned that he should see if he could get on at the Hamilton Ranch." Alma wrinkled her nose in distaste. "*Your* ranch."

She frowned. "Why would . . ."

"He said he was desperate to get out of Monarch so I told him to cash in on his connection to

319

his father," she said as if Livie was just plain slow.

"I'm sorry, I'm confused."

"His father was a ranch manager over in the Madison Valley." When Livie still didn't get it, she added, "For the *Broadwaters*. Isn't your step-mother a Broadwater?"

"I see you brought your bodyguard," Buckmaster said when Sarah climbed out of Russell's pickup in front of the Branding Iron Café.

"As you know, I don't have a vehicle," she said impatiently.

"Well, why don't I just buy you one?"

"Is that what you think, that I want your money?" She could tell he was in a mood. "Nor do I have a driver's license. Did you want to see me just to give me a hard time?"

"No." He softened his expression. "I thought we could have a piece of pie and talk. Remember before the kids were born when we used to come here and just sit and talk about the future?"

She remembered. He'd been so full of fiery ambition that she'd hoped it would burn out. She'd never cared about politics. The last place she'd wanted to live was the White House.

But she'd told herself she would never stand in Buck's way. "You did what you set out to do," she said as he stepped over to the café's entrance and started to open the door. "I'm proud of you. You'll make a good president."

He didn't seem to hear her as he looked back toward Russell, who was still sitting in his pickup pretending not to listen even though his window was down. "Russell, want to join us?"

"No, thanks." Russell turned his gaze to Sarah. "I have to pick up a few things at the store," he said, motioning across the street. "Holler when you're ready to go home."

Sarah saw that the word *home* nearly set Buckmaster off again.

"Home?" he said under his breath, and swore.

"Buck . . ."

"I can take you back to Russell's, if that's what you want," he said. "I don't like this, you acting as if I might hurt you."

Russell got out and started across the street toward the general store.

Sarah called after him. "Buck can take me back to your place after we have some pie. I'll call if I need anything. Thank you, Russell." She saw Buck grit his teeth, but he said nothing as she stepped into the café. The place filled her with memories of a time when she was young and happy.

When she'd met Buck that day in Yellowstone Park, he'd been so full of himself. He'd flirted with her as he unloaded a trailer full of horses. She'd loved hearing about his ranch. It had sounded like paradise. He was handsome and charming and irresistible. Was it any wonder she'd let herself fall in love with him? She'd told herself this was a man she could depend on. Montana had seemed so far away from the world she'd lived in before that. It was like being on another planet.

"Please don't take this out on Russell," she said once they were seated. "He's just being a friend."

Buck mugged a face. "Men and women can't be friends."

"Oh, Buck."

"I'm sorry, it's just that when I see you, it brings back so many memories. Then I see you with Russell."

"You have another *wife,* Buck. It isn't as if I could just move back into the house, even if either of us wanted that."

"What *do* you want, Sarah?"

"I told you. I just want to see my girls. I still haven't seen my babies." Before he could remind her that Harper and Cassidy were no longer babies, she said, "I know they are all grown up, but I still need to see them. You said they will be home from college soon?"

"A few days or so."

"You still haven't told them?"

"It's finals week. I don't want them blowing off the whole semester. Word is going to get out. I'm just hoping they don't hear until they're done with school this year."

"My timing wasn't very good, was it? I'm sorry even though I had no control over it—at least as far as I know. But then when would have been a good time to drop back into your lives?"

"Why now, Sarah?"

She shook her head. "I still can't remember, if that's what you're asking. I know it's hard for you to believe."

"You said you were going to see a doctor?"

She nodded. "At least I can find out if the memory loss is caused by something physical. Or if it is mental."

The young waitress whose name tag said "Cassie" came over and took their order. Buck chose apple pie with a scoop of vanilla ice cream just as he always had. She chose the lemon meringue, apparently surprising him.

"You used to always have the huckleberry," he said, frowning.

"Did I?" She could tell he was wondering in what other ways she had changed. She fiddled with her napkin, glad when the waitress returned with their order.

"I'm sure you need money to live on," Buck said after a few bites. He pulled an envelope out of his jacket pocket and slid it across the table.

She stared at it for a moment and then took another bite of pie.

"Sarah."

"I don't want your money, Buck."

"Then how do you plan to live?" he demanded.

"I don't know, but I will figure it out." She hadn't had a purse with her when Russell had found her. No identification of any kind. She'd been wearing slacks, a blouse and a pair of simple shoes. "I'm only fifty-eight. I can get a job."

He laughed. "Doing what? What are you trained to do?"

She had no idea. "I could be a nanny."

Buck shook his head as he reached across the table and took her hand. "Please, take the money. I'll set up a bank account for you and deposit money monthly. Let me do this, Sarah. I look at you and . . . you're still my wife in my heart."

She saw how hard the words were for him. "Thank you, Buck. But it's only temporary." She didn't tell him or even Russell, but at least some of her memory was starting to come back. She'd somehow survived for the past twenty-two years. Once her memory came back, she could go back to that life.

Unless she'd run from it as she had this one with Buck.

Chapter TWENTY-TWO

Livie drove back to the ranch, anxious to talk to her father. She'd tried to call him, but he'd apparently turned off his cell phone. It was something he never did, so she worried that there had to be something wrong at home.

He'd been acting strangely since their mother had returned. Not that she could blame him. She knew it was a shock. Add to that, his feelings for Sarah—and Angelina's obvious jealousy. Her stepmother had been seething since Sarah had returned.

Livie hadn't seen her mother since their meeting at the café. She wasn't sure how she felt. Sarah Hamilton was a stranger to her. She used to think she remembered her. But after seeing her again, she wasn't sure the memories had even been real.

When she reached the ranch, she entered the house and went looking for her father. She was still shocked by what she'd learned. Drake's father had worked as a ranch manager for the Broadwaters. Angelina hadn't lived on the ranch for years, but wasn't it possible that she not only knew Drake's father, Amos, but also Drake himself?

The house felt unusually quiet. She checked the kitchen, her father's den, and started down the hall toward Angelina's office. None of the staff seemed to be around today. Had her father given everyone the day off for some reason?

Her concern growing, she tapped on Angelina's closed door and then tried the knob. As the door swung open, she saw that the room was empty. Where was everyone? At the sound of laughter outside, she stepped to the window. Two of the cowhands were practicing roping in the back by the corrals. No sign of her father.

As she started to leave the room, her eye caught a flash of pale blue. The corner of a sheet of pale blue paper stuck out of the desk drawer.

Moving like a sleepwalker, Livie stepped to the desk. Her hand trembled as she slowly opened the drawer.

The sheet of paper fell back into the drawer, but not before she'd seen what was written on it. She stared down at it, her heart in her throat. It was the same color paper she'd received from her blackmailer. Only apparently this blackmail note had never been sent.

"Tell me about Angelina," Sarah said, surprising Russell later at the house after Buckmaster had dropped her off. He'd seen Angelina Hamilton leaving the guesthouse the other day when he'd returned with the sheriff. From the expression on the woman's face, he'd known that she and Sarah must have argued.

"Tell you about her? You met her," he said as he went into the kitchen to put on a pot of coffee.

"You could say that," she said, shedding her jacket and taking a seat at the kitchen table. The day had started out cool and never really warmed up. So like spring in Montana. "What's she like?"

He didn't know how to answer and said as much. "What do you want to know?" he asked cautiously as he busied himself with the coffee.

She got up to move to the counter next to him, studying his face as he worked. "You don't like her."

"I've never met her, not really."

"Why did Buck marry her?"

Russell let out a nervous laugh. "He didn't consult me at the time nor take me into his confidence."

"I'm sorry, I know I'm putting you on the spot, but I need to know."

The coffee began to gurgle. He scratched his jaw for a moment. "I can tell you what people say about her, I suppose."

Now it was her turn to laugh. "You really do have a hard time saying anything bad about anyone, don't you?"

He flushed with embarrassment. "I'm not as nice a man as you're making me out to be."

She leaned over and kissed him on the cheek.

"Yes, you are. If it makes you too uncomfortable . . ."

"No, I'm sure you're curious about her." He eyed Sarah for a moment. "But I would think you have a pretty good idea what she's like after your . . . visit."

"She doesn't like me and she wants me to disappear, I can tell you that much. She offered to buy me off."

He shook his head, thinking how sad the situation was.

"It's all right. I might not know where I've been the past twenty-two years, but I know I'm fairly resilient. I suspect I didn't have it easy." She pretended to swat him. "Stop looking so sympathetic and tell me what people say about her."

"All right." The coffee was ready so he poured them both a cup. "Given the Broadwaters' apparent connections, it would appear that he married her to help his political career."

She nodded, as if not surprised.

"I've heard she throws extravagant parties."

"For people who can help Buck, right?"

Russell nodded. He felt uncomfortable. "I've heard that they go through a lot of staff because they all hate working for her."

He could see that also didn't surprise her. "What kind of mother was she to my children?"

He chose his words carefully. "I got the

impression that she wasn't a mother figure at all."

"She's ambitious like my husband, isn't she?"

He nodded. "I believe her aspirations include redecorating the White House."

"She said I'm hurting his campaign. I hope not. I know how much it means to him. That's one reason I plan to see my daughters and leave."

"Where will you go?" Russell asked, dreading the day she would leave, but knowing it was coming. "What will you do?"

She smiled. "I have no idea. I'm hoping the neurologist will be able to help me."

"Is it possible you have another family some-where?"

"I've thought of that."

"Maybe they're looking for you," he suggested.

"Maybe. We should know soon enough. I'm surprised my return from the dead hasn't already been picked up by the media."

He saw her frown. Did she suspect as he did that if someone was looking for her, it wouldn't be a loving family?

At the sound of several vehicles coming up the road to the house, Livie stepped to the window of her stepmother's home office and looked out.

Angelina pulled up first, followed by her father. As they got out of their respective vehicles, they seemed to be arguing.

Livie turned and hurried down to the front

329

door. By the time she reached it, they were just coming in.

"I need to talk to you," she said to her father.

"Oh, more drama," Angelina said. "It is never ending, is it? Now what?"

"You might want to come along, as well," Livie said to her. "I found something in your office that my father needs to see."

"*My* office? What were you doing . . ."

"I was looking for you and Dad."

"And you thought we were in my office?"

Her father took off his Stetson, hung it on the rack off the entry and said, "Let's see what this is about."

Inside Angelina's office, Livie moved to the desk. "The blackmail threats I've been receiving were all on pale blue paper with matching envelopes." She opened the drawer. "Exactly like this. This is a blackmail note like mine, only it appar-ently was never sent."

"This is ridiculous. You can't possibly think that I've been blackmailing Olivia," Angelina cried, and looked to her husband. "That black-mail note came in the mail addressed to you," she said to her. "I stuck it in the drawer and was going to mention it to your father, but when the blackmailer was found dead and Cooper was arrested, I forgot about it."

Her father looked from Angelina to Livie. "Let me see that."

The note was short and sweet.

You owe me. Get me $100,000. I'll call to tell you where to meet me.

"Where is the envelope?" Livie asked.

"I threw it away. I kept the note because I thought it might be needed should any of this go to trial." Angelina looked again at her husband. "You can't seriously believe I was blackmailing your daughter, Buckmaster. Why would I do that? I didn't even know about her . . . indiscretion until recently."

Livie let the "indiscretion" go. She couldn't argue that she'd been stupid and careless.

Her father looked to her. "I suppose that does explain it, then," he said.

She didn't know if she believed Angelina or not. Admittedly, her stepmother had all the right answers. Was it possible she'd jumped too quickly to the wrong conclusion when she'd seen the blue paper?

Stepping to the desk, Angelina rummaged through it and said, "Someone's been in my desk drawer." She shot a look at Livie.

"I didn't touch anything."

"Well, someone has gone through my things," she accused.

"Who would go through your . . ." Buckmaster began, but she quickly cut him off.

"I'm not suffering from dementia. Someone looked through my things."

"I'm sure there's an explanation."

Angelina merely glared at him before slamming the desk drawer; the tension between the two of them was thick enough to cut with a chain saw. "This probably isn't the time to ask about the wedding . . ."

"Angelina."

"I have to know since I'm sure you're planning to have the reception here," his wife said.

"It's all right, Dad. Cooper and I are getting married as planned."

Her stepmother raised a brow. Even her father looked a little surprised, though he quickly said how glad he was, adding that he was sure Cooper would be cleared of the ridiculous charges long before the wedding.

"If that's all, I need to freshen up before dinner." Angelina waited until they left her office before she locked the door behind her and disappeared into the master bedroom.

"Maybe she's telling the truth, but there's more," Livie said as she and her dad went downstairs. Once in his den, she told him about her trip up north to talk first to Drake Connors's friend, then his mother.

"His father was a ranch manager for the Broadwaters. There's a connection." Her father rubbed a hand over his face. "It doesn't mean Angelina knew Drake. You know her, she doesn't even know the name of our ranch manager. She has no interest in ranching and I'm sure she didn't when she lived at home."

Livie groaned. "You have to admit that's awfully coincidental. What if she and Drake were in it together?"

"Why would she blackmail you?"

She thought about that and grasped at the first thing that came to mind. "For the money. I know she's worried about what's going to become of her now that Mother is back."

"I know Angelina is concerned. But your mother wasn't back when you got the first blackmail note, right?"

Livie had to admit that was true.

"Let's look at this logically. How would she even know about what happened to you in January?"

"Drake would have told her."

"Assuming she has that kind of relationship with her family's ranch manager." Her father shook his head. "Also if she were the blackmailer, wouldn't she be smart enough not to leave one of the notes in her desk where anyone could find it?"

Livie shrugged. "No one goes into that room but her and Lane, right? Usually the door is locked."

"Honey, all of this is quite a leap, you have to admit. You know that for such a large state, Montana is really a small world. Because the population is tiny by comparison, there are a lot of connections between people."

She nodded, knowing it was true. "But you have to admit, it looks suspicious."

"I think you're jumping to the wrong conclusion, but I'll ask her about Drake."

"Dad, she isn't going to admit to any of it if she is guilty."

"Then I'll ask her brother," he said, getting to his feet. "How is that?"

She stood on tiptoe to kiss his cheek. "Thank you. Did you hear when Cooper's bail hearing is going to be?"

"Four this afternoon. That was the soonest we could get it."

"Will the judge even grant bail in a murder case?"

"It will take a lot of talking and a lot of money, but don't worry, I'll do my best to get him out."

"Thank you so much." Getting him out on bail was a start, but unless the real killer was found . . . "Did you see Mother?"

He nodded. "I gave her some money to live on. I'm worried about her." He saw Livie frown and added, "It's going to be all right."

That's what Cooper kept saying. But Livie had her doubts.

Chapter TWENTY-THREE

As Livie drove into town for the bail hearing, she couldn't help worrying. What if her father couldn't get Cooper out of jail? Worse, what if they couldn't prove that he had nothing to do with killing Drake Connors?

Distracted, she realized she'd turned down the wrong street. Ahead, she saw the sign for the lumberyard. Asking Delia to be her maid of honor had been a mistake—childhood pact or no pact. But it was too late to do anything about that since she wasn't even sure there was going to be a wedding.

Driving past the place, she noticed how run-down the area looked. The outside of the lumberyard needed paint. So did the small house Delia lived in right next door. As far as she knew, business had been good, but Delia's family had to be a drain since she was the only one who worked the business.

She was almost past the place when she saw movement in the shadowed alleyway between the lumberyard and the house. With a start, she saw Delia talking to a man. The two seemed to be having a heated argument. They must have heard her vehicle because they both looked in her direction.

Livie fought her first instinct—to duck down. As they turned toward her, she saw to her surprise that the man was Hitch McCray. She quickly sped up.

Two blocks down, Livie pulled over in front of the courthouse even though it was too early for the bail hearing. Her hands were shaking. Delia and Hitch?

Delia had never liked Hitch when they were growing up. Had something changed? For starters, Delia had lost Cooper. She knew Delia was capable of doing anything to get Cooper back but would she use Hitch to do it? And what would Hitch get out of it? Could he harbor such bad feelings that he'd get involved in something with Delia to hurt her?

The sheriff had been worried that Hitch might be behind the blackmail. Seeing the two of them together arguing . . . Was it possible they had something to do with Drake's murder?

Livie knew she was clutching at straws. The sheriff hadn't been able to find any connection between Drake and Delia or Drake and Hitch. The only connection she'd discovered was to her stepmother. And Lane, she thought with a start. Lane and Drake were about the same age. If they'd all been on the ranch together . . .

Her head spinning, she climbed out, desperate for fresh air. Glancing at her watch, she saw she still had plenty of time. She decided to walk around the block and try to clear her head.

She hadn't gone but a short way, though, before she heard someone call her name behind her. Turning, she saw Delia. One look at her and Livie knew the woman had come looking for her after seeing her drive by the lumberyard. Or was Delia planning to go to Cooper's bail hearing?

"Let me guess, you're going to the bail hearing," she said.

Delia lifted a brow as she caught up to her. "Of course. I want to be there for moral support."

"For me? Or Cooper?"

With a sigh, Delia said, "Both of you. I'm your friend, too, even if you don't believe it."

"I just saw you with Hitch McCray. Is he also a friend?"

"Hitch?" She frowned. "You must have seen us discussing his bill. He is such a deadbeat. You were definitely smart to spurn his affections."

Livie doubted very seriously that what she'd witness had anything to do with Hitch's bill and said as much. "What were you really doing with Hitch? I know you can't be dating him."

"I'm sorry, but it really isn't any of your business."

"It is if the two of you are conspiring together."

"Conspiring?" Delia laughed. "To do what?"

"Keep me from marrying Cooper."

"How would we do that, Olivia?" The woman sounded as if she really wanted to know. "Unless

337

you're worried because you've done something? But I suppose you must have considering someone has been blackmailing you."

"How did you . . ."

"Cooper told me." Delia smiled when she saw her shocked reaction. "I told you. We're good friends."

"I'm not getting into this with you. Since there's time before the arraignment, I'm going to take a walk around the block," Livie said, and turned away.

"Come on, Livie, there's no reason for you to be suspicious of me," she said, catching up to her. "Don't you remember when we were best friends? We told each other *everything*. Then you went away to college and were too smart for me."

"That isn't true."

"I knew you were too good for me when we were friends. You saw how I lived compared to you. You never wanted for anything."

"You've done well all by yourself. You should be proud of that."

"I am. But I miss you. I haven't had a friend like you since."

Livie looked over at her as they walked. She, too, hadn't had a best friend since then. Delia sounded so sincere she felt her heart go out to her. "I miss that closeness, too."

They walked for a ways in silence. "How are you holding up?" Delia asked.

"As well as can be expected." It saddened her that they hadn't remained the good friends they used to be. She knew that she was partly responsible for that. While she'd gone away to college, Delia had gone to work at the lumberyard.

But when she'd returned, she and Delia hadn't been able to pick up the friendship where they'd left off. Then Cooper had hired on at the ranch. Livie hadn't even known that he and Delia had dated until she ran into her in downtown Big Timber and her "friend" had berated her for "stealing" Cooper. When she'd realized that Livie hadn't known the two of them had dated, she'd apologized, but the friendship was irrevocably broken.

Could two old friends who'd shared the same man ever be good friends again? Asking Delia to be her maid of honor had been partly the pact and also an attempt to mend those fences between them. It wasn't until later that Livie had realized Delia hadn't gotten over Cooper.

The question was how far would she go to get him back if she got the chance?

"Part of the problem," Livie said as they neared the courthouse, "is I don't know if I can trust you."

Delia sighed. "Cooper and I are just friends."

"I wish I could believe that you're okay with that and nothing more."

"I'm sorry you feel that way, but I've moved on."

She lifted a brow. "By dating Hitch?"

"Yes, why not?" she said with a wide smile.

Livie stopped walking. "Tell me this isn't a pathetic attempt to try to make Cooper jealous."

"Are you *that* insecure about your relationship?" Delia demanded as Livie started walking again and she had to catch up. "Cooper's marrying you, isn't he?"

When Livie didn't answer, Delia grabbed her arm to stop her. "You're the one who involved yourself in my relationship with Cooper—not the other way around. I *know* how he felt about me. Too bad you'll never know if it was your charm or your father's money that made him suddenly interested in you."

Livie had heard enough and said as much to Delia.

"If you want to pick someone else for your maid of honor . . ."

"I don't. Let's just get through the wedding without any more . . . trouble."

"What kind of trouble are you talking about? Why don't you tell me what it is you did that you're being blackmailed about."

They were passing a small burger place that had just opened on a side street. A fan blasted out the smell of burger grease and onions. Livie felt her stomach turn.

"This man Cooper is alleged to have killed," Delia was saying. "He's part of this somehow, right? Did you have an affair with him? Was that it?"

Livie fought the nausea. The smell of the frying burgers had her stomach roiling.

"What's wrong? Are you going to be sick? You're white as a sheet. Was it something I said?"

Turning, Livie ran back the way they'd come. She only made it as far as a vacant lot before she threw up. She was wiping her mouth with a tissue from her purse when she heard Delia behind her.

"Oh, my God. Tell me you aren't *pregnant*."

Cooper stood in court for the second time in his life. He'd seen Livie come in and sit in the back. She looked pale and his heart went out to her. He'd had no idea how sick she'd been with this pregnancy. The thought of the baby made his chest ache. He'd thought he'd feel better after he slugged Drake Connors. Instead, all he'd done was set himself up for a murder rap.

Delia had come in, too, but she'd sat alone in the back. She looked upset. Livie only looked pale and scared. Delia looked as if she wanted to kill someone.

He gave Livie a smile, one he hoped was reassuring, then had to turn around and listen as he was apprised of his constitutional rights.

"Has the defendant obtained counsel?" the judge asked.

"He has, Your Honor," attorney Patrick Forrester told him, and provided the clerk with the information.

He listened as he was told of the charges against him. One count of deliberate homicide.

"How do you plead?"

"Not guilty, Your Honor."

"We ask that bail be set at this time, Your Honor," Patrick said. "My client has strong ties to the community, will be wed in a few months to Senator Buckmaster Hamilton's daughter Olivia and is also employed by the senator and has been for several years now. Senator Hamilton will be posting my client's bond."

The prosecutor stood and pointed out the nature of the crime, including reminding the judge that the victim had been shot twice in the *back*. "Your Honor, Cooper Barnett has only lived in this community a short time. He is a horse wrangler with a questionable past, and because of his engagement to Senator Hamilton's daughter, he has the funds to not just skip the country, but disappear along with his future bride. I ask that bail be denied and the defendant be remanded over to custody."

Cooper heard a chair scrape behind him.

"May I be allowed to speak on the defendant's behalf?" Buckmaster's voice boomed in the small courtroom. He gave a short statement listing Cooper's qualities. Cooper was touched and felt again that bond with Livie's family that he'd fought just as ardently as he had when he was trying to keep her at arm's length.

"Bail is set at one million dollars."

He wasn't all that surprised, but he heard Livie gasp.

"A preliminary hearing is set for three weeks from today." The judge banged his gavel and it was over.

Cooper felt his future father-in-law's hand on his shoulder and turned.

"I'll have the bond posted as quickly as possible so you can get out of here," Buckmaster said.

Cooper was still stunned the judge had allowed bail at all. "You don't have to do this."

"You're family, son."

"Not yet, and the way things are going, there is a good chance I won't make the wedding."

"You will if I have anything to do with it," Buckmaster said.

Cooper thought of all the times he'd butted heads with this man. He was stubborn and arrogant and . . . He realized that could just as easily describe himself.

"I don't know how to thank you."

"Sure you do." The older man smiled. "Be good to my daughter. I trust her judgment so I know you didn't commit the crime. I have one of the top criminal lawyers coming to handle your case."

As Cooper was led back to his cell, all he could think about was Livie. Even with Drake Connors dead, he worried about her. He also knew that his freedom was only temporary. Unless the real killer was caught, he figured he was as good as convicted—high-priced legal attorney or not.

It had taken longer than Buckmaster had expected to get his hands on sufficient funds to post Cooper's bond. He felt as if he was failing Livie for not getting her fiancé out of jail sooner. He hadn't waited around for Cooper to be released since he'd been told he already had a ride. Buckmaster assumed Livie would be picking him up.

He worried about the two of them even before this latest development.

"I hope you didn't just throw a hundred-thousand dollars away," Angelina said when Buckmaster found her waiting for him on his return from town. "But it's only money to you, isn't it?"

Sometimes he forgot that while the Broadwaters had a name, they no longer had money. He knew it was one reason she'd married him, even with the prenup. That and the idea of him being president. He hadn't realized how much she craved both. It worried him now. What if she didn't get what she felt she deserved after fifteen years? He'd seen a side of her that scared him.

"I don't want to get into this."

"We *are* in it. Up to our necks. Have you seen the paper? The *Associated Press* picked up the story about Sarah. Reporters have been calling all afternoon, wanting to know if it is true about

Buckmaster Hamilton's first wife returning from the dead. Lane is off somewhere, God only knows where, and I have had to deal with all of it alone."

"I'm sorry. But what I was doing is also important," he said.

"Sarah called for you. I told her not to ever call here again."

Buckmaster sighed. "Was that necessary?"

"What do you even know about Sarah?"

He looked at her as if she'd lost her mind. "What are you talking about? I was married to the woman and had six children with her."

"She wasn't from here, isn't that what you told me? Where did she live before you met her?"

"Back East. Why are you asking me this? She was twenty-four when we met. She'd grown up in a normal family. She was an only child, so was I. After college and the death of her parents, she came out here to work in Yellowstone Park for a summer. That's when our paths crossed. I was twenty-five. I'd taken a load of horses up to the park. I stopped in the cafeteria at Old Faithful and there she was."

"What did she major in?"

He shook his head. "English, I think. Literature. I can't remember. How could any of this . . ."

"You said she was adopted, so maybe there is something in her genetic makeup that made her do what she did."

He realized where Angelina was headed with

this. "Is this about damage control? You're looking for some flaw in Sarah to explain her trying to kill herself and then taking off for twenty-two years?"

"Better than some flaw in you."

He shook his head. "Hasn't the woman been through enough?"

"That's just it, we don't know what she's been through, do we?"

"What do you have for me?" Frank asked his deputy as Jamison came into his office and closed the door behind him. He had Jamison working closely with the crime scene techs he'd brought in.

"That large round parachute you found? It's the kind used by paratroopers, soldiers, marines, any group trained in parachuting into an operation behind enemy lines."

"Military?" he asked as he motioned Jamison into a chair.

"Not necessarily. There are several dozen countries with paratroopers who use this type of parachute. This particular one is an older model, the T-7. It has a twenty-eight-foot canopy that is opened by a static line." When he saw Frank frown, he said, "A fifteen-foot static line runs from the parachute. The prop blast blows the parachute open and snaps the cord between the static line and canopy."

"How long does that take?"

"Approximately three seconds, allowing a low-level jump."

"So the person wearing the parachute wouldn't have had to release the jump cord or necessarily have any parachuting experience," the sheriff said. "The person wouldn't even have to be conscious at the time."

"I suppose not."

"What does it take to get out of the harness?" Frank asked.

"The T-7 comes with a single release box with three locks. You give it a quarter to a half turn, hit the top of the release mechanism and . . . you're free. Or in this case, Sarah Hamilton was free. The lab rushed the tests. I did as you suggested and talked to her daughter Kat. She was more than willing to offer her DNA so it could be compared to her mother's. Sarah Hamilton's DNA was on the harness. Also when we searched the area, we found a jumpsuit, combat-type boots and a helmet, all in her size hidden under some logs."

Frank sat back and let out a long sigh. "So much for me speculating that she might have been unconscious when she was dropped from the plane. She'd changed clothes before she'd started out of the woods. So she had to have remembered what was going on before she collided with Russell Murdock's pickup. She lied."

He'd been lied to his whole career as sheriff so it shouldn't have hit him as hard as it had. "She seemed so . . . sincere about her memory loss."

"Maybe she was. We don't know how long she'd been in the woods."

He studied Jamison for a long moment. "Long enough to forget she'd jumped from a moving plane, climbed down from a tree and changed her clothes?"

His deputy shrugged. "Anything is possible."

"It brings up the question of who was operating that plane." He had tried to keep a lid on this, not even letting it out within the department. Calling in the crime techs had managed to do that—at least temporarily. He hated to think what would happen when this finally got out.

"Whoever put her out had to know she would crash in the trees," he said. "There weren't any open areas where she was dropped. She could have been killed. Which leads me to believe it wasn't her first time jumping out of a plane."

"Dropping her in a field would have attracted too much attention. That area where the chute was found was so isolated that ranchers farther away wouldn't think much of a low-flying plane in the distance. But one in their field . . ."

"See if any one of the ranchers in a ten-mile area heard a plane that night," Frank ordered. "And keep this under your hat. Her return has sparked enough attention. If the press found out how she made her reentry . . . Is there any way to track that parachute?"

"I doubt it. They're pretty common."

"So who dropped her off and why use such a covert method?"

"Good question," Jamison said. "The timing is the concern with her husband having only recently announced his candidacy for the presidency."

"More than ever we have to find out where Sarah Hamilton has been for the past twenty-two years," Frank said. "Someone was flying that plane. Someone knows where she's been and why she's back."

"I don't like anything about this. If she was just some woman who maybe had an affair and took off twenty-two years ago, we should be able to find out who she is and where she's been."

Frank agreed. "Let's start with putting out a missing persons on her. See if we get any hits. We need her fingerprints. We have her DNA from the parachute. But let's ask her for a sample anyway and see what she says."

Jamison raised an eyebrow. "Do you really think she will do that willingly?"

"If she has nothing to hide. She says she's as anxious to uncover her past as we are. Let's see if that's true."

Chapter TWENTY-FOUR

After his argument with his wife, Buckmaster had gone for a horseback ride. He needed to get away for a while to think. Before his ride, he'd taken a call from Sarah that had upset him. She'd been contacted by Harper and Cassidy. Both girls were furious with him for not telling them about her. Sarah said she'd tried to assure them he was just looking out for them. However honorable his motives, he kept finding himself the bad guy. They would both get over it, though. He wasn't so sure about the others.

Ainsley was the exception. She'd always been the one he could count on. It had disappointed him when he'd heard that she'd dropped out of law school. For so many years she'd stayed at the ranch, running things. He'd wanted her to have a life of her own.

Before she'd left for her television series job scouting locations, he'd asked her about her sister Bo. "Is anything wrong that you know of?"

"Like what?"

"She hasn't said much about the foundation."

"Dad, don't you think Mother returning has her wondering what will happen to it now? You started the foundation in her name because she died."

He hoped that was all that was going on with Bo as he recalled the way she was drinking at Livie's engagement party. As he returned from his ride and entered the house, he stopped in the entryway when he heard voices. The television droned in the background. He recognized his own voice and the newsman's who had interviewed him. Angelina and Lane never tired of watching old footage of his run for Senate. They spent hours dissecting interviews.

Buckmaster felt as if he was about to walk into another trap. He started for the stairs, not up for talk about the upcoming election, when he heard Angelina say, "Your father is amazing at these interviews," pride dripping from her voice along with . . . a wistfulness.

Your father? Which of his girls was here? He stopped to listen.

"He did well, didn't he, Lane," Angelina was saying. "He knew exactly how to play it. Just like his latest interview. He gave nothing away."

"I don't understand why he kept saying he didn't know if he is going to run for president for so long," Kat said from the living room. "Every-one knew he was. Isn't that what the three of you have been working toward all these years?"

"He couldn't throw his hat into the ring too early," Lane said. "It's all about timing."

"He had to have the right people behind him with

donations and support first," Angelina chimed in.

"Also he needed contributors with deep pockets," Lane added. "If they want him for president, they have to come up with the coin. Running for president costs a fortune. Your father would be bankrupt if he tried to finance it himself."

"Great. No wonder I hate politics," Kat said in disgust. "Doesn't it make you feel dirty? Why spend all that money when you could be doing something important with it like helping the poor or putting it toward cancer research?"

"You don't seem to mind being a senator's daughter," Angelina said pointedly. "As I recall, he got you out of a few scrapes because of his political power and now he's saving your sister's boyfriend."

With a sigh, Buckmaster knew he had to break this up before the mud started slinging. "Hi, sweetheart," he said to Kat as he walked into the room. "Angelina, please turn that off," he said, motioning to the television. "No politics now."

Turning to Kat, he said, "I want to hear about your photo exhibit." Ainsley had told him about it earlier.

"It's nothing," Kat said as Angelina and Lane excused themselves, clearly bored by photo talk. "I only stopped by to pick up a few things."

"Your own exhibit *is* a big deal," he said, but she merely shrugged. "What are you picking up?"

"I'm going on a road trip. I need more photographs. So I thought I'd take a cooler and a tent. I'm not sure where I'll end up."

"Sounds like fun. I could use a road trip myself," he said, thinking of his wife and brother-in-law. When he saw Kat's expression, he quickly added, "I wasn't looking for an invitation."

"I can understand why you might want to take off right now," she said, following his gaze in the direction that Angelina and Lane had gone.

"Believe me, I'm tempted," he said with a laugh. "Maybe some island in the middle of nowhere. No cell coverage, no internet, no television." No Angelina and Lane Broadwater tag teaming him to do something he wasn't ready to do. "I would just sit on the beach and watch the sunset. I might never come back. You'd have to come visit."

She stared at him as if she didn't recognize him. "That doesn't sound anything like you. You would be miserable within a day. Maybe sooner."

"I might surprise you."

Kat shook her head. "You're going to be president of the United States. It's been your dream for as long as I can remember."

"Dreams change."

"Is this about Mother?" When he didn't answer, she said, "Now you're starting to worry me. This will all blow over. You're a fighter. You can't let this get you down. The country needs you."

He laughed. "What did you do with my daughter Kat?"

"I'm serious. You'll be disappointed someday if you don't go for this," she said, surprising him even more. "You'll be a good president." She smiled. "I would even vote for you."

He dragged her into a hug. It had been so long since she'd let him hug her. But this time, she hugged him back. "Good luck with your photos. Let me know when the exhibit is scheduled. I want to be there."

When the sheriff and his deputy drove up, Russell realized he'd been waiting for the other shoe to drop. Sarah's sudden appearance had been like a stone dropped in a still pond. The ripple effect had rocked her family. Now that the media had gotten hold of it, waves would be lapping soon at even his door.

"Afternoon, Sheriff," he said, opening the door. "Deputy Jamison. I would imagine you're here to see Sarah."

"Mind if we come in?" Frank asked.

"We just finished breakfast. Come on in the kitchen. Sarah made pancakes. There's some left if you're hungry."

The two lawmen declined, but followed him into the kitchen where Sarah was washing the dishes. Pleasantries were exchanged.

Russell watched Sarah drying her hands on the kitchen towel. She looked calm enough, but he'd seen her hands shaking only moments before.

What did she have to hide besides the way she'd returned to Beartooth? The past twenty-two years?

"How about some coffee?" he asked Frank and Bentley.

"We'd love some if the two of you will join us." The sheriff and the two others pulled out chairs at the table as if this visit were a social one.

"Let me pour," Russell said when he saw how nervous Sarah was.

When they were all seated with their cups of coffee, the sheriff said, "How are you feeling, Sarah?"

"Better. Russell has been so kind as to let me stay out here in his guesthouse. It is so pleasant. I have a beautiful view of the Crazy Mountains from my window."

Russell saw the sheriff watching her closely as she lifted her cup with two hands and took a drink.

"Has any more of your memory returned?" Frank asked.

She shook her head without looking up at him.

"I'm sure that must be horribly frustrating. I was hoping I could help."

Sarah raised her eyes slowly. "I'm seeing a neurologist as soon as they can get me in. Not that I expect he can do much, but maybe he can tell me what caused this."

"I had another thought. I'd like to take your fingerprints and DNA. I know it's a long shot . . ."

Sarah dropped her cup. It caught the edge of the

table, shattering into dozens of shards, hot coffee splashing over her.

Russell was on his feet, grabbing the kitchen towel. "Are you burned?"

"A little," she said, trying to hold her sopping wet shirt and slacks away from her skin.

"Go change. I'll keep our guests company until you return. Here, let me help you." He walked her to the door. Once out of earshot of the two in the kitchen, he said, "You don't have to do this."

She looked confused for a moment as if she thought he was referring to a change of clothes.

"Tell them no, Sarah," he said with a shake of his head. "You've done nothing. They can't force you."

"You're afraid of what they might find."

He met her gaze. "Aren't you?"

When he turned back to the kitchen, he saw that the sheriff had cleaned up the broken cup and spilled coffee. But as he walked back in past his trash can, he couldn't be sure all of the broken cup pieces had ended up in the trash.

Delia couldn't believe it. Olivia was *pregnant*. No wonder Cooper was miserable. He felt he had no choice but to marry her.

She knew the last thing he wanted right now was a baby. He was in the middle of building a house and working at the Hamilton Ranch. She'd seen how exhausted he was most days when he'd come into the lumberyard.

She'd wanted so badly to help him. To save him. He'd been blinded by the Hamiltons. Tricked by Olivia. Delia had tried to warn him.

Livie's not like that, he'd said.

Ha, she thought now. Livie was a Hamilton. She got what she wanted any way she could get it. Delia had grown up on a chicken-scratch plot of land down the road from the Hamiltons. Buckmaster had tried to buy them out, calling the place an eyesore. He'd offered her father a whole lot of money for that eyesore.

She could laugh about that now. But when her father had finally caved and sold them the land, she'd been devastated. The truth was that she'd loved living so close to the Hamilton Ranch. She could pretend she was one of the Hamilton girls. She spent enough time at Olivia's house.

For a while, she'd felt like family. Looking back now, she realized it had just been charity. Olivia gave her cast-off clothes and Buckmaster had insisted she learn to ride. He'd been kind enough to give her a horse that she could call her own, as long as she didn't try to take it home.

Back then she'd been thrilled to have Olivia's old clothes. There was nothing wrong with them. Some of them still had the tags on them because she'd never even worn them. She'd just decided she didn't want them anymore.

Delia had loved horseback riding and still did. But now she realized that Buckmaster had only felt sorry for her. Poor little Delia Rollins.

After the sale of their place to him, she and her family had moved into an apartment in a large old house in town. Buckmaster had her old home and the barns leveled. She drove by recently and couldn't even tell where her family had lived.

You're just jealous of her, Hitch had said last night before she'd thrown him out. He'd hit too close to the truth. She wanted to be Olivia. She wanted all of it—the huge ranch, the nice clothes, the adoration, but mostly she wanted Cooper.

Livie had *everything* and now she was having Cooper's baby. It was too much. As if struck by lightning, she suddenly remembered the blackmail threat. What if this baby *wasn't* Cooper's?

Her vision blurred with fury. That had to be it. Livie had cheated on him! The baby wasn't Cooper's and yet the wedding hadn't been canceled? Cooper would go through with it. He would raise this child as his own. He was that kind of man.

She couldn't let that happen. She had tried to stop the wedding every way she knew how. But now she had no choice. She couldn't let Cooper marry her. Livie would ruin his life. Delia loved him too much to let this happen.

There was only one way to stop it. She told

herself that Cooper would thank her one day even if it meant the two of them might never be together.

If Frank had been worried before his and Jamison's visit to Sarah Hamilton's, he was even more concerned now. Sarah had come back after changing her clothing and declined to give them her fingerprints or her DNA.

"I'm only here to see my daughters. Once I see the twins," she'd said, "I'm leaving."

Frank had tried to change her mind, saying that if anyone should want to know who she'd been, it would be her.

"I'm not interested in what has passed. All care about is the future, surely you can understand that."

"She was nervous the moment she saw us," the deputy said as they drove back to Big Timber. "It could be a simple case of her not wanting the life she's been leading the past twenty-two years to catch up with her."

Frank had thought of that. "If she wasn't the former wife of possibly our next president, I wouldn't worry about it. But after finding that damned parachute . . ."

"It would help if we knew why she drove her car into the river all those years ago in an attempt to kill herself. Unless you think it was staged."

He shook his head. "Who in their right mind drives into the Yellowstone River in the middle of winter and expects to survive that? No, I think she was trying to kill herself. But then who did she call when she'd survived? Lester indicated that she was upset for failing."

"She sounds like a flake. She tries to kill herself, fails, gets a friend to pick her up and disappears, letting everyone think she's dead. She makes a new life—new husband, kids—that goes sour and she thinks, 'Hey, that old one wasn't so bad,' especially since there's a good chance she can get rid of the current wife and live in the White House. She thinks, 'Why not go back to it?'"

"I might buy that if she didn't just drop back into this life like a paratrooper." Frank shook his head. "As much as I hate to do it, at some point I feel I have to warn Buckmaster."

"She's the mother of his children. Do you really think he's going to believe you?"

He shook his head. "We have DNA from the parachute. With luck, we'll be able to get a print from the piece of the coffee cup I rescued." He'd never done anything illegal since joining law enforcement, but he had to know who Sarah Hamilton was. He felt like Homeland Security throwing out the rules. But this could be a risk to national security. "I want all my ducks in a row before I go to the senator."

Livie had been so disappointed when Cooper had been taken away again after his bail hearing.

She'd hoped they would let him go once bail had been set. But one million dollars? Her father had promised her he would take care of it. Now she had no idea how long it would take.

To make matters worse, when she had gotten back to the ranch pickup she'd driven into town, one of the tires was flat. She'd had to call a service to come change it. While the tire was being changed, she'd got a little something to eat, hoping it would help settle her stomach.

She'd mulled over her run-in with Delia while she waited. In a way, she was glad she'd confronted her. It had cleared the air at least for a short while. That was until she'd gotten sick to her stomach and Delia had guessed that she was pregnant.

Now, as she headed home, she kept seeing Delia's expression when she realized that her once best friend was pregnant. What gave her a chill was the pure hatred she'd seen in the woman's face.

She shuddered now to think about it. Clearly, Delia thought she stood a chance with Cooper as long as he wasn't married. But now that she knew about the pregnancy . . . She also knew about the blackmail—had Cooper really told her? Had Delia guessed that given the blackmail that the baby might not be his?

Livie didn't want to think about Delia's reaction to that news. The woman actually thought she would make Cooper a better wife. Maybe she was right, Livie thought. She'd definitely let him down.

She'd reached the cabin and had just gotten out of the ranch truck when she heard a vehicle coming fast up the road behind her.

The truck was old, a lot like the one that Cooper drove. Squinting she watched dust boil up behind it as it roared toward her. Who in the world . . .

The driver skidded to a stop just yards from her. Livie took a step back as Delia Rollins climbed out of the pickup, a gun in her hand.

Chapter TWENTY-FIVE

"It's not even his baby, is it?" Delia called as she advanced on her, the gun pointed at Livie's heart. "Admit it."

"What are you doing?" Livie cried, and took a step back as Delia charged at her.

"What does it look like I'm doing? I'm going to save Cooper from making the biggest mistake of his life."

"Delia, you're talking crazy. The baby is his. We're getting married. Cooper . . ."

"You're not getting married. I never was going to let that happen. I left the price tag on my maid of honor dress so I could take it back. I had hoped that Cooper would come to his senses. Since he hasn't . . ." She motioned with the gun. "Come on. I have a plan."

Livie took another step back. She thought about turning and making a run for the cabin, but she feared that Delia would shoot her in the back. "I'm not going anywhere with you."

"Fine. I'll kill you where you stand so it will be the first thing Cooper sees when he comes home. He should be getting out on bail by now."

Livie realized the reason she hadn't heard anything from him was that she'd turned her phone off while in court and forgot to turn it back on. She'd been so upset over Delia and the large amount of bail her father had to put up for bond.

She pulled her phone out of her purse.

Delia jerked it out of her hand. "Yep, two messages from Cooper that you will never hear." She dropped the phone and smashed it under her boot heel. "Is this where you want to die, Olivia?" she asked as she took aim at her heart.

"No." The last thing she wanted was for Cooper to find her in front of his cabin. Also she believed that if she could stall for time, Delia would come to her senses. "Delia, if you want to be with Cooper, you can't kill me. You'll never have him if you do that."

"I'll never have him, anyway. But then neither will you." She grabbed Livie's arm and, keeping the gun pointed at her, pulled her toward the new house Cooper had been building for them.

• • •

The moment Cooper was free, he called Livie. Her cell phone went straight to voice mail. "That's odd," he said to himself. He left a message that he would get a ride and meet her at the cabin.

Buckmaster had offered to pick him up, but he'd been so sure he could reach Livie to let her know. He thought about calling the ranch, but decided to call his friend Rylan West. "Any chance you could give a jailbird a ride home?"

Rylan laughed. "Glad to hear you're out."

"Just until the trial."

"I'll be right there."

A man of his word, Rylan drove up not twenty minutes later. As he climbed into his friend's pickup, he said, "I couldn't reach Livie. She must be at the ranch. Would you mind taking me there? That's where I left my pickup."

Cooper tried Livie once more. It went straight to voice mail again. He left another message telling her where he was going and that he would be home soon.

"If you're worried, we could go by your place first," Rylan said.

"No, I need my truck and, like I said, she's probably at the ranch, anyway." He couldn't help his disappointment. He'd thought for sure she would be at the cabin waiting for him. It worried him, her phone going straight to voice mail, but he told himself he would see her soon.

As they climbed the steps into the skeleton of the house, Delia pulled a roll of duct tape from her pocket, "Here," she said, thrusting it at Livie. "Wrap some around one wrist."

"Delia, don't throw away your life. The lumber-yard is doing great and . . ."

"You have no idea what my life is like. My family left me in so much debt, I'll never be able to dig my way out. Without Cooper, I have nothing to live for."

"That's not true. I thought you said you were dating Hitch."

She laughed. "You didn't believe that."

Livie had managed to wrap the tape a couple of times around one wrist. Delia grabbed the tape and, forcing both of Livie's wrists together with-out lowering the gun, wrapped the tape around a half dozen times. She ripped the tape and shoved it into Livie's hand again.

"Now your ankles. You should be able to do it even with your hands bound."

"Delia, what are you planning to do?"

"I told you. Make sure you don't ruin Cooper's life any more than you have already."

"By killing me? You're not a murderer."

"Not yet. Start wrapping your ankles. I don't want Cooper to come home too early. I would hate to have to kill both of you."

Just the thought of Delia turning the gun on Cooper made her bend over to start the tape. But as she did, she saw Cooper's hammer where he'd dropped it that day she'd come out to the house to talk to him.

Desperate and sensing that Delia *did* have what it would take to kill her, she dropped the tape and grabbed for the hammer.

Delia must have seen the hammer about the same time Livie had. She kicked at it, sending the hammer skittering across the floor. Livie dove for it, hitting the floor hard. She rolled into Delia and knocked her off her feet to hit the floor.

Livie tried to get back onto her feet, but she struggled because of her bound wrists—while Delia was faster.

She saw that she had only one chance. She threw herself back down and rolled toward the gaping opening that dropped into the basement—the one Cooper had warned her about.

Delia screamed for her to stop, but it was too late. As Livie started to fall, she grabbed for the edge of the floor, caught it in her hands. Her body swung down, her grip on the floor gave and she dropped the ten feet to the basement floor below her.

Back in his office, Frank looked again at what he'd found out about Cooper Barnett's juvenile record. He'd had to get a warrant to have the file unsealed, but he was glad he did.

According to the police report from the small town in Oklahoma where Cooper had grown up, he and a friend had been in a convenience store when the friend pulled a gun and demanded the clerk hand over everything in the cash register.

Cooper had tried to stop the friend. The clerk was wounded in the skirmish that followed. Both youths were arrested. Cooper was sent to a boys' ranch. The other youth did time.

That was Cooper's last brush with the law—until now. It didn't surprise him that Buckmaster had come through with the bond and bailed Cooper out. Frank had his doubts about the young man's guilt, as well. But the evidence against him was still strong. They had proof that the fatal shot had come from his gun. Even without the gun, they had a good case.

He saw that he had a message. Calling voice mail, he listened as Olivia Hamilton told him about what she'd found in her stepmother's desk drawer and the connection she'd found between her and Drake Connors.

Angelina Broadwater Hamilton and Drake Connors? He thought about what Olivia had told him about Drake saying he had bigger fish to fry. His pickup had been found on the way to the Hamilton Ranch, but had Drake gone there to try to strong-arm the senator or his wife?

Frank quickly put in a call to the Broadwater Ranch manager. It didn't take long to get Amos Connors on the phone.

"This is Sheriff Frank Curry over in Sweetgrass County," he said. "I'm calling about your son."

"I already heard from the coroner that he was dead," Amos said. "Just surprised it didn't happen sooner."

"Why do you say that?"

"Are you kidding? I heard that he was black-mailing people over there. Wouldn't be the first time someone took after him with a gun. There's something wrong with him, has been since he was born. Quite frankly, I'm not even sure he's mine."

"Did he get in trouble over there on the Broad-water Ranch before he left?" Frank asked.

The man hesitated. "I work for the Broadwaters so I can't . . ."

"I can have you dragged into court if I have to. Was he involved with Angelina Broadwater?"

The man swore. "Not just Angelina."

"Who else?" Silence. "You might as well tell me since it is all going to come out. I can subpoena you and will."

"Drake was nineteen. Angelina was in her thirties. I guess that's where he got the idea of going for older women with money. Her father found out what was going on and ran Drake off with a shotgun. After her father found out she'd been funneling money from the ranch to pay Drake to keep the affairs quiet, he threw her and her brother off the ranch without a cent. The two of them got political and went on to greener pastures. Does that answer your question, Sheriff?"

"You said affairs."

The man groaned. "Angelina wasn't the only Broadwater my so-called son was blackmailing. That answer your question?"

It did. He hung up.

Frank pulled out the file and the two blackmail notes he'd been given. Olivia had thrown the first one away, but she'd written down for him what she remembered from the note.

He compared the first three to the last one that Olivia had been referring to in the phone call. According to her, the blackmail note had been mailed to the house and Angelina had intercepted it. She'd apparently thrown the envelope away and hadn't thought it was important since Drake was dead.

"I wouldn't be surprised if she's thrown the note away as well by now even though she swears she kept it in case it would help Cooper in some way if this has to go to trial," Olivia said in her message.

Frank looked at what Livie told him had been

written on the fourth note. The tone and every-thing was completely different. This blackmail note hadn't been meant for Olivia Hamilton at all, he thought as he reached for his phone. When the judge answered, Frank told him about the warrants he was going to need.

Delia moved to the edge of the flooring and looked down into the dark basement. She'd expected to see Olivia splattered on the concrete. When she didn't she bent farther over the opening. No Olivia. What the . . .

Hurriedly she looked to see where the stairs came up from the basement. There was only one set and they looked temporary. She picked up the hammer that had slid into the corner and moved to the stairs.

"I know you're down there, Olivia. I'm betting you're hurt from your fall. As lucky as you are, you must have landed on your feet." She swung the hammer. The stairs shuddered as the top plank split in two. One piece fell into the dark basement, landing with a loud *clink*.

She knocked off the rest of the top stair, then the next one. Balancing on just the two-by-four frame, she knocked off another step. The wood clattered to the basement floor.

"How are you doing down there? Trying to get that tape off? Better hurry." Delia put the hammer down and hurried to her truck for the two full cans of gas she'd brought. The matches were in her pocket.

"I know how hard Cooper worked on this house. I hate to do this," she called down to Olivia. "But he wouldn't want to live here. It would always remind him of you. We can't have that, now can we?"

She began to splash the gas onto the wood subflooring and the wood struts. The wood was dry, it would burn fast. She was counting on that. She didn't want Cooper to get out of jail too early and spoil everything. If only he had listened to her. If only he had dropped Olivia right away. If only he had realized that the right woman for him was the first one he'd met. She and Cooper could have lived in this house and been happy.

She struck a match and watched it burn for a few seconds before she dropped it onto the gas-soaked floor.

Livie tried not to panic. She'd landed hard, twisting her bad ankle, but thankfully landing on her feet. She could hear Delia walking around on the floor over her, then heard hammering before boards began to drop into the basement.

All she knew was that she had to get her wrists free and find a way out of here before Delia came looking for her. She'd discovered some rough metal and was busy cutting the tape from her wrists—just as Delia had guessed she was doing.

Livie had no idea what time it was, but Delia was right. Cooper must be out on bail. He'd called her, she was guessing for a ride. Her heart broke at the thought of him leaving the message. He would probably think she was at the Hamilton Ranch, safe.

She just didn't want him showing up here now. While she told herself that Delia couldn't kill him, she realized that she'd thought Delia couldn't kill her, either. But it appeared that's exactly what she had planned.

She sawed at the thick tape faster. She could feel the clock ticking. Once she had her hands free, she thought she might be able to climb out. The basement windows weren't in yet—just holes in the wall above the concrete—but they were too high for her to reach. If she could find something to stand on . . .

The tape started to give. Just a little longer. With a start, she realized she hadn't heard Delia walking around upstairs for at least a few minutes. She'd been surprised when she hadn't come down the basement stairs after her. Instead, it sounded as if she'd destroyed the top steps. Was Delia's plan to leave her down here?

It didn't make any sense—until she heard her up there again and smelled the gas only moments before she smelled the smoke.

●　●　●

Delia hurried away from the burning structure, chased by flames licking across the dry wood. The house had gone up faster than she expected. She'd had to drop one of the gas cans, even though it was still half-full.

Now she stood on the other side of her truck to wait. Once those flames got to that can of gas, there would be an explosion. Ablaze, the first floor would drop into the basement. There was no way Livie could survive. This was going to work out better than she'd planned.

While arson would be suspected, wasn't there a chance that they would think Livie had burned the house and gotten caught in her own crime? All Delia had to do was leave and get back to the lumberyard. Hitch would give her an alibi. What choice did he have? She smiled as she recalled how she'd got him worked up and drunk enough that he'd gone to find Livie and settle an old score, as he called it.

The next day he'd told her how he'd found her eating at the Branding Iron. He knew where there was an old farm truck with the keys in it. He'd taken it and waited outside of town for her— and run her off the road.

He'd been worried that she'd seen him and that he'd be arrested at any moment. He'd been so glad that he hadn't killed her. She'd realized then that he would be worthless to her for anything else. He didn't have the fortitude to do what had to be done. She did.

One more thing had to be done before Olivia Hamilton could be erased from Cooper's life. She grabbed the third gas can and walked toward the cabin.

Warrants in hand, Sheriff Curry drove out to the Hamilton Ranch with two deputies. He expected trouble, but to his surprise Buckmaster let them in.

"I have nothing to hide," the senator said, and glanced toward his wife. "Where would you like to start?"

"Why don't we start with your wife and her brother's office," Frank suggested as he handed him the two warrants. "Is your brother here?" he asked Angelina only a moment before Lane came from down the hall.

The moment he saw the uniformed men, he started, looking like a deer caught in headlights. "What's going on?" he asked.

"We have a warrant to search not only the Hamilton Ranch premises but also yours, as well." Frank motioned for one of the officers to take Lane to his room on the ranch, but Lane balked.

"What are you searching my place for?" Lane asked, looking scared. "I told you whose room you should be looking in."

"You're the one who told them you saw Ainsley take the gun from under Cooper's pickup seat?" Buckmaster demanded. "You're fired."

"I just told them the truth. Have you searched her apartment?" Lane demanded. "That is what you're looking for, isn't it? The murder weapon?"

"We've already searched her apartment," the sheriff said. "I'm sure this won't come as a surprise to you. We found the murder weapon hidden in the back of one of her drawers." As Buckmaster got to his feet, Frank waved him down. "You aren't familiar with guns, are you, Mr. Broadwater?"

Lane looked confused. "What does my ability with guns have to do with—"

"Cooper Barnett kept an unloaded .45 under the seat of his pickup along with a box of cartridges," the sheriff said. "I'm sure you were careful to wipe all your prints off the gun before you put it in Ainsley Hamilton's apartment, but you weren't adept enough with firearms to load the gun with gloves on, were you?"

All the color drained from Lane Broadwater's face.

"What is he talking about, Lane?" Angelina demanded. "What have you done?"

"What have *I* done?" Lane shouted as he turned on his sister. "It's what you did with that . . . that . . . ranch manager's son. That blackmail note wasn't for Olivia and you know it. It was for *you*. Drake Connors showed up here at the ranch demanding the money. One hundred thousand dollars or he was going to . . ."

"Stop!" she cried. "Don't you dare blame me for this. What about your part in all this?"

Lane looked as if he might break down. "He wasn't going to go away, Angelina. If I didn't come up with the money, he wasn't just going to Buckmaster. He was going to the press." Lane's gaze went to the senator. "You hired me to run interference for your campaigns. That's all I was doing. I've worked too hard to let that little prick ruin everything. When Angelina told me that the man who'd been blackmailing Olivia was Drake Connors, I knew what it would take to stop him. A .45 slug."

"Or two in the back," Frank said. "Lane Broadwater, you're under arrest for the deliberate homicide of Drake Connors. Read him his rights," he said, and handed Lane off to one of his deputies.

"You better get me out like you did that saddle tramp you call a horse trainer," Lane called to Buckmaster. "Otherwise, I'll be the one going to the media with my story. You hear that, Angelina?" he cried as the deputy pushed him out the door. "I'll tell them *everything*."

"Did you really find fingerprints on the casings?" Buckmaster asked after Lane had been led away.

"I'm sure the crime lab will, but a confession is even better," Frank said. "Especially one in front of such distinguished witnesses. Will you get him out?"

The senator shook his head. "Not a man who shot another man in the back."

After the sheriff and his deputies had left, Buckmaster stood at the front window looking out at the ranch. He'd inherited much of the land and money and made more and bought more land. He wanted to leave it to his children.

"What now?" Angelina said behind him. She hadn't said a word since her brother had been taken away in handcuffs.

The past week had ripped the cover off their perfect little universe and exposed them all in ways he could never have imagined. Where *did* they go from here? He had no idea.

He thought of Sarah and felt that old familiar ache. She would always be his first and only love. But could he ever trust her again?

He turned slowly to look at Angelina. She'd given him fifteen years. He owed her. But he wasn't sure he could give her what she wanted. "You knew when you heard the name Drake Connors that he would eventually show up at your door," he said.

She straightened, her chin lifted into that regal

look. The Ice Queen. Unless you looked closer and saw her tears.

"It was after my divorce," she began, her voice breaking. "He made me feel young and alive, sexy and desirable." She looked away. Her gaze came back to his, this time filled with defiance. "I needed him and he needed my father's money. It ended badly. I didn't know then that Drake and Lane . . . I'd put it behind me. A learning experience, I suppose. I'm not that woman anymore."

"I need to know something, Angelina, and I need the truth." Was she capable of the truth? He couldn't be sure. "Did you send Lane to kill him?"

"You heard what my brother . . ."

"I heard his story and yours. But I also know how protective he is of you. Did you take the gun out of Cooper's pickup and give it to your brother to kill Drake Connors?"

The tape gave as Livie sawed through the last strand. She pulled her wrists apart, freeing herself, and ripped off the remaining tape. Overhead she could hear the crackling of the fire. The air was thick with smoke above her and she could feel the heat.

Where was Delia? Had she left? Livie wouldn't have been able to hear the pickup engine over the sound of the fire roaring above her. It didn't matter where Delia was. She had to get out of here.

Looking around for something to stand on, she spotted a large old wooden toolbox of Cooper's. If she could pull it closer to one of the basement window openings . . . The box was much heavier than she'd expected, but she managed to move it a few inches. She tried again, moving it closer. Just a few feet.

She put all of her strength into it and was able to push it closer. One more shove. Above her she heard something break. Part of the flooring support fell on the other side of the basement. Burning wood crashed to the concrete. Sparks flew into the air.

She shoved the toolbox again. Close enough, she thought as she hurriedly climbed up on it. The entire structure above her was on fire. Any minute it could come crashing down. She grabbed the edge of the concrete below the window opening and pulled herself up. Once she got an elbow under her, she slid through the opening just moments before the flames licked downward.

As she dropped through the window opening, she fell into the cool grass below it on the opposite side of the house from where Delia was parked. She laid there for a moment trying to catch her breath. The smoke was thick, the flames so close she could feel them scorching her face.

Getting to her feet, she saw the horses in the corral. They were trying to get out, panicked by the fire. As she ran toward them, past the corner of the house now in flames, she saw that the cabin was also ablaze. All she could think about was letting the mustangs into the pasture. If the grass next to the cabin caught fire and spread to the barn and corral, all of the horses would die.

She tried not to think about how hard Cooper had worked on the new house or how much he loved the cabin he'd built. Both of those could be replaced. But she wouldn't let anything happen to his mustangs, especially Blue, the one he was training for her to ride one day.

Livie was rushing to the corrals when the burning house exploded behind her. The blast almost knocked her off her feet. The explosion panicked the horses. She limped toward them as the sky behind her turned black with falling ash.

Cooper saw the flames miles from the turnoff. A funnel of black billowed up into the late-afternoon air. At first he thought one of his neighbors must be burning an old haystack, but the closer he got, the more afraid he was that the fire was on his place.

He'd thought for sure that Livie would be at the Hamilton Ranch, but Buckmaster had told him that she'd gone home to the cabin to wait for his call. Earlier he'd been so worried about her. She'd looked pale and scared and there was no doubt that she and Delia had gotten into it before his bail hearing.

As he reached the turnoff, he saw flames shooting up into the air, smoke rising above his small ranch. His heart fell. The new house was on fire. So was the cabin. Where was Livie?

He stomped on the gas pedal, the old pickup fishtailing as he raced toward the fires. His mind galloped ahead of him. How could a fire have started in the house? It couldn't and yet . . .

It didn't matter. All his work. All the hours he'd put into the building to have it reduced to ashes. None of that mattered. He just prayed that Livie was all right, even as he knew that if both buildings were on fire, Livie was in trouble.

He called the sheriff as he drove. "My place is on fire. I don't know where Livie is. Please hurry!"

Livie reached the corral and quickly opened the gate into the pasture. Her ankle was killing her. She knew she'd reinjured it in her fall. But that was the least of her worries. Past the horses, she could see the cabin in flames and Delia standing in front of it, staring at her handiwork.

Opening the gate to the pasture, the horses stampeded past her away from the fire. The corral emptied out, and she saw Delia look her way. Her old friend seemed surprised at first, as if she didn't believe what she was seeing. Then she pulled out the gun and started walking toward her.

Livie turned toward the barn, but she knew trying to hide in there would be futile, not to mention suicidal. Cooper's shotgun was in there, but she also knew she couldn't shoot Delia. She had to save the mustangs before the fire spread. That's if Delia didn't find her and shoot her.

She'd been so sure that her once best friend wasn't capable of murder. Delia would have let her burn to death. She was acting like a woman with nothing to lose. All those long hours trying to keep the lumberyard going . . . Had she seen Cooper as the one good thing in her life? And now she believed that Livie had taken him from her. Nothing would convince her otherwise.

Livie looked out at the mustangs. Most of them were still running to the far side of the pasture. Only one horse had stopped and now stood standing broadside looking at her.

Blue. She turned to see that Delia was only yards from her. She hobbled toward the mustang, expecting Blue to take off with the others when she got too close. But he held his ground, nickering softly as Livie approached.

"I wouldn't do that, if I were you," Delia called

behind her. "That horse is wild. You could get your neck broken." She laughed. Behind Delia, smoke billowed up, shutting off the last of the day's sunlight. The sound of flames crackled in the air. Delia wasn't close enough to be a dead shot with a pistol. But if Livie waited much longer . . .

She saw a large rock. Stepping on it, she grabbed a handful of Blue's mane and swung herself up onto the horse's back. She'd expected the mustang to buck her off. A gunshot filled the air. She wrapped her arms around the horse's neck and dug in her heels. Blue took off at a dead run toward the other horses.

Livie could almost feel the bull's-eye on her back. She lay over the horse and spurred Blue on as she heard the whine of another bullet whiz past.

Cooper saw the old pickup parked too close to the burning house only seconds before he saw Delia out by the corrals. He roared up in his truck, but she didn't seem to hear him over the fire. Leaping out he ran toward her. Past her he saw Livie riding off on . . . Blue.

He couldn't believe it as he leaped from the truck and ran toward the corrals and Delia. Livie had been so afraid of the mustang. He'd wondered if she would ever ride the horse he'd been training for her.

When he swung his gaze back to Delia, he saw the gun. She raised it and took aim at Livie. "No!" he screamed as he slammed into her. The shot went wild as he knocked her to the ground and wrestled the gun from her. "Have you lost your mind?" he demanded as he looked into her face.

She was crying, tears running down her face. "I love you. You can't marry her. She'll ruin your life. She already has tried. Please, Cooper, we can run away, far from here. You'll forget about her." She grabbed his shirt with both hands and tried to pull him down. "It will be her word against ours."

He broke the hold. "Delia, what have you done?"

She began to cry harder as the wail of sirens filled the air. Following the sheriff's patrol cars were fire engines. They would be too late to save the house or the cabin, but they might be able to save the barn and corrals.

He hadn't realized he was still holding Delia down until the sheriff took the gun from his hand and helped him up.

"She's wrong for you, Cooper. You would have eventually gotten over her. I'm sorry about your house and cabin, but they would only have reminded you of her," she said before the sheriff handcuffed her and locked her into the back of his patrol car.

The firefighters were putting out the blaze and

watering down the grass near the barn as Cooper walked toward the pasture.

Livie and Blue had stopped just short of the other horses. As he neared them, she slid off the mustang, dropping to the ground. He could see that she was limping badly, but she was alive. He ran to her, thanking God.

Lifting her into his arms, he held her tight. She clung to him. Nearby Blue nickered softly before running off to join the other mustangs.

EPILOGUE

When everything came out, the media frenzy followed. Frank had known that would be the case. The stories were too juicy. The press couldn't get enough of the dirt.

He'd held a news conference, shocked at how many news vans were parked outside the sheriff's department. He'd confirmed that Lane Broadwater had been arrested for the deliberate homicide of Drake Connors and was being held without bail, but because it was an ongoing investigation that was all he could release at that time.

They also had questions about Delia Rollins. He confirmed that she, too, had been arrested for attempted homicide and was being held until her trial.

The reporters fired questions at him.

"Was Drake Connors blackmailing the senator's wife as well as the senator's daughter?"

"What was the nature of that blackmail?"

"Are Olivia Hamilton and Cooper Barnett still getting married?"

"What about Sarah Hamilton? Is it true she's come back from the grave?"

He refused to answer their questions. He felt sorry for Buckmaster. The senator had to post guards at the gate to keep the press off the ranch.

Russell had called to say that Sarah had moved to an undisclosed location and that he'd had to run the press off his property, as well.

Frank didn't know where Sarah Hamilton was hiding. Nor did he know where Angelina was. Nettie had heard from Mabel Murphy that Buckmaster had thrown her out. No one had seen her, so he couldn't be sure that was just what everyone wanted to believe.

He was glad that he'd been right about the lab finding partials of Lane Broadwater's prints on the casings in Cooper's .45 that he'd used to kill Drake Connors. But there was a second print, as well. The county attorney would decide if more charges would be pending.

Meanwhile, the investigation into Sarah Hamilton continued. The lab was able to get her fingerprints off the broken piece of cup he shouldn't have taken, but had. Both her DNA and prints were run through IAFIS, the national fingerprint and criminal history system.

Nothing came up.

But Frank wasn't giving up. Sarah had been somewhere for the past twenty-two years; he had a feeling, given time, they would find out where—and why she'd come back to Beartooth.

"I never thought your father would let us elope," Cooper said as he came up behind Livie and encircled her in his arms, his hand going to the slight rounding that was their baby.

He'd told her that day, smoke still in the air, that he didn't care who the father was. He loved her. He would love the baby because it was hers and he meant every word. After almost losing her, he knew what was important.

But he hadn't been sure she still wanted to marry him. "Livie, I love you, but I have nothing to offer you. The house, the cabin, it's all gone. I don't know what you see in me, but whatever it is, you make me want to be a better man." When she seemed to hesitate, he said, "Do you still want to be my wife?"

Now the sea breeze blew across the lanai bringing with it the sweet smell of flowers.

"It's beautiful here," she said as she leaned back into him. "I'll be sorry to leave."

"Are you sorry your sisters didn't get to come to the wedding?" he asked.

She shook her head. "They're too happy for us to complain. Given everything that happened . . . this was the perfect wedding and honeymoon."

A week before when she'd told him about the DNA test the doctor could run on him and the baby, he'd told her it wasn't necessary.

"Drake Connors was a liar, but I think about this he was telling the truth. I want to do the test."

He'd agreed to give her a DNA sample. "But, Livie, I don't want to know. Like I told you. It doesn't matter. That baby growing inside you is part of you. That's good enough for me."

But when the test results had come back, he'd known the moment she'd opened them. She'd lit up from inside. For the first time since that January night last winter, Livie looked as if she was finally free of the past.

She'd thrown herself into his arms. "Yes, Cooper Barnett, I will marry you."

Livie looked out at the ocean. She loved the sound of the waves. They reminded her of the sound of the baby inside her. Her and Cooper's baby. They were waiting, wanting to be surprised, but she knew her father was hoping for a grandson, although he said he'd take a granddaughter.

"We fly home tomorrow. Are you sure you're ready?" her husband asked.

Husband. She liked that. She nodded. She would miss Hawaii, but she also missed Montana. It was home and always would be.

Cooper placed his hand on her stomach. The hand was large, sun-browned, scarred from years of hard labor, a strong hand. The kind of hand a father should have.

"So much has happened," she said, amazed that they had weathered the storm.

"But we made it through." She turned to look at him. His dark eyes were shiny with emotion. "If we could get through all of that, then we can get through anything."

She nodded. "I'm so sorry about your house and cabin. But we can rebuild."

He shook his head. "You aren't going to have to wait for me to build us a house. I told your dad that we would appreciate the help he offered along with that land by the creek. It's a beautiful spot for a new beginning and it's adjacent to my property."

"Why would you do that?" Livie asked in surprise.

He met her gaze. "For us. I let my pride get in the way before. Now I have a wife and a baby coming."

"You don't have to do that. We can put a trailer on your land. We can manage. I know how you feel about my father helping us. I don't want you doing something . . ."

"I didn't want people to think I was marrying you for what your father could give me," Cooper said. "After everything that has happened to us? I don't give two cents about what people think." He cupped her cheek in the palm of his hand. It felt warm against her skin. She leaned into it. "I love you. I'd love you if you were an orphan without a dime."

She laughed. "You just wish I *was* an orphan. I know marrying into the Hamiltons isn't easy."

"No, it's not," he agreed. "But they're all beginning to grow on me, especially your father. He didn't hesitate to come up with a million-dollar bond for me. I will never forget that." He bent to kiss her sweetly on the lips. "Still glad you married me, Olivia Hamilton?"

She smiled up at him, tears in her eyes. "More than ever."

He swung her up into his arms and started toward the bedroom. "I'm going to make you happy, Livie. I promise."

"You already do."